Praise for *Sonny's Revenge*

"If Philadelphia is in your DNA, this book is mandatory. Many have waited patiently to see justice served and I am sure the revenge will be sweet. I especially enjoy John's encounters with other people, especially the romantic encounters because they are both accurate and hysterical. This is Philadelphia sarcasm and wit at its best and makes me proud of my roots."
— Bill Rosen, Author

"Another winner! Michael has once again given us the pleasure of his captivating writing. Having lived in the areas he is bringing to life, I love that he can invite all to come along on this amazing journey and introduce us to the real and the raw of South Philly's Italian culture including the food, the humor, the mob, the honor of family. This is a page turner you cannot put down."
— Ruth Archer, South Philly native and fan of Sonny's

"'You kiddin' me?' To be able to follow up the first story with this one is amazing. I did not think it would be possible to be more drawn into a story than I was with *Sonny's Vendetta*. The connection to the characters make you feel like you want to be part of an Italian family. Michael Attiani's storytelling talent is a gift to anyone who reads his work. I only hope there is more coming!"
— Dean Bianchini, Philadelphia native and entrepreneur

"After the cliffhanger ending of *Sonny's Vendetta*, I couldn't wait to read this next installment, *Sonny's Revenge*. Continuing the wild, humorous romp through South Philly's Italian neighborhoods, characters and culture, the excitement and twists continue. Attiani delivers another winner, and leaves the reader breathless and ready for the third book."
— Martin Bullen, avid reader

"I thought this would be like *The Godfather* or *The Sopranos*. This wasn't that — it was more fun. Michael writes with an extremely sharp wit and sarcastic style that makes this book series a darkly funny take on the mob genre. But you didn't hear that from me."
— Amy Allsop, COO of an Italian restaurant chain like Sonny's. But not.

Sonny's REVENGE

Sonny's REVENGE

MEATBALLS, MAGICIANS AND MORTICIANS IN SOUTH PHILLY

MICHAEL ATTIANI

For more information, visit www.sonnysvendetta.com

Edited by David Aretha
Book design by Christy Day, www.constellationbookservices.com

ISBN (paperback): 978-1-7372794-2-6
ISBN (ebook): 978-1-7372794-3-3

Printed in the United States of America

Dedicated to Alfredo, an inspirational grandfather
and a great chef, who was never too saucy.

KILL OR BE KILLED

"Here's how this is going to work," the old man waving around the hand-cannon explained to his captive audience—two goons who were *literally* his captives, duct-taped to a pair of chairs in my sister's garage. They had been sent here to kidnap my sister's kids but were captured in the process, and now they're being restrained by duct tape, *pink* duct tape because my sister bought it years ago as a joke, and it's the only thing Guido (the well-armed old guy) or his own goons could find for the job at hand in the garage.

"I'm going to offer you both the opportunity to speak. If neither of you volunteers, I will randomly volunteer one of you. I am going to ask the volunteer questions, and if there are *any* delays or if I think he's lying, I am going to punch his partner in the face. Fair enough?"

The two men smirked.

"But wait," he continued before they could respond. "Just to be fair, if a guy gets punched in the face, *he* gets to answer the *next* question, and the same rules will apply the other way around. Any reluctance or lying on the *second* guy's part, and I'm punching the *first* guy in the face."

"See how this works? Back and forth we'll go, punching guys in the face until I get the information I need," and the old man swung the gun back and forth in front of them like the weighted arm of a metronome—tick, tock, tick, tock, tick, tock.

"You each have your buddy's fate…and *face*…in your hands." He giggled a little at the unintended, impromptu humor he'd injected. Guido was not a giggly guy. This was all for show. Then he continued, "and if your friend's fate doesn't matter to you, just realize *he* will have the opportunity to return the favor in due time."

"So, who wants to go first?"

Guido, my uncle, was calm and in charge. Clearly, he possessed vast experience interrogating assholes. He'd been doing it longer than I've been alive, and I've been around since the 1960s. He was wasting no time on small talk with his guests who were seated in a garage only about fifty feet and three rooms away from a preoccupied babysitter who was reclining in my sister's and brother-in-law's family room.

My sister and brother-in-law were downtown at the time having dinner with me and a few others.

Under normal circumstances, Guido's interrogation would have to be conducted someplace desolate because such things can become rather loud, but that wasn't necessary tonight because the music in the babysitter's earphones was blasting away, and she was singularly focused on her phone screen, sexting her tortured boyfriend.

She was so oblivious to everything else around her, she had no clue two potential kidnappers had been captured in the back yard and restrained in the garage, nor that an interrogation was taking place. Hell, she was so singularly focused on her phone, the interrogation could have been happening on the sofa next to her and she wouldn't have noticed.

As for my sister's two boys sleeping upstairs, a marching band could perform in their room and they wouldn't wake up. It takes forever to get little kids to sleep, but once these two were out, they were *out*.

Although the occupants within the house were comfy and safe, the two guys in the chairs were not to be envied. Guido is an old-school, badass "organizer" who runs our South Philly neighborhood and protects my family like a wolverine protects its cubs. He is eighty years old, but don't kid yourself. He'll kick your ass all by himself.

Guido and his crew maintain order in my neighborhood as well as a few others surrounding us, and after finding out his best friend was murdered tonight by the same group of assholes who were trying to kidnap my sister's children (unsuccessfully) and my girlfriend's children (unfortunately successfully), he was on the warpath to find the remaining kids and discover who *specifically* was behind these plots, even though he had a hunch.

Ordinarily, Guido doesn't resort to violence. He resolves situations with cunning and threats. But there was no time for that right now and he wasn't in the mood anyway, so he got down to a business he deplored, and that began with him addressing his captives.

Fools that they were, they initially failed to grasp the gravity of their situation. Both men stared forward with nothing but contempt for Guido on their faces, unimpressed by his threat of repeatedly punching them in the face, especially since they were both sitting there, duct-taped to chairs after being apprehended and manhandled by Guido's bigger and far more physically imposing minions.

Guido's crew was basically comprised of human mountains who dwarf Mister Universe contestants, so by comparison, it's understandable a punch to the face by an old man wouldn't be considered much of a threat.

Since no one volunteered to go first, Guido randomly picked a candidate. "You." He pointed to the one to his right whose gaze at an imaginary spot on the garage wall hadn't wavered since he was seated and secured to a chair. Guido menacingly waved the ubiquitous, government-issue Browning M1911 .45 caliber handgun in the guy's face and informed him, "You're going to tell me where the other children are, and who put you up to this, and you're going to do it now, or I'll shoot you squarely in the face. Is that clear?"

Suddenly the guy's gaze straight ahead was broken and he flinched at what his captor had just said, turning his full attention toward Guido. "Wait! You said you'd punch *him*. Shooting *me* in the face wasn't the deal. You said you were going to *punch him*."

"Yeah. You're right. I did say that. I also lied. I mean, you're the one bound and strapped to a chair, and I'm standing here with the gun. What are you gonna do, sue me for breach of contract?"

The man was slack-jawed and didn't answer, probably assuming Guido's question was rhetorical.

It wasn't. Guido leaned forward like he was looking for an answer, shrugged, and pulled the trigger of the bombastically loud gun, shooting the man in the foot (not the face).

Such an injury wasn't necessarily fatal, if addressed soon, but it was excruciatingly painful, and would definitely affect the guy's long-term ballroom dancing career because everything in front of the heel of his left foot had been pretty much vaporized. That caliber of shell is destructive, especially when fired from such close range. The guy, and the chair he was strapped to, instantly fell to the floor, and he proceeded to scream in obvious agony.

This was all unfolding in my younger sister Angela's garage, which was designed to accommodate two full-sized vehicles comfortably, but could have easily been designed for situations like this as well. Two guys strapped to chairs left plenty of room for Guido and his crew to mill about.

Beyond space, though, the garage was perfect for the task at hand. The garage door was to Guido's left. The only physical connection to the house was the wall on his right. There was nothing but roof above the garage (no rooms), lawn behind it (stocked with an occasional deer or twelve), driveway to the side (where Guido's black Cadillac was parked with its motor running), and lawn and street to the front. The house itself sat in the middle of a suburban acre and was very private, with no one within ear shot to the back or to the driveway side of the large residence. Shrubbery hugged the front wall between the garage and the street, providing effective, if not unintended, sound insulation.

Two windows, which could have been liabilities if curiosity-seekers were nearby, faced the street, but black-out shades adorned them both to keep the sun from bleaching the paint on the cars usually parked in there, and those same shades provided exceptional visual privacy. Since Angela's car was in the shop, thanks to her being run off the road by these very cretins a couple days ago, and her husband Tom's car was in the city with him and Ange attending our celebratory dinner, the garage was left completely devoid of automobiles. Guido didn't have to worry about mess either, because the ground was raw concrete, and there was a hose hanging from the wall to spray any bodily fluids spilled out into the driveway through the large expanse of the two-car-wide door when it's opened.

Honestly, garages are great for privately kicking the crap out of guys for information. Keep that in mind! If you're ever looking for a good place to conduct an interrogation, think "garage."

"Rats. I appear to have missed his face," Guido said jokingly.

This was theater. One guy always gets shot. That's why G always tries to abduct at least two captives. The first guy has a chance to talk, but he's usually too stupid to seize the opportunity, believing for some reason the man with the gun won't actually pull the trigger. G's method removes all doubt for the second man, and it does so loudly. The louder the gun the better, which is why a Browning M1911 is Guido's weapon of choice. It's rather LOUD. An added bonus is the garage is an echo chamber, making everything seem even louder.

The noisy, pathetic wailing of the wounded man on the ground only added to the theatrics, and helped ply the cooperation of the other, as-yet intact hostage.

Guido turned his attention to the bound assailant to his left who had predictably pissed his pants when his cohort suddenly and in perpetuity became known as "hop-along." This meant Uncle G had chosen the correct guy to shoot. He pointed the .45 at Man #2 and before Guido could inhale, his captive started babbling everything from where he grew up, to how much his mother will miss him if he never sees her again because he's dead, to his theories on Jimmy Hoffa's whereabouts. Somewhere in the middle of all that blathering, he mentioned where my girlfriend's kids could be found, and whose plan it was. That second part *was* the primary goal of Guido's endeavor, after all, because it also told him who killed his best friend, our family attorney Joe Acchione.

Total time elapsed? Under three minutes.

Just an hour ago, a different old man, this one being quite dapper, especially in contrast to Guido's typical state of dishevelment, grabbed a dinner mint from the hostess station on his way past it, but never broke stride. He departed the South Philly restaurant where my family, friends and I were having dinner, and stepped into his awaiting limo. He had just dropped an atom bomb of a newsflash at our table and was feeling smug.

He informed us of his retribution for his son being killed earlier in the afternoon at Sonny's, my family's former Italian restaurant. I say "former," because my parents sold Sonny's a few months back and the guy who got shot was the one who bought it, well more like stole it because he never paid for it, at least not in full. Once they gained control of Sonny's, he and his band of frauds shuttered the place and dismantled it in an attempt to break my family's spirits. It was all part of a vendetta they had against us, but we'll get to that in due time.

The dapper old man let us know, while we were dining and celebrating, his people had murdered Joe Acchione and kidnapped my sister's kids, and my girlfriend's kids.

Before he arrived, we were all minding our own business, concluding a celebratory meal in honor of my heroics thwarting the vendetta and saving our entire family from imminent peril, but then his news put a predictable damper on everything.

Hours earlier, I *might* have shot the old man's son in the face. Okay, I *did* shoot him in the face, but he had it coming! You see, while I was being restrained by two of his henchmen, and after a painfully long-winded and baseless dissertation on why he hated my family, the old man's son revealed his plan to kill us all, starting with me.

He figured sharing his plan with me didn't matter because his thugs were about to pull me outside into the alley and murder me, but he wanted me to know the impending fate of my family before he ended my life to make me suffer a little more in my scant remaining moments. Well, uncle G, that wonderful man, rescued me, and that rescue provided me with the opportunity to come back in from the alley and shoot the old man's son right in his fucking face before he killed my entire clan.

For some strange reason the old man was taking the murder of his son rather personally and was almost giddy about informing us of his family's subsequent and swift retaliation against us.

There are two things to report here. First and foremost, his family started the whole thing. *We* were retaliating against *them*, not the other way around. They were the ones enforcing a century-old (and might I add, *canceled)* vendetta against my unsuspecting family, and that vendetta was entirely based on a teenaged girl's lie anyway, so *we* were the wronged party, not them.

My family did absolutely nothing to these people, and they knew it. One would *think* such a revelation would have inspired them to call the whole thing off, but au contraire. They maintained their course of destruction, even after their failed attempt to murder my grandfather in the 1920s.

More about that later, too.

Secondly, the old man had been misinformed.

Oh sure, his people murdered Joe Acchione, our ninety-five-year-old family attorney. Joe was dead, and there's no getting around that.

And yes, his crew successfully kidnapped my girlfriend's two kids. He got that one right too, *but* his crew *failed* to kidnap Angela's kids. That's where he was wrong, and it proved to be a very crucial oversight.

Angela and Tom's little cherubs were never even in danger. They were both snuggled and warm, sleeping in their respective beds, just as they had been since the babysitter dumped them there earlier that evening.

Once she got them to bed for good, the babysitter landed with a thud in Angela's plush family room sofa, bored to tears, listening to music through her earphones and eating a half-gallon of Breyer's mint chocolate chip ice cream (a delicious Philadelphia staple), one big spoonful at a time, right out of the container. She still possessed a teenager's metabolism, so she didn't have a care in the world about consuming several thousand sugary calories in one sitting.

Just wait, kid. Just wait. Your day of calorie-counting will come, and so will hot-flashes.

Meanwhile, her white-athletic-sock-swaddled feet were folded beneath her, stretching her yoga pants to near translucence at her kneecaps. Her torso was swallowed up in an oversized white hoody, which hung below her knees when she stood up. Shiny blue block letters spelled out "PENN STATE," the university her freshman boyfriend attended, across her hoody's chest. She was a very cute young girl who was downright pretty when she was made up and ready for a date, but when she's babysitting two prepubescents, her hair is pulled back, there's no makeup, and instead of perfume, she smells slightly of dried, sour ice cream.

Her aesthetic goal this evening was comfort. Mission accomplished.

While she sat quietly biding her time, awaiting Tom and Ange's return, she was completely unaware of the plot that had been foiled on the back lawn not one hundred feet from where she was blissfully texting her horny boyfriend. For the record, a boy his age really doesn't care if his girlfriend is wearing makeup, has her hair done, or smells pretty. He wanted to sneak over and with what little time was at their disposal before Angela and Tom return, at least get between her and the inside of that hoody he gave her (if not those yoga pants).

About a week ago, while my family was under attack by the psycho I shot in the face and by his partner in crime, my former friend and recent paramour Gina, Uncle Guido had posted a couple members of his crew at Angela's house to keep an eye on things. So, not only had the two assailants assigned to kidnap Ange's kids failed, they had been captured and detained in the garage, awaiting my uncle's arrival.

Unfortunately, although my sister's kids were safe and snuggled, my girlfriend, Indi's children were not so fortunate. They *had* been kidnapped from their father's place fewer than ninety minutes ago and were still at large. Although that's not a very long time under normal circumstances, when it comes to abduction, it's an eternity. If we imagine a ninety-minute radius drawn from the nucleus of a circle, we quickly realize that circle is huge, and the kids could be anywhere in it. Worse yet, that circle grew as every second passed.

No Time to Hesitate

Once Guido heard all he needed to hear, he turned his attention back to the man writhing on the floor who was *still* screaming and crying and otherwise making a ruckus and said, "Would you *please* shut up?" Guido leaned over, grabbed a dirty garage rag off the floor and shoved it into the guy's gaping mouth.

Fortunately for the guy on the ground, there wasn't a spider egg sack waiting to hatch in that rag. There could've been, and that would've been worse than being shot in the face. But did he pause from making noise long enough to thank his captor? No. His sobbing, though muffled, never subsided.

The cooperative guy didn't stop blubbering, either.

Guido dialed his phone as he turned to his men and calmly listed their next steps, which included collecting all the weapons they'd confiscated, throwing both guys in the trunk of Guido's crew's car parked up the street, and then hosing down the garage so it would be clean when Tom and Angela arrived home. Then they were to wait for Guido to call them and confirm the information he'd received was good before doing anything else.

No one wants to imagine what would happen if the information he received was not good, so let's not go there.

Guido then addressed the two men who were still taped to chairs, and asked a question: would they rather be dropped in the middle of fucking nowhere, naked and still bound up by duct tape, where they'd probably die and get pecked by buzzards, or would they like to be dropped at the local hospital for medical treatment?

They unanimously chose the latter option. Well, the cooperative guy chose that option. The guy with a rag in his mouth just nodded his head vehemently. Guido added a single codicil. He would only drop them at the hospital if they agreed to keep their mouths shut with the authorities, because if they didn't, the next time they were all together, and yes, there would most assuredly be a next time, the two of them would start coming apart piece by piece.

This time, there was no reason to doubt Guido's sincerity. Both men nodded their heads with equal parts approval and terror.

Guido actually liked survivors. They told stories to other would-be scumbags, which enhanced his lore. The more his reputation spread, the less he had to do what he did tonight.

Like the Canadian Mounted Police, or Scotland Yard, or the Pinkertons, or Elmer Fudd, or *some* famous character or organization whose motto is more memorable to me than who said it, Uncle Guido *always* gets his man…or kids. Whatever. You get the idea. In this case, he had gained the precise location of where the kidnapped children were being held, and who was behind this mess.

The party on the other side of the phone picked up and Guido shared the location of the missing children and detailed what should be done to immediately reacquire them. He walked out to the driveway where his Cadillac and driver awaited and headed back to the city. In the meantime, he called my old friend Rocco, who was also part of Guido's crew, to swing by the restaurant where I was having dinner and collect me, and then he called Angela to put her at ease about her children.

By the way, in case you were interested, the babysitter's boyfriend got the green light to come over. Guido's guys were concealed around the side of the garage but didn't engage once they figured the teenager wasn't a threat to anyone besides the babysitter's baby-maker. Ange and Tom walked in on the two teenagers about twenty minutes after the boyfriend arrived. The babysitter was still dressed, assuming you consider wearing socks "dressed," and the boyfriend was completely bare-assed naked and hopped to his feet when my sister and brother-in-law stepped into the family room. My sister looked at him, in all his aroused glory, shook her head, said "I've had enough surprises for one night. Tom…?" and turned to go upstairs and check in on her kids. Tom tossed the babysitter some cash, announced he and Angela were going upstairs for the night, and the sitter and boyfriend could leave when they were finished.

The boyfriend was thrilled by the prospect of finishing what he'd started, but the sitter was already wearing most of her clothes as well as a fresh new "Are you fucking kidding me?" facial expression. She was *more* than finished.

Mr. college boy was halfway home before he stopped looking like a human sundial.

The Night That Wouldn't End

Even though Guido was already working on this when we first heard about it, the old man's news of killing Joe and kidnapping my sister's and girlfriend's kids was fresh news to us, and we feared the worst.

There was panicking.

Joe Acchione was a ninety-five-year-old lawyer who had just helped us recoup our family restaurant. He was an old man, and friend of the family, who posed absolutely no threat to anyone. Killing him was utter bullshit.

In the moment, I was numb hearing Joe was gone so nefariously, but it didn't take too many seconds before the pain began to swell and keep getting worse. He was Guido's best friend, and although there's much more to say about Joe, I'll start by noting the world is much worse off without him in it, and Guido was going to be simultaneously woefully bereft and maniacally vengeful.

If you ever want to blow up someone's universe, don't attack them directly. People tend to endure direct attacks with remarkable resilience. If you really want to get under their skin, attack their closest friends or family. That will launch your targets into a frenzied orbit. I certainly felt a hole in my heart knowing they had killed Joe. I can't even imagine where Guido's head was, and the thought of him being unbalanced was horrifying.

The attack had a similar effect on Indi, my former girlfriend, and Ange, my sister, when they learned their kids were in jeopardy.

Indi (her real name is Swati, but I call her Indi) immediately called her ex-husband. It was his night to have the kids, but when Indi called him and he ran up to make sure the kids were still asleep in their room, he noticed the window to their room was wide open and they had been abducted. Indi screamed frantically at me to recover her children, but even over her screams, I could hear her ex-husband yelling even louder through the phone speaker.

Angela sat at the table in shock, watching Indi and grabbing Tom's forearm so tightly, her fingernails were drawing blood. She kept repeating, "Tom, call the house. Tom, call the house," which he did. He held and dialed his cell phone with his one free hand and called the babysitter.

As you already know, she was too busy texting her boyfriend and eating ice cream to answer Tom's call, so she let the call go through to voicemail, which she never set up in the first place and would never check anyway, because she's sixteen years old and those people don't *do* voicemail.

Unfortunately, neither Tom nor Angela knew what *you* know, so they immediately jumped to the worst possible conclusion—their kids were gone and possibly dead, or worse.

Tom set his phone down, looked blankly at Angela, almost paralyzed with fear, and said "I...I can't reach the sitter!"

Angela was in a full panic. "Where can Ashley possibly be? Keep calling, for God's sake! If my babies have been stolen and harmed in any way, I will fucking *kill* somebody!"

She was staring directly at me when she said that.

Angela's panic and threats only fueled the flames of Indi's meltdown. She was freaking the hell out about her *own* missing progeny. She was already sobbing uncontrollably, and Ange's comment sent Indi into full wailing mode. It was deafening. Her hysteria would be interrupted just long enough for her to scream at me about how it was my fault her children had been kidnapped and how she'd never forgive me.

Every time I stupidly tried to defend myself, she returned to alternating between screaming and convulsively blubbering.

The previous night, Indi and I had a heart-to-heart about the status of our relationship, and she told me she could never commit to me because I was immature, self-absorbed, and unstable. Obviously, the events of this evening were going to be a setback to me convincing her otherwise.

What a mess!

Just then, Ange's phone rang. It was Guido.

"Uncle Guido. Where are you? Some bastards kidnapped my kids! Swati's too!"

"Not your kids—never happened," he soothed her reassuringly. "I never called off the detail I had assigned to watch your house. My boys spotted two men crossing your backyard and we captured them. We questioned them in your garage and have the information we need to get Swati's children back. These assholes never made it inside your house, Angela. No one inside is aware of what went on, so don't go nuts when you get home because you'll just frighten your kids and that little blonde girl watching them. I have men in your driveway waiting for you to come home, so don't panic or hurt yourself rushing back here. Your place is being protected. In the meantime, do me a favor and tell your brother to get his ass outside so he can help my guys retrieve the other kids. Swati's kids will need to see a familiar face with us, and I imagine their mother is in no condition to be a calming element."

"Uncle Guido, I have no words…"

"I told you, Angela. I protect this family. Go home. Your boys are safe and tell Tom to catch his breath."

Angela was immediately visibly relieved and almost giddy. We all looked at her impatiently.

"*So?*" I asked. "What did Guido say?"

"Oh, he said they never got to my kids. They're fine."

Indi stopped waling for a moment, a glimmer of hope on her face, and asked, "My kids too?"

Angela replied, "Oh no. They got yours, but Guido thinks he knows where they are."

Indi exploded right back to the level of hysteria she'd been exhibiting a minute earlier. Everyone else glared at Angela with the universal "what the fuck" shrug and she just acted like she didn't understand what our problem was, then dismissively added, "I'm sure her kids are fine."

I didn't think it was possible, but Indi actually got worse with that comment.

"Oh, John, I almost forgot. Guido told me to tell you to get outside right away and get in a car he's sending so they can take you to where he thinks Swati's kids are being held. Hopefully you'll get there before something happens to them."

Indi looked at me with an expression of absolute horror, and even though we didn't think it was possible, her hysteria leaped to an all new level.

I got up and ran out the door to the parking lot, smacking Angela across the back of the head on my way by. Raj, Indi's brother and my best friend from childhood, was able to coax Indi out of the restaurant and then took her home, which was a relief because her abusiveness, as justified as it was, had become intolerable.

The four of them—Raj, Indi, Tom, and Angela—exited right after me.

I stepped outside and was greeted by Rocco, my enormous friend from grade school who now doubled as one of Guido's henchmen and my protector. He was waiting beside one of G's Cadillacs.

"What took you so long?" Rocco asked. "We've been waiting out here for a few minutes already, and time could be running out for those kids!"

"Angela forgot to tell me you were waiting."

Rock rolled his eyes. Even *he* knew how stupid Angela was being, and that speaks volumes, because he has an IQ of something around 12. We sped off to retrieve Indi's kids.

I didn't know it at the time, but thankfully, before Guido called Angela, he had called two more teams to recover Indi's kids. By the time we arrived where the kids were being held, G's other guys were already standing outside the house, relaxed. They had Indi's kids with them, and as we approached, they directed me inside.

I asked if everything was secure, and Guido's guys shrugged and said the door was unlocked when they got there, and the kids were inside alone watching TV. They handed me a sticky note which had been stuck to its screen: "Kids were never in danger, but you are" and it was in Gina's handwriting.

I called Indi to let her know we had her kids and they were safe, and then we drove the children home. Indi opened the door and dropped to her knees, grabbing her kids in the process. All three of them hugged and sobbed and consoled one another. She stood up, glared at me with virtual laser beams shooting out of her eyes, turned her back to me, and walked away, slamming the door in my face. It was in that moment I realized I *probably* wasn't going to be invited in for sex.

The door re-opened and Raj appeared. "Dude, let her get over this. She's a *little* emotional right now. Give her room and time and she'll come around." He tried to sound reassuring, but I'm not sure even he believed what he was recommending. Regardless, Indi's recovery was hers to process, and at least her kids were safe and home with her.

Then Raj looked at me desperately and said "Dude, take me with you. I really don't want to be near her tonight." I patted Raj on the arm and shrugged and let him know I hoped this was the end of the craziness for a while, and I'd catch up with him tomorrow.

G's men asked where they could drop me, and I had absolutely no answer for that question off the top of my head. The only thing I could imagine was to go back to our restaurant, Sonny's, and start putting it back together again so we could open soon, but I honestly wanted to put some real estate between me and that place right now. After thinking about it for a second, I wanted to put some real estate between me and *everything*. I wanted to get the fuck out of Philly, get away from Ange and Indi and Raj and G and everyone else and just disappear.

I asked for a ride back to Mr. Acchione's. The boys in the front seat didn't need to know why, but once I got to Mr. Acchione's, I planned to immediately get into my car and get the hell out of town. They obliged, and I sat back and savored the quiet commute, which only took about three minutes because we made all the lights.

REMEMBER PITTSBURGH?

I believe my exact words before speeding off were *"FUCK THIS PLACE!"*

And I meant it.

After a very full day, which included getting the shit beaten out of me for the second time this week and then being informed our family lawyer had been murdered, and my girlfriend's *and* sister's kids had been abducted (even though the latter statement turned out to be exaggerated), I'd had more than enough of our fair city to last me a lifetime and decided to run away from South Philly and never look back. I reversed out of the garage where Joe Acchione (the aforementioned dead lawyer) let me park, pointed the nose of my car westward, stepped on the accelerator and did not plan to lift up until I had put a thousand miles between me and here.

I'm John Valmonti and I drive a 1970 Dodge Challenger, which I purchased with money my parents gave me from the sale of Sonny's, our family's former Italian restaurant. It's been updated with a modern muscle-car engine, transmission, suspension, and other hot-rodding goodies. It's what one might call "a ten-footer." From ten feet away, it looks perfect, but the closer you get, you more you'll notice patina.

That's a nice way of saying stone-chips and little scratches in the paint and other ordinary wear-and-tear from ordinary use. It may not be pristine, but it's my single extravagance. Every one of my other material possessions fits into a Hefty bag I carry with me as luggage. The Hefty bag goes in the trunk of the Challenger. One of the most wonderful attributes of this car was when I buried my right foot in the accelerator, I left Philly quickly. In a hail of dust and loose gravel well after midnight, I had every intention of driving through the daylight hours until sunset, undeterred!

Chicago, or St. Louis, or Indianapolis, or wherever is that far away, here I come!

At least that was the plan when I set out, fueled by rage. I loudly screamed to myself in the car, banging my hand against the seat and the steering wheel for close to an hour– *Who the fuck do these people think they are? I don't need to take this shit! I'll be good and god damned if I'm going to stick around and keep getting attacked by Gina's fucking family for something my family didn't even do! And I'm sick and fucking tired of being beaten up!*

Getting beaten up so many times, I felt like one of those punch-ing-bag-things I had as a kid. The kind that's about the height of a kindergartner, shaped like a bowling pin and had the full-height image of a smiling TV clown on the front of it. Remember those? They were filled with air and were weighed down by sand in the base, so whenever you'd punch the clown in the mouth (something adults in the 1960s thought kids should know how to do), the bottom-heavy inflated bowling pin would tip over backward or sideways, but always come right back up, ready for the next punch. The only difference for me was my body was leaking badly and wasn't bouncing back up quite as quickly anymore.

After a week of that garbage, today was the last straw. I was pissed off, and it's a well-known customer service tactic, when a customer is pissed off and ranting, don't interrupt or try to calm the person down.

That tends to make things worse. No. The best option is to let the rant run its course. Ultimately, the flames of rage dwindle down to little more than a glowing ember of angst, at which point the customer tires out, stops ranting and is ready to listen to reason, hopefully.

In my case, I ranted to myself until I was hoarse, and although it took me an hour to get there, I had only made it as far as the Downingtown exit on the Pennsylvania Turnpike, not even the western-most edge of the Philadelphia suburbs, before I flamed out. I was finally quiet. I harrumphed now and then, but otherwise, I had exorcised my demons and now had little choice but to settle in and drive.

Unfortunately for me, except for a half-hour nap before dinner, I had been awake for twenty, very active and exhausting hours, and once my adrenalin had subsided, thanks to my tantrum, those hours were taking their toll on me. I kept driving, but I grew more and more tired by the mile, trying every trick in the book to stay awake, like pinching myself, plucking hair from my nostrils, singing loudly to whatever songs I could find on the radio, Slapping my thighs with my palms, driving with the windows down hoping the frigid night air would shock me into being alert—everything!

That all worked well enough for a while, but after a few hours, I had nothing left in reserves and realized there were lengthy stretches of road I had just covered but couldn't remember. I only snapped back to consciousness when my car passed over rumble-strips—the tires making that unmistakable gargling noise and the steering wheel vibrating in my hands. If those strips didn't do the trick, I'd have been destined for some impromptu and unintended off-road excursions.

Sitting on my ass for six hours, driving across the seemingly endless and perpetually dark Turnpike, I finally conceded victory to exhaustion and called Pittsburgh today's ultimate destination.

That's okay. Even though I was still in Pennsylvania, at least I was outta Philly!

Of course, you can't just pull over on the shoulder of the Turnpike, or sleep in your car at a rest stop. Those are great ways to get propositioned by lonely truckers, *not* to get restful hours of shut-eye, so I exited the interstate and set out to find a convenient and affordable hotel, preferably not one charging by the hour with the headboard in the neighboring room banging against my wall all night, if you know what I'm sayin'.

Lucky for me, I found the kind of cheap-ass hotel weary travelers crave. One whose owners are so frugal, they don't even bother buying new signs when they purchase the place from a name brand hotel chain. They just shuffle the letters around to avoid copyright infringement, like rebranding a former Hilton into a brand new Holtin, or a Sheraton into a Shoretan.

This one had sunken to new depths and was rebranded a Motel 9.

And signage wasn't the only place where the owners economized. When I stepped through the lobby doors, I thought I'd stepped back in time into the Golden Girls' living room. There was a lot of mauve, Kelly green and brass, a lot of it.

I didn't really care about décor, or fancy names though. This stop had a single purpose: sleep, and I knew when my eyes finally closed, I really wouldn't care if I was in a 5-star hotel penthouse, or the back of a White Chevy cargo van with an "Old West" mural painted on the side and thick shag rugs on the walls. As long as where I rest my head is clean and safe and I'm asleep, all is good in the world.

The good news here is, by all indications, housekeeping was doing its job. To their credit, the hotel looked clean inside and out, and the air smelled of disinfectant—maybe not a particularly sexy aroma, but a reassuring one nonetheless. I didn't want a mama cockroach laying eggs in my ears while I slept, or anything. I also didn't want to lie in bed, wide awake, *worrying* about a mama cockroach doing that.

During my brief encounter at the front desk, I bribed Chad, the hotel desk clerk, with a crisp hundred-dollar bill because his hotel's policy forbade him from renting rooms to anyone without a credit card. I don't have one of those, so the hotel is earning nothing from my stay. Instead, pimple-faced and portly Chad ended up with a pocketful of ill-gotten cash. I suspect his hotel's policy also forbade him from renting rooms and pocketing the cash, but he didn't seem quite as persnickety about that rule.

Thank goodness for fungible ethics!

Exhausted to the point where I seriously considered lying down in the elevator, I stumbled out when its doors opened onto the second floor lobby and trudged like a zombie to my room all the way down at the end of the hall.

I never trust hotel access cards. Technology and I are rarely on the best of terms, so when I dropped the card into the slot and the light changed from red to green, I wasted no time turning the lever and entering the room before the lock changed its mind and switched back to red. Something working, let alone on the first try, in this hotel seemed less likely than Jesus being the bellhop, so I didn't want to tempt fate and have to unlock the door twice.

As expected, the retro-'80s ugliness didn't end in the main lobby, or even in the elevators or the corridors. The theme had spread in the hotel room itself like an unattended fungus across the floor and up the walls. Everything the vile décor touched looked arguably more tired than me. Who cared? All I wanted was a hot shower and several hours of uninterrupted sleep, so as far as I was concerned, the clash between mauve walls and Kelly green carpeting could continue on to its heart's content once I was in sleepyland.

Once the fluorescent bulb over the bathroom mirror finally flickered to life, I was bathed in a pink glow from the floor tile, all the way up the shower walls. The toilet was pink. The sink was pink, but counter top was green. The walls without tile were covered with floral vinyl wall paper and guess which colors were featured. Go ahead, guess. I'll give you a hint: green and pink.

It looked like someone threw up all eight years of the Reagan administration in the bathroom, but I reminded myself what was important: "shower and sleep! Shower and sleep!" and I soldiered on.

I turned both shower knobs on full blast to start drawing hot water through the building's labyrinth of old pipes, and then proceeded to peel off my clothes. Sitting naked on the cushioned pink toilet seat, waiting for steam to appear through the shower door, I knew I was in the home stretch to falling asleep on that big beautiful king size bed awaiting me in the other room.

Nirvana was within reach!

I gazed into the mirror from my seat on the commode and saw a very tired fifty year old man looking back at me, bags under his eyes, and cuts and bruises from the week's pummeling very visible.

I was born and raised in South Philly, which is where Philadelphia tends to keep most of its Italians. My entire life has revolved around the *dynamic* world of food service (that, for the uninitiated is what we call sarcasm). I work mostly as a cook or bartender, but depending on the night, and who doesn't show up for their shift, I occasionally fill in as a dishwasher or server in my family's very small Italian restaurant. Well, I did all that until they recently sold it.

If I was strolling through Lilliput, passersby might stop and stare, but in my neighborhood my appearance is unexceptional. I look like any other dark-haired middle-aged Italian guy. I'm a little more than an inch over six feet tall—not fat, not skinny, but normal. Like most people of Italian descent, I have big brown eyes, tan easily, and if I don't keep up with them, I get those weird wolfman-like eyebrows which look like someone glued fat caterpillars on my forehead.

In addition to the physical characteristics I just mentioned, this week I have added a vast array of technicolor hematomas all over my body, courtesy of multiple intensive beatings. Let me assure you, this has been one hell of a shitty week. Remember Pompeii and Mount

Vesuvius? Remember Hiroshima and the A-bomb? Remember the pennant collapse of the 1964 Phillies? If those lucky bastards wanted to experience real suffering, they could've been me for the past seven days!

My grade-school classmate, friend since birth, and childhood next-door neighbor Gina Gianetti (AKA "GG," AKA "Geez," AKA "psychotic *bitch*") had betrayed me and conspired with her creepy uncle from the old country to defraud the Valmonti family (*my* family) out of our legacy: Sonny's, an Italian restaurant nestled in beautiful (which we pronounce locally as: BEE-YOOOO-DEE-FOOL) Philadelphia, PA.

Even after the huge head start I gave it, the shower in this dump is still taking forever to find warm water somewhere in this hotel's pipes, so I have a little time to reflect on the recent seven-day debacle. Not that I haven't been obsessing over that subject every second in the car while I drove here.

Sonny's was opened nearly eighty years ago in its current location by my father's father, Alfredo (AKA Al Valmonti, as I'd always known him, and apparently Fredo Mantelli to those who knew him in his youth in Italy). Why did he have two names? Well, because some little tramp he grew up with named Isabella, who not ironically bore a striking resemblance to my old pal Gina (because Gina is actually Bella's great-granddaughter), framed Alfredo for something he never did.

More than a century ago, Bella was a teenaged girl who got herself knocked up by some coward who ran away the instant he found out she was pregnant. But instead of facing the music for her own bad choices when pressed for answers by her parents, she shifted the blame for the burgeoning bambino in her belly onto someone else. Did she blame the spineless lout who hit-and-ran? Of course not. She blamed someone who was entirely innocent.

In the meantime, while Isabella's lie was percolating in southern *Italy*, Fredo, my grandfather, who was completely unaware of Bella's impending motherhood, was on a boat from Genoa headed to south

Philly to begin his new life with a new adventure in a new land where he intended to make something of himself. He would do just that... after a couple slight detours, like when a member of Bella's family tried to kill him a few years after he landed on our hallowed shores.

Why would anyone try to kill Fredo?

Because meek and sweet Fredo was the entirely innocent person upon whom Bella tried to pin her pregnancy. She literally blamed her best friend in the whole wide world for her own fuck up. That was the thanks he got for being a good friend. She told her father that Fredo had raped her and then ran away to America to escape his responsibilities. Much to her chagrin, this lie didn't get her entirely off the hook, but it did put an imaginary noose around Fredo's neck.

Bella's father detonated when he was informed of this unforgivable transgression against his family. Although the rape of his daughter would ordinarily be more than enough justification to react the way he did, the rape was secondary to the "big picture."

Bella's father had toiled much of his life with one goal in mind: getting his daughter married to a wealthy landowner. He was so obsessed, he and his wife only continued to have children because he needed a daughter. After having two boys, they finally produced a daughter. He felt like he had hit the lottery. His diligence had finally been accompanied by good fortune and everything was falling into place as planned. The child-bearing period had finally ended with success.

Once Bella was born, it was only a matter of a few days before he successfully arranged her betrothal to the only son of a wealthy family whose sole desire was to perpetuate their name. Bella's father spent the ensuing years nurturing that family relationship, ensuring nothing and no one could come between him and that marriage.

Although her older brothers labored heavily every day with their father, cultivating their small plot of land to produce enough crops to support the family, Bella's sole responsibility in life was to survive to her fifteenth birthday. Then, the wedding would go off as planned. She would produce children, but most importantly, her entire family would have wealth and property.

With this news of her pregnancy, her father's entire universe and life's effort were instantaneously turning from gravy to liquid shit. News of this impropriety would get out, and the wealthy family who anxiously awaited the grandchildren she was destined to produce would instead shun her and her family for being dirty and unworthy. Bella lost more than her virginity. She lost her family's entire legacy. Banging that no-good lout who ran off when he learned of her pregnancy shot her family's entire future squarely in the proverbial ass, or at least it would have had it not been for Bella's mother.

Bella's mother instinctively stepped in and pulled enough strings with her family in Spain to preserve her daughter's betrothal. Sending Bella away to live with an aunt and have the child there would ensure no one locally would be any the wiser of her pregnancy. Bella could return home after bearing the child and still get married, as long as they all contended she was a virgin, and she left the child behind in Spain.

But that solution did little to quell Bella's father's obsessive rage. He wanted blood. He was angry toward Bella for being pregnant, but he held Fredo, the supposed rapist, responsible for destroying the family's future and rendering a life's work moot.

Of course, Fredo never would have done what Bella accused him of doing, not in a million years, but he was not around to defend himself when accused, so the accusation stuck to him like a "kick me" sign taped to his back. Worst of all, as is often the case with kick-me signs, he had no idea it was there.

In her defense, Bella believed blaming something on Fredo would be a harmless means to escape culpability for what she and her *actual* sperm-donor had done, because Fredo would be across an ocean and completely untouchable. In early 1900s Italy, in the moment, that logic was sound enough, but it didn't take long before things like telephones and air travel and world wars made the world much smaller, and Fredo and everyone else on the planet gradually became *very* locatable.

In his fury, believing his only daughter had been defiled by Fredo, Bella's father placed a vendetta to kill every Mantelli, and the primary target was naive, innocent Fredo. You'll hear more about this all later, but suffice to say, Fredo survived the murderous plot against him and ultimately became my grandfather…but not before having his name changed from Fredo Mantelli to Al Valmonti in hopes of throwing vendetta hungry assassins off his trail.

About a century later, my good buddy Gina learned of the ancient vendetta and revived it when she also discovered she was related to Bella. Armed with that knowledge, she became a power-hungry psycho-bitch.

It's hard to come down on Bella like a bag of sledgehammers simply because she tried to cover her own scared young ass with a lie. It was a character flaw, sure, but not rooted in evil. Besides, she was a fourteen-year-old kid and she naively believed Fredo would be out of reach of any possible retribution. And she never declared a vendetta against the Mantellis. She merely put a target on Fredo. Bella's *father* was the one who declared the vendetta.

Gina, conversely, is an evil sociopath. She's in her fifties and should know better than to try to execute a vendetta designed to wipe out my family, but she carefully crafted a lie to kill us anyway, all so she could ascend her family's power structure.

That shit, my friends, is fucked up.

Armed with her pathology, Gina and her uncle connived to swindle my family out of Sonny's and then dismantle it piece by piece in front of us. The goal was to torment us by systematically unwriting our family history by dismantling our single legacy—Sonny's—and then kill us, because what fun is it to simply kill your prey when you can tease it first?

Assholes.

Anyway, my family had no idea what had happened or why. In the beginning of the recent scourge, we thought someone had purchased Sonny's. End of story. We may not be collectively smart, but when ownership of the business and the building were transferred and installment payments failed to arrive, we were savvy enough to realize something was awry. With the assistance of my "uncle" Guido and Joe Acchione (our incredibly shrewd, charismatic, and wonderful family attorney) we were able to uncover and navigate Gina and her uncle's gauntlet of treachery.

Guido and Joe identified the vendetta connection and got us on the right track to recoup Sonny's, but even more importantly, they helped us diffuse the threats on our lives and live beyond next Tuesday.

A little over a week ago, I was happily working in a New Orleans restaurant, sharing a small apartment with a very attractive woman.

Since being summoned home by Uncle Guido, it has been a violent week of beatings and attempted (and successful) murders, but in the end the Valmontis prevailed. We recaptured our Sonny's flag and vanquished our foes in demonstrative fashion, and when it came time to celebrate, a small group of us—me, my on-again/off-again girlfriend Indi, her brother and my best friend Raj, my sister Angela, and her husband Tom—descended on a nice little Italian joint around the corner from my parents' South Philly row home and ordered a lot of food.

Enough obsessing about shit I can't change. The shower is finally hot, and I'm sitting here naked.

AHHHHH…

The hot water blasted out of the showerhead and beat down on the top of my head as I closed my eyes and imagined all the day's atrocities washing off me—getting beaten in Sonny's, watching a dozen or so guys get gunned down in an alley, shooting a guy a couple times, learning my girlfriend's and sister's progeny were kidnapped, all while our attorney was smothered to death in front of his bound and gagged nurse. There was a *lot* to wash off.

It took a while for the magical pulse from the showerhead to wash away those nightmares, and I gave it all the time it needed before I lathered up. I wasn't exactly in a hurry. The full effects of the shower needed to soothe me before I could enjoy nocturnal splendor between the sheets of my king-sized bed. Tranquility was my only pathway to hours of slumbering bliss in sleepy-land, and a long, hot shower was the perfect means to a desired end.

I finished rinsing, dried off, wrapped the towel around my waist, and headed to my bed. The warmth of the shower had relaxed me to the point where I had just about enough consciousness left in me to make it to my pillow before I collapsed.

...SHIT

I was two steps out of the bathroom when I heard her voice.

"Hey sexy, miss me?"

My eyes opened and there, seated in the room's lone upholstered chair, was the old man from earlier in the restaurant. Gina was standing next to him, leaning against the bureau, holding a gun with a silencer, and it was pointed at me.

The relaxing benefits of that glorious hot shower were rendered moot in a "poof."

"Are you *fucking* kidding me? What are you *doing* here? How'd you find me? More importantly, how'd you get *in* here? I'm going to punch Chad right in his pimply fucking desk-clerk face when I get outta here."

Gina replied, "*If* you get outta here you mean, and don't be too hard on the kid. He just told me where to find you. We got in here on our own. These electronic hotel door locks are a joke. I swear hotels hand out cards just to make the guests feel safe." She held up a contraption smaller than a pack of cigarettes and said "two seconds with this little electronic beauty and no more lock."

"...once, twice, three times a lady," I interjected.

"And we followed you out of Acchione's driveway. I thought following that hot rod of yours was going to be hard, but you must've been really exhausted. You barely went five miles over the speed limit the whole way here. Sometimes you were so far *below* the limit, we wanted to start pushing you with our bumper because we were getting bored waiting for you to decide when and where to stop."

She added a little chuckle and said, "Right, Grandfather?" with a great big, toothy smile.

The old man didn't like that. He didn't like any of her little monologue. I don't think he was prepared to be introduced that way, and he sure as hell wasn't in a sophomoric, giggly mood. He shot her a terse stare and ground his teeth.

I retorted, "Well, congratu-fucking-lations on your stellar surveillance skills. I'd applaud if I wasn't so fucking tired, so if you'll excuse me, I'm going to sleep now." And with that, I dropped my towel, flashed my bare frame at her and the old man, and dove on top of the bedspread, face-first into my pillow, and shut my eyes. "If you want to shoot me, go ahead," I said into my pillow. "I'm just too goddamned tired to give a shit right now."

The old man spoke up for the first time.

He was still neat as a pin, to borrow a phrase from his era. It was the wee-hours of the morning, but his shirt was still buttoned to the top. His tie was tight to his neck. His jacket was still on and a little handkerchief was still folded so a triangle of itself protruded from his breast pocket. His clothes were unrumpled; his hair was perfectly in place and he looked refreshed. If anything, he looked fresher now than he had earlier in the evening when he interrupted our dinner to tell us his crew had killed and kidnapped members of my family.

"If you two are finished trying to impress one another with your mutual nonchalant banter, I would like to get down to business so I can leave this disgusting room and this disgusting hotel and this disgusting country. And before we go any further, son, stop acting like you're asleep. Sit up and cover yourself. You are not a boy. You're a man. Act like one."

I spitefully continued to lay there, acting like he wasn't talking to me, and made fake snoring noises like I did when I was a kid and my mother was trying to wake me for school.

The old man stood up, methodically unwove his belt from his pant loops, doubled it up, held it above his head in his right hand, and lashed it one time across my ass. The leather smacked *loudly* and I grabbed my stinging butt cheeks and jumped up.

"What the absolute *fuck*, old man! Get out of *my* room, you crazy motherfuckers!"

Gina was laughing hysterically, but the old man never broke character. He calmly reversed the entire belt process, re-wove it through the loops in his pants, and sat back down. "If you want to be treated like a child, I will oblige; however, I came here hoping to speak with a man. I am hoping *you* will oblige." And then he gestured with his hand for me to go to the bureau, get clothes, and then dress.

I glared at him, continued to rub my stinging ass, and walked to my Hefty bag. I foraged for a few things, all the while glaring at the deranged duo of uninvited guests in *my* fucking hotel room.

Gina spoke up. "Maybe we should have included a little S&M in our times together, Johnny. I kinda liked watching you get whipped like that."

"Shut the fuck up, bitch," I wittily and dismissively retorted.

Her demeanor changed from playful joy to fury, and she pointed her gun at me again, only more menacingly this time.

The old man calmly raised his own hand to Gina's and, without ever moving his gaze from me, physically lowered her arm back down to her side. "Calm down, my dear. This man saved your life earlier this afternoon, remember? The least we can do is not kill him before he puts on his pants."

I was still stinging from being whipped. I hadn't been hit like that since my mother did it to me as a kid. Back then, toward the end of her term as my punisher, I would defiantly stare her down when she hit me as if to say, "Is that the best you got, bully?" But I wasn't prepared for tonight's attack, and now that the shock had worn off, I was pissed at myself for acting so juvenile. I should have taken that belt and choked that old fucker, but instead I had danced around like an organ grinder's trained monkey.

Lesson learned.

"Look, it's not like I don't cherish these times together, but what's it going to take for you two to get the fuck outta here? I think I have another hundred bucks in my wallet, if you didn't steal it already. Will that get it done?"

"Watch your language, boy, or I'll soap your mouth, just as I spanked your bare behind. Sit down when you're finished dressing. Gina, put the gun away before something regrettable happens. I don't think Johnny is going to go anywhere or do anything. He's too curious right now to interrupt our visit."

The old man misread the situation. I was too tired at this point to be curious. All I wanted to do was sleep, and I was so fatigued by this entire epic with this old man and his family, I'd have gladly taken that gun from Gina, killed them both right there, and gone to sleep, leaving clean-up for the next morning. Unfortunately, I wasn't so stupid to believe I could move swiftly enough to overtake her before she turned the gun a few degrees to the right and shot me in the process. Pointed directly at me or not, I was held in place by her weapon. Curiosity was the *last* thing I was feeling in that room at that moment.

Uncle G did teach me a few things over the last week, though. I was listening more to the "why" and "how" things were being said, instead of just listening to the words, but I still had to work on shutting the fuck up.

The old man, for all his careful wardrobe choices and formality, was playing a role. He believed I was hanging on his every word because he was used to being the most important guy in every room. He had become accustomed to being the boss, having everyone wait for him to share his pearls of wisdom and advice. He was arrogant and self-important. I hoped to be able to use that against him…assuming I didn't get shot first, which was still a very real possibility, so I played along.

"Oh, please, tell me a story, grandpop," I responded sarcastically.

He glared at me again.

"The only reason we're speaking at all right now, why I followed you to this godforsaken cesspool of an excuse for a hotel instead of merely having you exterminated like an insect, is because I recognized something of value in your behavior this afternoon outside your family's former establishment. After being betrayed, beaten, humiliated, and sentenced to death, you spared my granddaughter's life and granted her safe passage. At your lowest point, when vengeance would have been entirely understandable, you exhibited tremendous character and a capacity for compassion and forgiveness. I think our families need more of that between one another, and I am hoping you can be the fulcrum to bring us all into balance.

"Just so you're aware," he continued, "I was prepared to accommodate your family and compensate them for what my son had done to you and your business."

He paused. Closed his eyes, breathed in deeply and slowly, looked me in the eyes, and finished. "Then you killed my son in cold blood."

He left that last sentence hanging in the air for a moment, and glared, thinly veiling his anger. He stared at me for what seemed like an eternity.

I remember talking to a guest at the bar at Sonny's one night, years ago. He was a salesman, in town for the evening. He had dinner and a few drinks by himself and watched a Flyers game on the twelve-inch tube TV on the wall above the cash register. As the dining room emptied out, the kitchen staff cleaned everything and the last of the bar patrons left. I turned off the TV, hours after the game had ended, and went to settle up with the sole remaining straggler.

Sometimes in life, a lesson is shared, and it's your choice if you want to listen to it. That night, I had nowhere in particular to go but upstairs to sleep in my apartment. It was cold outside and the bar was warm, so I entertained the semi-inebriated salesman who shared one of his selling techniques with me, which basically broke down to this: When there's a moment of silence in a conversation, the one who breaks it loses control to the other person, so "Shut the fuck up and be patient."

Salesmen will use this tool all the time. They'll ask you a question and just sit there, waiting for you to speak. Most people will feel uncomfortable and compelled to fill awkward silence with words, and they'll start yammering, sharing all sorts of valuable information about what they really want, or are really willing to spend, or, in the case in my hotel room, making excuses for what had happened.

I stared right back at the old man. If he wanted to say something else, he could go right ahead and do so, but I wasn't going to make this any easier for him. Besides, I was so tired I was literally falling asleep—gun pointed at me or not.

Our eyes were casually locked and the side of his mouth slowly rose in a smile, as if acknowledging that the stupid short-order cook standing before him may be more savvy than he thought. Either that or maybe he had some spinach stuck in one of his molars and he was trying to suck it out of there.

By this point in the day, I honestly had no clue. I was beyond exhausted.

Gina was the first to flinch. She raised the gun again and filled the dead air, blurting out, "Nothing! You murdered my uncle, and you have *nothing* to say?"

The old man grabbed Gina's wrist, squeezed, and jerked it down-ward, causing her obvious and immediate discomfort. If fire could come out of his eyes, he would have burned her face off her skull. She was disrupting his theater. He carefully drafted this script and didn't need her ad-libbing. This was the first time the old man had lost his temper since we met earlier in the evening.

How about that? He's human and vulnerable after all. Thanks for the lessons, Uncle G, and old drunk salesman guy.

The silence broken, he turned his attention back toward me. "Why would someone exhibiting such compassion mere moments earlier in that filthy alley commit murder immediately after re-entering your own restaurant? What could my son have possibly said to you to inspire such a severe response?"

Again there was silence. He was used to getting his way, and not answering would anger him. I wanted to see that rage again. I wanted him a little less balanced, a little less controlled. I didn't have much to lose. They were probably going to kill me in a few minutes anyway… and maybe *then* I could finally sleep! Satisfying his curiosity was my only remaining currency, and I wasn't about to squander it.

The old man burst halfway out of the chair and yelled "ANSWER ME!" before catching himself and settling back in the chair, breathing deeply and clutching the upholstered arms of the chair with a death grip.

Hey, if I'm lucky, the old fart will have a coronary and then it's one-on-one between me and Gina, and I don't care how many shots she'd get off. I'd kick her bitch ass! Chances are she'd hesitate before pulling the trigger anyway. Amateur.

I gave it another moment. I tilted my head and raised my eyebrows in a nonverbal cue, and asked the old man, "Are *you* finished acting childishly, yet, or shall I spank you? I'm not sure what you want from me here. What's done is done."

"I want to know why you killed my *son*! My *SON*!"

The old man was exasperated. Kidnapping kids, lighting a fuse with us at the restaurant, trailing me to Pittsburgh, the death of his son, the late hour, missing the Early Bird Special at the senior center buffet… Whatever the final straw was, the day had finally gotten the best of him. He sprung to his feet all the way this time, and that was my chance and I didn't hesitate. I plowed into his chest, pushing him to the side, into Gina. They both fell backward, landing against the bureau. Gina's natural reaction was to put her hands back in search of balance, palms facing the wall. Doing that made grabbing the gun away from her easy.

I swiped the gun and stepped back to a safe distance in the middle of the room while the two of them were on their asses on the floor, the old man in Gina's lap, looking shocked and embarrassed. For the first time, he looked rumpled and human. He had completely forfeited control to me and seemed to age ten years in the process.

Even in his eighties, he was strong. Thirty years earlier, if I'd lunged at him, he'd have cast me aside without so much as an increased pulse rate. Strong or not, his reactions were slow. This evening reminded him how old and mortal he was. He went to press himself against the floor to get back to his feet, and I waved him off with my new handgun.

"Not so fast there, big daddy. Why don't you just stay down there where it's safe, on top of Gina. She's used to having men on top of her, so she won't mind."

Gina knew better than to say anything. Her interruption was the first step toward taking him off his game, and not putting the gun away when asked is why they'd lost control to me, and she knew it. He did too. He should have never brought her. She's a devious spy, but a lousy soldier.

"Now what? You shoot us like you shot my son?"

"As you noted earlier, my tendency is to show compassion, but I'm also willing to do what needs to be done. So, as long as you two cooperate, I'm not going to do anything to you except make sure you don't leave too soon and follow me. Now, get up slowly and sit your old ass in that chair, and do not move. Gina, get up and stand here, front and center."

The old man begrudgingly squatted and slid into the chair, and GG stood up and moved toward me. She was a half dozen feet from me when I told her to stop.

"Take off all your clothes, Gina, and put them on this bureau."

"You sick fuck. If you think I'm going to let you do something sexual to me in front of my *grandfather…*"

"Lighten up, granny. This ain't foreplay. After all you've done to my family this week, I wouldn't touch you with your *dead uncle's*…well, just do what I'm telling you to do and be quiet."

She finished disrobing and covered herself with her two hands.

"Really? *Now* you've discovered modesty? Move over to the bed and lay on your stomach—nose pressed into the pillow, arms at your sides, palms facing up on either side of your ass. DO IT!"

She did as she was told, and the old man was already standing up and disrobing. He understood the drill. He finished, shrugged, and tilted his head, nonverbally asking if there was anything else.

"Go to the bathroom and turn on the shower, full blast, old man." I followed him to the bath, keeping myself between him and Gina, and watching her all the while to limit any risk of pointless shenanigans. He leaned his ancient ass over—a view I may never forget, no matter how much I try—and turned the shower spray on. I waved him back into the room with the gun barrel and told him to assume a similar position next to his charming granddaughter.

My gun was trained on them while I grabbed their discarded clothes and threw everything—shoes, socks, underwear, pants, shirts, even the old man's pocket handkerchief—into the bathtub where the shower was running. Everything was quickly becoming saturated, everything except the old man's belt. I doubled that up and smacked them both on the ass with it before I tossed that in the tub. They weren't going to put those clothes back on anytime too soon, especially because I didn't bother turning the shower off before I left.

"You know what, Gina? You're right. I sort of like beating your ass, figuratively and literally. Now don't go anywhere for a while, and let's not *ever* see one another again, okay?"

"Oh, and you asked why I killed your son, sir. It's simple. Even though he was a sadistic fuck who smiled while he described what he had been doing to my family, I could have overlooked his decision to torture and kill me because I got away. What he wanted to do to me didn't happen and was water under the bridge, but when he told me he was going to kill my sister and her children just for the sake of hurting my parents, I knew he was too dangerous to keep around. Keep that in mind, both of you. I don't know what sort of bullshit you think my family ever did to you. Again, what's done is done, but if you go after my family again, I will end you and everyone you care about."

I grabbed my shit and left. Chad wasn't at the front desk, or I'd have shot him in the ass on my way by for good measure, but instead I stepped outside to get in my car and leave. On the way to my car, I spotted the old black, stretched Cadillac limo, the same one that had been parked in front of the restaurant earlier in the evening when we'd been told Indi's and Angela's kids had been abducted. It wasn't one of those embarrassing casino limos with LED lights in the ceilings, wraparound sofas, and a full bar inside. It was old, elegant, and immaculate, much like the old man it carted around. The motor was running, and even though the windows were tinted so dark I couldn't see anything inside, I knew at least the driver was in there waiting for Gina and her grandfather to return. Other guys could've been in there too. There could've been a half dozen guys in there with bazookas as far as I could tell, so I ducked away cleanly, got in my Challenger, and made a mad dash out of the lot. Against my better judgment, I headed back to the

Turnpike to retrace my path to Philly, because I realized no matter where I went, this shit was going to follow me until it was concluded, so I might as well cut its head off now.

Once I was clear of the hotel, I called Guido.

God *damn*, what a week!

What a *day*!

THE LONG RIDE HOME

Once again, I was driving home to Philly to deal with family crap. Exactly seven days ago, I had just finished frolicking in a New Orleans restaurant's salad greens with the owner's naked wife and returned to the kitchen when a call came in from Uncle Guido that changed my life forever. Since then, I had become reacquainted with my childhood bestie and next door neighbor, Gina, killed her uncle, and now left her and her grandfather laying face-down and naked on a hotel bed with their saturated clothes sloshing around in the bottom of a half-filled bathtub.

I was on the phone with Guido again, except this time, *I* was calling *him* with an emergency. Before I could utter a word, Guido interrupted: "Kid, before you say anything, are you free to talk?"

"Yeah, I'm in my car, and I ..."

He interrupted again. "I want you to do the following, exactly in the order I'm telling you, and I don't want you to say another single word. Capice? Number 1, meet me at the same place we met when you first came home a week ago. Number 2, hang up the phone. Number 3, after you hang up, snap the phone in two pieces and throw them both out the window. Number 4, hurry up. G'bye." And he hung up.

I did as Guido instructed, and with the exception of the sonorous growl of the big V8 under the hood, the ride back to Philly was a quiet one. I'm not a big "talk on the phone" guy anyway, but somehow, I craved talking to someone, *anyone* once I tossed my phone out the window. If I had a phone, I probably wouldn't have used it, but without it, I felt lost. I actually considered pulling into a rest stop and buying a replacement burner, but G was clear. I wasn't to talk to anyone until I saw him, and I inferred from his "hurry up" comment I wasn't to stop unless it was an emergency.

What I *really* wanted to do was call Indi. I had this nagging urge to try to patch things up between us, even though it had only been a few hours since she slammed her door in my face, which probably means she doesn't want to talk to me, possibly ever, but certainly not tonight.

Like having a cell phone, if my relationship with Indi was fine, I'd probably be content not speaking to her for months, but knowing I couldn't call her made me crave hearing her voice. She occupied an important space in my life, and her absence created an uncomfortable void. As my mind fixated on Indi, my subconscious drifted off into daydreams. The concrete ribbon of Pennsylvania Turnpike passed beneath my muscle car, the tires making a *ka-thunk, ka-thunk* over every seam of every road panel for three hundred miles. I drove in that semi-conscious state for hours before I realized I had been driving in a semi-conscious state and had no recollection of anything between Pittsburgh and Harrisburg.

The last time I returned to Philly was last week to meet with Uncle Guido for the first time since my parents sold Sonny's to these conniving jackals. Here I was again, returning to Philly to meet G, only this time I was only gone a few hours, and once again, I was driving when I should have been sleeping.

If I was tired hours ago when I headed *west* on the Turnpike, I was catatonic now, heading east and completing an impromptu twelve-hour round trip. The road occasionally blurred in front of me. I think I actually fell asleep with my eyes open a couple times. Ordinarily I worry about getting speeding tickets, but sometimes on this return trip I actually noticed I was barely going twenty miles per hour because I was so tired and mentally disengaged.

The car meandered across the dotted lines between lanes a few times, interrupted only by the rumble strips PENDOT had installed to keep idiots like me from drifting off to sleep, and then off a cliff, and the harder I tried to stay focused and awake, the more I unwittingly lolled into a stupor.

It was early afternoon by the time I returned to the City of Brotherly Love. Unlike the night before when I drove past an illuminated and sleeping boathouse row, the place was now awash in fall sunshine, and rowers were on the river practicing their craft before the seasonal weather turned too cold for all but the most obsessed rowers to be out there. Traffic was heavy, especially inbound with me, and that was good news because the volume of cars heightened my attention, which quelled my sleep-deprived dozing, at least for a while.

After several *long* hours heading in the opposite direction from last night, I pulled the Challenger into a parking space in front of the Melrose Diner, just as Unc had instructed me to do on our brief call a few hours ago, and as I parked the car, I failed to notice Uncle G and two of his guys approach me from the side of the diner. I was so tired, Guido's tap on my window with his pinky ring nearly gave me a heart attack.

As I regained my composure, G spoke to me and then to Marco, one of his henchmen.

"Johnny, give Marco your car keys. Marco, take the car to the shop and check it and everything in it for devices, but don't leave here until I give you this bag 'cause I want you to check what's in it, too."

He handed me a bag: "Here. It's a change of clothes. Go to the men's room and take off *everything* you're wearing and put what you take off into this bag."

I did as I was told, swapped what I was wearing for what was in the bag (Levi's, a T-shirt, and flip-flops—no underwear) and put the stuff I was wearing in the bag. I handed the bag to G and he handed it to Marco, who left immediately.

"What was *that* all about?" I asked as I went to sit down in a booth.

He grabbed my arm and spun me around before I could get past him. "I'll tell you as we go. Follow me," and he pulled me out the door.

We stepped outside into the afternoon sun as shadows began to get longer on the pavement below our feet. Uncle Guido started talking. Listening helped distract me from my freezing toes. Midday or not, it was still November. Seriously, what adult would wear flip-flops outside in Philadelphia this time of year? Of course, just wearing a T-shirt wasn't a whole lot of help either. I coulda cut glass with my nipples, they were so cold and hard!

"Bad shit happened around here last night, kid, but before I tell you where we stand with any of it, I wanna hear about *your* night after you left town, and you'll have plenty of time to tell me about it. Right now, though, we need to go someplace private so they can't find you. If they were alone with anything you have, they could have installed listening or tracking devices, so we had to get rid of everything. Your car will be fine, but everything else you had had to get tossed."

"Unc, that's everything I own in the world in that car. *EVERYTHING!*"

"And you'll get the car back."

"But what about all of my stuff in it?"

"Was any of it irreplaceable?"

"Well, no, but …"

"Then be a man, for Christ's sake, and stop complaining. Some things are not replaceable—*people*, for example—but I'll buy you new stuff. Will that make you happy? I would think staying alive might be a little more important than a couple concert T-shirts and a pair of

'Home of the Whopper' joke underpants, but I'm not a whiny little bitch, so what do I know?"

"How'd you know about my 'Home of the Whopper' underpants?" I asked. Marilyn, Mr. Acchione's live-in nurse, had helped me out of them the other night after my first beating. I told her I'd gotten them as a joke to wear for Valentine's one year.

"How do you think? Marilyn told me and Joe about them the night she saw them, and the three of us laughed our asses off at your expense. She said you got them for Valentine's, but after she got a look at what you were concealing with them, Marilyn suggested Halloween might've been more appropriate—a trick more than a treat."

He had another little chuckle at my expense and said, "Let's get past this. Time is limited and we need to be sure we're prepared for what's coming. Tell me *everything* that happened since you left last night."

I told him the whole story, about me driving to Pittsburgh, getting the room, grabbing a shower, being surprised by the geezer and Gina, about how I escaped—the whole thing. It was a rare sighting, but when I mentioned spanking the two of them with the old man's belt, Uncle G let his guard down for a moment and smiled. Then he realized what he'd done and wiped it off his face as quickly as it appeared, like he somehow wasn't allowed to smile, not today, not the day after Joe had been murdered. Regardless, the smirk was there. I saw it.

"Thank god you're okay. If you ended up like Joe, your parents would never forgive me. *I'd* never forgive me."

"For the record, I'd probably never forgive you either," and I punched him in the arm. It was like punching a tree trunk.

We headed down the block and ducked into a row house I'd never been in before. He had safe havens stashed everywhere. He told me we'd be staying there for a while, watching the Melrose parking lot. I could get something to eat or drink from the kitchen, or just crash on the sofa, but I was strictly instructed not to open any curtains or otherwise draw attention to the place, meaning not turning on any lights, or a television, or anything. G wanted to remain incognito.

The house was typical—old, narrow, decorated in "early garage sale" style. The weird thing was this was actually someone's home, and not my uncle's safe house. G had a key, but there were photos of someone else's family in little frames everywhere, and there were drawings made by little kids, on the fridge. I was stumped. There was no reason on this Earth why *he'd* have access to this place, but there we were, key-holding guests in someone else's home.

"Shhh…don't wake the house."

"There are people sleeping here?"

"Yes. Upstairs. The husband works days. The wife's a nurse. She works the night shift and gets home in time to get the kids off to school in the morning. Then she sleeps. She's upstairs asleep right now, directly above us, so…*SHHHH*!"

"So, we're in a guy's house. He's out and his wife is upstairs asleep, and he'd be okay if he knew this?"

"Does 'shhh' mean something different today than it did when I was your age!"

"Fine. Whatever. I'll be sleeping too, then. Have fun 'spotting deer' or whatever the fuck you're doing."

"Watch your mouth. There's people upstairs."

"'There are' people, not 'there's people.' 'People' are plural, G. Besides, if just the wife is upstairs, it's 'There's a person upstairs.' Singular. Learn grammar, you old dago."

"I will come over there and kick your short-order-cook ass if you don't shut the *fuck* up," and he looked at me, crossed his eyes to let me know he was messing with me, and didn't intend to actually kick my ass, at least at the moment. Every now and then, the old man would find his sense of humor. It stayed well-hidden, but when he let it out, he was actually sorta fun to be with.

"What are we looking for?" I asked, this time in a very hushed tone.

"*I'm* watching to see if they followed you. I have this sense they left a bug on you, and I want to see if I was right."

"Would that be a good thing or a bad thing?"

"Believe it or not, a good thing."

"So them stalking me would be considered good?"

"In this case, yes. If they put a tracking device on you, that means they had a purpose for you and they had planned to let you go from the very beginning. If there was no device, then they won't be following you, they had no intention of letting you go, and you're on their hit list. Being marked for death is considered a bad thing in most circles of polite society. And these people are serious."

Suddenly, my interest in this surveillance game was renewed. "No shit?"

"You made good time getting back. They had to organize before they could get after you. Their guys probably didn't realize you had escaped and the old man's and that little bitch's clothes were soaking wet. That was a nice touch, by the way. I'll have to keep that in mind for any time I want to slow someone down. All that taken into consideration, you probably had a thirty-minute head start. You got here, got changed, we came over here…they're probably still about ten minutes out if they're coming at all. We'll stay here for an hour or so and…or not."

The elegant limo I'd spotted in Pittsburgh rolled past the front of our safe house and the rest of the neighborhood and pulled into a stall in front of the diner. A Cro-magnon refugee of a thug hopped out from the front passenger seat and lumbered inside the structure. He was gargantuan, and even from a half-a-block away, you could see he had a face that looked like it had been beaten by a large mallet, and then left that way. His nose was about two inches left of where it belonged. He had one, single, long eyebrow stretching across his entire forehead, and it was nearly as thick as it was long. His eyebrow (singular) was so hairy, it almost looked like it needed to be parted to the right or left, and it looked even more ridiculous because the top of his head was completely bald. His eyes were uneven. His mouth was crooked and only featured one lip—the bottom. If this hideous creature walked up to you and you shrieked, you'd try to convince him (it?) you were shocked by how handsome he was, because there's a very good chance he'd eat you if you made him angry.

We could see him duck through the six-foot-eight-inch high doorway and walk through the dining rooms and into the restroom corridor and even look behind the line at the cooks and kitchen staff. The Melrose employees all looked at him with a collective "What the fuck?" expression on their faces, but they knew better than to confront a guy who looked like this, so they just stood and watched him go about his business. He walked back outside and grunted his report to the old man and Gina, who were standing outside the car in the parking lot.

The old man was as dapper as ever in an entirely different (and dry) suit. He must've had luggage in the limo's trunk. Gina wasn't quite as lucky. She was standing in the parking lot wearing only a buttoned-down men's shirt that had been tailored for the old man but was a couple sizes too big for her. She had rolled up the sleeves to her wrists and the shirt's tail stretched to halfway between her knees and ankles. She was also barefoot.

If my feet were cold in flip-flops, hers must've been frozen solid coming in direct contact with the pavement. Her whole body looked like it was freezing. Her chin was in her chest and her shoulders were up around her ears. Her arms were crossed in front of her like she was trying to conserve heat, and she was spastically hopping from one foot to the other. She was clearly uncomfortable and standing outside only because she was told to do so. She had fucked up earlier, and now she was being taught a lesson in humility. Even from here I could see the rage on her face.

Guido's phone buzzed and the screen lit up. He'd received a text:

"Found device in pants and bag. Brought both back and left them in dumpster."

G nodded and smiled and looked back out at the lot. We couldn't see or hear the actual discussion, but one occurred nonetheless. The goon who searched the diner got back in the front seat, the old man and Gina returned to the back of the car, and it backed out of the lot and left.

"Ah, kid. Whatever would you do without me?"

"Well, I'd have probably stayed in New Orleans where I was living with a great-looking blonde nurse who loved parading around our apartment naked when she wasn't working and bringing in more money than me, but besides that…I'd still be happy."

Guido ignored my response. "Well, we know they want you alive. I can only imagine for what purpose. Come on. Let's get out of here so we don't wake anybody up."

Just then a woman appeared at the bottom of the steps and half-shrieked. G announced himself to her and she visibly relaxed. He put a hand on her shoulder and handed her a roll of cash, gave her a kiss on her cheek, and summoned me to leave.

I didn't ask. I just dutifully did what I was told to do.

GUIDO

"Where to next?" I asked. "Not for nothin', but I'm guessing Joe's place isn't an option..."

Guido was quiet for a moment and took a breath before answering, like in all the maneuvering this morning, he had momentarily forgotten about Joe. "No," he sighed. "Joe's won't work. It's an active crime scene. I'll take you back to my place."

"Ah, because your place is an *in*-active crime scene? If those walls could talk, am I right?" I kidded, but Guido didn't crack a smile. Losing Joe was hitting him hard, especially with the wound being so new and raw.

I'd known this man all my life. I'd been to his place exactly twice during those five decades—once as an infant, and once when I was in kindergarten. At this point, I couldn't even tell you with any confidence where he lived, not even what block it was on. That's exactly the way he liked things to be—anonymous.

Once he arrived in Philly, he never relocated again, not once. He wasn't exactly fancy either. He was the type of guy who probably found a "crash pad" when he first arrived on these shores, figured it worked, and then stayed there for the rest of his life. It wouldn't have surprised me if his dump wasn't even furnished, just a mattress on the floor and an orange plastic milk crate next to it as a night table. I envisioned long strips of wallpaper peeling off the walls from the ceiling to the floor and a 1950s refrigerator humming along in a corner filled only with a half-consumed carton of milk that expired twenty years ago, and a bag of lunch meat from a company that went out of business in 1977.

We pulled up to his row home which was a block away from my parents' row home. I couldn't believe he was a block away all these years and I had absolutely no idea.

The Cadillac sat at the curb in front of his place, engine idling like it was on a launch pad waiting for the word to take off. The front door of G's house opened and one of his crew stood there and nodded, indicating everything was good inside.

At the gesture, the guy in the back with me, but behind Guido in the passenger seat, got out of the Caddy, stepped to G's door, and waited for the old man to tap his window to exit. The driver remained at the wheel, in case we needed to make a quick escape. Guido, almost out of reflex, tapped lightly on the window glass with the back of his right hand. His big gold pinky ring made the impact, and its clinking was very loud within the confines of the car's interior. By this time, the guy sitting on the other side of me, behind the driver, was on the sidewalk surveilling the street, and he and the other guy from the back seat stood on either side of G as he exited the car and walked quickly up his front steps. I followed the three of them up the steps and into the house.

Guido's path from the car to the house was so well-orchestrated, the Secret Service could have taken notes to refine their process for protecting the President. Of course, nobody flanked me, because no one gave a shit whether or not I made it into the house safely, fuckers.

Once we were in and safe, one of the guys from the car remained with us and the other returned to the Caddy which slowly pulled away and rolled down the street.

One step into Guido's rowhome and it was like coming home, probably because the place was exactly like my parents' place, which was exactly like nearly every other row home in this neighborhood. The stairs to the second floor were directly in line with the front door, and the living room, dining room and kitchen ran front to back in that order. Everything was visible too, because like many other locals, Guido had removed all the walls dividing the rooms on the first floor. It was the "open concept" all the cool kids love these days, except homeowners like Guido didn't do this because it was trendy. They did it out of necessity.

A hundred or so years ago, when these places were built and smelled of newly cut wood and fresh plaster, there were walls separating these rooms from one another, but splitting this narrow, small floor into all those rooms made them uncomfortably small, like "Superman would be cramped getting changed in them" small. So, folks did what made sense. Instead of having to wait in line for someone to leave a room before entering, they just removed the walls so everyone could be together at the same time. Aesthetically and practically this was a great idea, and so far it has worked. I say "so far" because I don't know a single homeowner who consulted an architect or engineer to make sure none of those walls were holding up the second, or in some cases third, floors.

Naturally, when I stepped across the threshold, I scanned the open room. There were lights on under the cabinets in the kitchen and on a lone end table in the living room, which may not sound like much light, but in an area this small, it was plenty. Side-to-side the place was less than twenty feet wide, including the width of the stairs, and front to back it was probably about fifty. A big dog could come in the front door and be out the back door into the alley in probably three seconds. That's why so few neighbors have big dogs.

Speaking of which, the one man I would never suspect would have a pet had a ... thing sleeping, or maybe dead, on his living room sofa.

I say "thing" because I couldn't immediately determine without close inspection what it actually was.

"What is *that*?"

And then the scariest, most-serious man I've ever known squealed like a school girl and skipped over to he sofa.

"*This* is *Zippy*!" he announced in a sing-song way, dropping to his knees in front of the sofa so he could look the thing directly in its cataract-glazed eyes. He cupped Zippy's tiny head in his two catcher's mitt-sized hands and continued "Hiiii buddy."

If a big dog's time in through the front door and out the back could be measured in seconds, this thing's trip could be measured by a calendar—days, maybe seasons. Its body wasn't quite as long as a cheesesteak, but it moved about as quickly, which is to say "not at all."

Zippy never moved or acknowledge Guido or anything else. Its little tongue stuck halfway out its closed mouth, probably because there were no teeth to hold it back. Its skin was pink with grey patches here and there, and puckered everywhere like a chicken's skin after you pluck out its feathers. I could tell all this because it only had about a half dozen long hairs on its entire body, and they looked like they'd been teased up, for an overall appearance of cotton candy.

"That thing looks like an old man's ball-sack. You should call him Scrotum."

Guido never took his eyes off Zippy, though he had moved his right hand from cupping the thing's head to petting its tiny body, which probably felt like petting a deflating rubber balloon.

"The Zipster is sixteen years old, and he's been with me since he was a pup—first and only dog I've ever had."

"So, it's a dog?"

"Fuck you. Yes, it's a dog. What the hell else would he be? He's some sort of Jack Russell Terrier mixed with a bunch of other shit. One of the people in the neighborhood's dog got knocked up by a stray and I begrudgingly agreed to take the last pup of the litter off their hands. Best decision I ever made. This guy was full of energy as a pup, lemme just tell you."

"Well, it appears his battery is on low-charge, because I'm not entirely sure Scrotie isn't dead."

"Well, what do you expect? Do you think you'll be doing cartwheels when you're a hundred-and-two? Every time Joe would complain about getting old and all his aches and pains, I'd tell him it could be worse. He could be as old as Zippy. I mean, at least Joe could control his pee."

"Scrotie can't control his bladder?"

"No. He's a hundred-and-two for fuck's sake. It's okay. I make accommodations. I set this absorbent pee-pee pad on the sofa for him every morning before I leave. I have to replace it now though. For a little dog, he sure pees a lot."

"Well, that's a relief. I was worried that urine smell was coming from you, and did you really just say 'pee-pee pad?'"

Then I heard the squeak of a fart and bristled. "Please tell me that was him, not you."

"He's old, kid. He farts and pees. It's about all he does these days."

"Doesn't he shit, too?"

Guido looked behind Scrotie and nodded. "Yeah. It looks like he made a little one today. Good boy, Zipster."

I honestly couldn't believe what I was witnessing, and after this display, I was seriously rethinking my decision not to stay at Joe's, crime scene or not.

BE IT EVER SO HUMBLE

South Philly is a densely populated enclave established a couple centuries ago, predominately by the Irish before it became overrun with Italians a little more than a hundred years ago. Back before the Irish were settling here, it was bucolic, but then about 150 years ago, the city's borders were stretching in all directions and South Philly was incorporated into the city. Over time, the swamps to the south and east along the river were filled in and converted to docks for ship building and cargo loading and off-loading. Railway lines were run and industrial businesses opened and operated within close proximity to the river. The labor force to operate all that had to live somewhere, so the rolling fields to the immediate north and west of the Delaware River were gobbled up and became neighborhoods with offices, storefronts, and homes—lots of homes. Space was scarce, and so was money, so no acreage was squandered. Block after block of row homes whose sidewalls were connected to one another forming a continuous façade from street corner to street corner comprised neighborhood after neighborhood throughout the region. Building neighborhoods became a massive construction undertaking, and South Philly was "ground zero." The older homes were closest to the river, and the growth sprawled out from there.

Every block, everywhere you turned in South Philly, was lined with strings of narrow, two- or three-story brick row homes. This was typical for cities like New York and Baltimore, and was common elsewhere in Philly as well.

In the 1800s and early 1900s, wealthy city dwellers had massive country homes constructed a few miles outside downtown on expanses of acreage with rolling pastures and unimpeded views of nature. Regional rail lines were constructed to convey those affluent citizens to and from the city because roads barely existed, if at all. The urban center seemed a thousand miles away back then. By the 1920s, most of those homes within five miles of Center City were bulldozed and converted into row homes and manufacturing plants and distribution centers. People today look back on this as an architectural genocide, but in reality, the city had nowhere else to grow but through those architectural treasures, and it did so with the soulless discipline of a machine.

In most cases, those grand estates and magnificent palaces, filled with handcrafted woodwork and libraries and ballrooms and twenty-foot ceilings, were replaced with homogenized, modest, plain-faced row homes, filled with low-waged parents, their ten kids, and immigrant relatives seeking a place to land until they could get themselves on their feet.

The row homes were small and absolutely identical—kitchens in the basement (yes, the basement), living rooms and dining rooms on street level, and bedrooms above. Some were built before the days of indoor plumbing, so each was equipped with an outhouse in its tiny backyard.

Over time, these homes were renovated. Most would see their kitchens moved to the first floor and bathrooms added upstairs. Basements were typically converted to rec rooms, or apartments for older children, or even dormitories for the aforementioned familial immigrants. In many cases, and I can only imagine the multitude of civic palms that had to be greased to permit this to happen, street-facing living room windows were replaced by storefronts and families would sell cheesesteaks, or bread, or desserts, or other family specialties to the public directly from their homes. In other cases, entire homes would be converted to restaurants or dry goods stores.

Ironically, even though the castles of the wealthy were built to endure a thousand years, it would be these drab, crappy row homes that would linger indefinitely. A hundred years later, most of those neighborhoods were still intact, and some of them, like pockets of South Philly, had thrived and look better today than they did when they were new.

If you were like my uncle, had money, and wanted to live in something more fitting of your station, however, you had little choice. Since there was no vacant land nearby where one could build anything of substance, and there was nowhere to expand a row home except straight up, those who came into money moved to the northern or western suburbs, or east across the river to New Jersey, where big houses sat on acreage.

Somehow, Guido figured out a third option. He stayed humble. He bought an ordinary row home decades ago, and then bought the one next door sometime later where both his body guard and his housekeeper could stay. His was essentially a bachelor pad with the first floor set up for entertaining and eating, the entire second floor redesigned with a single master bedroom, a small office and a large master bathroom, and a basement where I'd be spending the evening—essentially an efficiency apartment without windows.

"Fairly humble digs, unc. I guess you can't afford anything a little bigger?"

"Very funny, junior. This neighborhood is ground zero for my enterprise, so it's important I live here. It's so ordinary outside it's practically invisible. It's plenty big for just me, and my personal security detail is next door. This is sort of like my own personal White House—part residence, part office, part dormitory with the guys living next door. Who knows? Maybe someday all of this will be yours and you can load the place next door with hot and cold running bimbos."

"Ahhh, a boy can dream, Unc. Not that I'm not grateful for you putting me up, but I *can* stay at Joe's if it's easier for you. Someone should probably keep an eye on his place."

"Place is an active crime scene, kid. It's crawling with cops and forensics and the place has been redecorated with caution tape. There are plenty of eyes on it. Trust me."

He breathed in and out. The gravity of that statement merited time to be absorbed. He also needed a moment to regain his composure because news of Joe's death was only a few hours old and Guido was still visibly stinging.

"They murdered him there. While you were at dinner and those fucking animals were kidnapping children, Gina and another guy—not her grandfather, because I asked—went to Joe's house, bound Marilyn, and strangled Joe in front of her. That sweet, smart, gentle man lives ninety-five years, *never* hurts *anyone*, rubs shoulders with presidents and other leaders of the free fucking world, and that little bitch invades his home and murders him like he was nothing. That piece of shit you spared murdered my friend. That's why I was so worried about you last night, kid. If she could do that to Joe, she could certainly do it to you. That's why I wanted to know if they had other plans for you, or if they intended to murder you too."

"I had no idea if anyone else is at risk, or what to think besides the old saying that keeps playing in my head—'win the battle, lose the war.' Once I found Joe, I put armed details on everyone else, including your girlfriend and her pygmy brother. I'll do everything possible to keep everyone safe, but I can't be everywhere all the time. We need to cut the head off this snake."

"I'm so sorry about Joe. I had…*have* the utmost respect for him. He was an amazing man and I was looking forward to getting to know him better. It's my fault. If I hadn't let Gina go, none of this would be happening."

Guido looked at me calmly and seriously and said, "You're right. If not for your mercy, Joe would be alive, but you did exactly what he would have done, and he'd have thought less of you if you did otherwise. That's the difference between him and me. He would have shown her mercy, too, but you can't treat a lioness like a domestic kitty cat, kid. She's a killer, and you let her go. Let's fix that error in judgment, shall we?"

He was pissed, and wanted revenge, and you know what? I was good with that.

Guido was a strong and serious man. Everywhere he went, he went a hundred miles per hour and with authority. He stomped, no *stormed* when he walked. He always seemed to be on his toes, ready to pounce on whoever or whatever confronted him. Even when he sat, he'd lean forward, like he was waiting to lunge at whoever was in front of him. I always swore the chairs in his house could have done without their backs, because I never saw him lean back and relax, ever. He is also one of those fortunate Mediterranean people whose skin is perfect—not a wrinkle, not one. The man defied time.

Although he and Mr. Acchione were physically different, they were cut from the same cloth. They were tough grinders who never made excuses. They accepted setbacks as part of the game and worked them into solutions. They were old-school, the best part of that school.

Back in the late '50s, Guido arrived in Philadelphia with virtually no ability to speak the local language. It didn't matter. Just as he overcame every other obstacle in his life, he quickly learned to communicate in English, at least enough to meet his needs. He didn't become a linguist, mastering the tongue of his adopted home, ensuring his grammar and usage were always perfect, shaving off pieces of his accent every day of his life, trying to disguise himself as a local. He learned the language so it could be a tool for him to do what needed to be done. If he used an incorrect tense, or conjugated something incorrectly, or used the wrong word or pronunciation, he'd assume you knew what he was saying, and if you didn't, you could ask, but if you derided him for being wrong, he'd glare at you and not say a word, and you'd shit your pants in fear for being an impertinent, pedantic jackass.

Over the years his verbal skills became as good as almost anyone else's. No one would ever mistake him for an Ivy-Leaguer like Mr. Acchione, but anyone who would infer he was somehow intellectually inferior because of his "everyman" speech would be making a very grave tactical error.

"Kid, siddown. We gotta talk."

"You tell me what needs to be done, Unc, and I'll take care of it. That old man was a treasure and it's my fault he's gone. If not for my stupid compassion for Gina, he'd still be with us. I want to fix this. I *need* to fix this."

"That's not the point here, John. If it hadn't been Gina, it would have been someone else on that crew. And remember what I told you when you first came home last week and learned about the deception of your parents. It's not your fault when someone else does something despicable. It's *their* fault, and *they* need to be held accountable. Taking care of Gina, although definitely on the agenda, is not our main purpose. We need to resolve the root of this problem, and it's time for me to tell you what's really going on."

"Gee, Uncle G, are you sure I'm ready? I mean, I've only been beaten to a pulp a couple times this week because of this fiasco."

"Shuddup and listen, kid. No. Better yet, lemme ask you a question. Did you ever wonder why Gina got married so young, or why she started poppin' out little Ginas when she was only fifteen or sixteen, or why you, her next door neighbor and probably closest friend, not only wasn't invited to the wedding but only found out she had gotten married after she dropped out of school?"

"Do we have to start this conversation talking about Gina, Unc? The thought of her makes me physically ill."

"That's not my point. I'm only using her as an example. Try to stay with me, here. Did you ever wonder about those things or not?"

"I hadn't really given them much thought, to be honest with you, but now that you mention it, yeah. I guess it always seemed a little strange. I mean, girls got knocked up in high school. It happened, but Gina was the only one who got married first and had kids on purpose. One day she was going to school with me in the morning, and the next she was married and dropped out. We were close. I mean, our houses shared a wall with one another. We literally slept headboard to headboard on either side of the wall separating our houses, yet her house always seemed somehow secretive. Why? Was she in, like, Federal witness relocation or something?"

"Sort of. Would it make more sense if I told you she was Romani?"

"Not really. I mean, I'm half Roman, too—half on each side of the family as a matter of fact. I think the rest is Neapolitan."

"Not 'Roman,' you uncultured dolt. *Romani*. Some people call them Gypsies, but no one says that in polite company anymore. It's politically incorrect."

"She's a gypsy?"

"Didn't I just tell you no one says that word anymore?"

"Sorry, but still, no shit? Well, I guess that *could* explain things—married young, kids young, not a lot of formal education. I get it. I mean it's sort of stereotypical, but yeah. I see it. How'd you know?"

"Because I'm Romani too."

"You're a *gypsy*? Get. The. Fuck. *Outta* here! I didn't think we had gypsies in this country. I mean, aren't they like all shrouded in secrecy, telling fortunes, and living in fringed caravans in weird parts of Europe or something?"

"Well, obviously not, since I'm sitting right here in front of you, and Gina grew up next to you for about sixteen years, dumbass. You wanna hear a little story? Do you have the time? You wanna dazzle me with more stereotyping first? Maybe call me a gypsy again?"

"No. I'm fine. I want to hear this, but I am a little peckish. I haven't eaten since last night's dinner."

"Enrico," Guido called to his man in the kitchen. "Any chance you can throw something together for us to eat for lunch?"

Enrico responded, asking if sandwiches would be okay, and Guido approved. By the time we walked twenty feet into the kitchen and sat down, there were already two *magnificent* hoagies waiting for us. I have no idea how Enrico did it. It's as if he froze time, spent twenty minutes conjuring the perfect sandwiches, and then snapped his fingers for time to resume. Any other mortal would have spent all morning assembling these beauties.

In case you're not familiar with hoagies, they're sandwiches, but not just any sandwiches. They are as much a Philadelphia icon as the vaunted cheesesteak. If local lore is to be believed, the hoagie originated on Hog's Island, a small island off the southeast corner of the city where they built boats for the second World War and where the Philadelphia airport now stands (and probably sinks, because that whole area is a soppy marsh). Back when it was still a shipyard, it was littered with Italians who ate the local, meat-filled sandwich, called a Hoggie, which ultimately became known as a Hoagie.

In its most basic form, a hoagie is a long, seeded Italian roll filled with cheese, lunch meats, lettuce, tomato, onion, sweet peppers, maybe pickles, but definitely olive oil and oregano. There's an overabundance of sandwich shops throughout the region that will sell you a hoagie, but that doesn't mean you should buy them from just anywhere. Although some are downright delicious, others are affronts to your tastebuds—lacking quality ingredients or including such things as tuna fish salad, or worse yet, mayonnaise instead of olive oil.

On this occasion, Enrico made his case for sainthood. His hoagies were perfection—Sarcone's rolls (everything starts with the right roll), drizzled but not drowned in olive oil, layered with freshly sliced lunch meat and cheese from a local 9th Street deli (capicola, prosciutto, dried salami, *sharp* provolone), fresh leaves of iceberg lettuce (*never* that shredded shit), a fresh, juicy New Jersey beefsteak tomato (how he got one of these so beautiful and ripe in November defies all laws of time and space), a generous layer of sweet peppers, a half a palm full of cubed red onion, salt, pepper, a *light* dusting of garlic powder, a sprinkling of oregano, and finally a quick stripe of good balsamic vinegar for a surprise of sweetness for our fortunate palates.

These are the basic ingredients, but much like a blank canvas, a brush, and a pallet of paints are tools for creating a portrait, it takes the touch of an artist to bring it all together and create a masterpiece. Enrico is the Michelangelo of hoagies.

All hail Enrico, the culinary maestro who now quietly stood by with a dishtowel draped over his forearm and his arms folded humbly across his chest, his white apron exhibiting subtle stains of pride from errant tomato juice squirts. He was awaiting our verdict as Guido and I each took our first bites. Guido bit down, nodded his head in affirmation and didn't stop biting and chewing until the entire sandwich was gone, making yummy sounds and rolling his eyes the entire time. I, on the other hand, merely placed my sandwich back on the plate after my first bite, stood up, and applauded.

We finished our hoagies without uttering a sound, then Guido picked up where we left off.

"Good. Now, try to stay awake, and please shut up."

"Romani are very hierarchical—patriarchical, matriarchical, that kinda shit. It's very family-oriented, and leadership comes from elders, period. For years, Gina's great-great-grandmother, Isabella, was the leader of the family. She came from the same hometown as your grandfather Al. She was about his age, too. Like you and Gina, they were friends since they were little kids. Unlike you, though, only Isabella's father was Italian. Her mother was Romani. Bella's mother ran away from her family and escaped her arranged marriage to marry Isabella's father, and as a result, she was considered contaminated and banished from the Romani.

Isabella was destined to marry well for the benefit of her family's future. Romani or not, in those days, marriages were pre-arranged by parents, and children did as they were told, unlike today when they're belligerent assholes, like you."

"But, didn't you just say her mother ignored the pre-arranged marriage thing? And by the way, it's 'patriarchal' and 'matriarchal'" I added, with just a note of sarcasm and irony.

"Would you like me to punch you in the face with all the correcting the way I talk? And yeah, as it turned out, the fruit didn't fall far from the tree. Isabella was betrothed at birth to a man much older than her, because her father spotted an opportunity to combine the families and expand his land holdings. This sort of arrangement was very typical. Marriages then were not liaisons between two lovers. They were business arrangements—liaisons between two organizations who would benefit mutually from combining two families. The Romani continue this practice to this day. It's what happened to Gina. Even though the Romani weren't involved with Isabella, at least not before she got pregnant, they would have approved conceptually of her father's plan for her marriage. Isabella's mother's Romani family may have shunned her, but they still kept tabs on her."

"So what, my grandfather was hot for this Isabella and she spurned him for this pre-arranged guy?"

"No. Not even close. If you'd like to know what happened, I'll tell you, but not if you interrupt me, so stop it."

"Sorry, yeah. Go ahead."

"… anyway, Isabella's parents had made arrangements with her future husband's family right after she was born. She and this man were to be married right after her fifteenth birthday. Isabella never really knew the details, though, and she didn't care. She was very headstrong, and considered herself to be a modern woman and didn't want anything to do with the old ways. So without her parents' knowledge, just before she turned fifteen, she was out looking for her own husband—typical romantic shit: fall in love, blah blah blah. She didn't want an arranged marriage. Like most girls her age, she craved love and didn't see herself as a chip in a business deal.

"Al wasn't looking for love or anything marriage related for that matter. He was a teenaged boy. Like you, he dreamt of traveling—seeing the world or settling in America and finding his fortune."

"But that wasn't going to happen because he was going to knock up Isabella and screw everything up, right? Am I right?"

Guido just stopped talking and stared at me. He stared for about ten seconds, which feels like absolutely *forever* in real life, especially from him.

Anyway, when Guido was finally convinced he had my undivided attention *and* silence, he spoke again.

"If you want to hear this, stop interrupting me. You have no idea what the fuck you're talking about, so stop trying to anticipate a plot twist. Just stop it. Am I making myself clear? *STOP* it!"

He made a persuasive point, so I shut up and listened.

"As I was saying, they were two people on very different trajectories. Did they teach you that word in business school, college boy? 'Trajectory'? Look it up. Anyway, they were both teenagers and one day they were heading to sit under this huge shade tree where they sat every day. Isabella was unusually quiet and anxious, and Al was giddy. He could hardly wait to tell his best friend his amazing news. He had finally saved enough Lira to book steerage on a steamer to America and was leaving in a week. A friend of his had arrived in the U.S. a year earlier, and was offering to sponsor Al. His boat was destined for Philadelphia, not Ellis Island, but that's really all he knew. He really was a lot like you—incapable of staying put, and I can't tell you how much I miss that son of a bitch. He died *way* too young. I'll tell you all about Al sometime—his *real* story. The one your own pop doesn't even know.

"But getting back to Isabella, she had a secret of her own, and she needed to share that burden with her best friend.

"She had met a young man recently and became smitten. It was a fast romance—a little too fast as it turned out, because she was pregnant—at fourteen. While she was sneaking around behind their backs, her parents were literally planning her wedding day to the guy they'd arranged for her to marry. Carrying some other guy's kid was going to be a problem. If that wasn't bad enough, when she told her lover she was pregnant, he panicked and without telling her, ran off to fight in the war—World War I. You've heard of it? It was in all the papers. Anyway, Isabella was pregnant and she *thought* her parents *might* kill her, but she *knew* they would probably disown her. Her only relief was the belief her lover would scoop her up and take her to some fantasy land. What she *didn't* know was she was about to be abandoned by her family *and* her lover, and a global war was just getting started.

"She was terrified about her father's reaction and needed to talk to someone, and Al was the only one she could turn to. If the shit hit the fan, and she was left alone, she hoped Al would figure it out, and at the very least convince the local convent to take her in. He was going to be her safety valve."

"Holy crap! She must've been scared to death, and she was just a kid! I know. I interrupted again. Sorry. Please continue."

"… anyway, they meet up that day, like they did most days. Al used to get all nostalgic whenever he would tell me this story, which was often. You could see him imagining his home as he spoke.

"The fact is, by the time he was telling me about it in the '50s, the town of his youth only existed in his mind. Allied bombs in World War *II* had decimated Valmontone, leveling nearly eighty percent of the city. The ancient buildings and city gates still existed for him, though, in his mind, and they would until his death. He was never able to return."

Guido continued, "Both Al and Isabella were quiet on their walk, and barely said two words to one another on the way up the hill. Al noticed her uneasiness.

"'I know I've been a little strange lately,' Al told her, 'but that's because I've been waiting to tell you my big news. You remember how I've been talking about going to America?'

"'Of course,' she replied, even though she only half-heard him. She was miles away, obsessed with her own predicament.

"Al turned to her and grabbed her hands in his. When she turned to face him, he looked her in the eyes and said, 'It's finally happening. I have enough money now. My papers are all in order and I've reserved a spot on a steamer. I'm leaving for the port tomorrow. The ship departs the next day. I'm going, Isabella. I'm finally leaving on my adventure! I'm getting out of here. I'm going to find the world!"

"Al was so wrapped up in his own plans, he never once thought how his leaving would affect his friend. The only thought in his adolescent head was how excited *Isabella* would be for *him*, and how great this whole situation was for *him*. He was blissfully ignorant of the feelings of others, just like every other fifteen-year-old boy in the world.

"Isabella looked at him in disbelief, because she was a fourteen-year-old girl, and she was only thinking about herself, too. This was the worst possible news she could receive. She was hoping to come on this walk and convince him to shelter her if necessary, be there for her. Instead, she was losing the only ally she had. The world felt like it was closing in around her, and she broke down into sobs, got up, and ran home. Al called after her, asking her to stop, but she yelled for him to leave her alone and go away, that she never wanted to see him again.

"She got her wish. That was literally the last time they were together.

"Of course, being a self-absorbed teenager, Al misinterpreted her outburst as that of a young girl who secretly loved him and hoped they'd be together forever, never imagining there could be something else going on in her life that could inspire her to behave that way. It wasn't until a decade later he learned why she was crying, and it had nothing to do with any amorous feelings on her part for him.

"Teenaged boys are morons.

"Isabella ran home, and even though Al came by to see her again when he got down the hill and stopped by the next morning as well before he left, she wouldn't acknowledge him. In her mind, his assistance was no longer a viable option for her, and she had to move on. She was furious with him, even though he did absolutely nothing wrong.

"Al, still completely oblivious to what was going on with Isabella, made the long trek to the port, carrying the entirety of his worldly possessions in a beat-up, brown, cardboard suitcase with a broken clasp. Although he didn't have a car, he traveled like you, except the world had yet to invent Hefty bags."

"—cheapest, most replaceable luggage there is," I interjected.

He looked at me, tilted his head, and then rolled his eyes. Apparently, he wasn't a fan of my interruptions, *or* economizing.

"There she was," he continued, "this young, terrified girl. She was so afraid of how this was all going to end up, she hadn't slept more than a few minutes in a row in days, maybe weeks, and when she did, her dreams were filled with nightmares of how her father was going to react when he found out she was pregnant. One day, not long after

Al had left for America, she found the nerve, in what she believed to be an opportune moment, to confide in her mother."

"That was a mistake, I'm guessing," I blurted out accidentally.

"Yup. Her mother became furious and dragged Isabella, who was barely five feet tall and was waifishly thin, to the kitchen to confront her father with the news.

"It did *not* go well.

"You know the rest. She blamed Al for her being pregnant. Her father swore vengeance against your family, and the vendetta was born, blah blah blah."

"Wait. I thought you said her father was Italian and her mother was *shunned* by the Romani, so how do the Romani figure into all this?"

"Ahhh. We're not quite done yet, are we? Well, in order to conceal Isabella's pregnancy and hopefully salvage the arranged marriage, which would bring her family wealth and position, her mother knew what had to be done. She needed her Romani family to care for Isabella during the pregnancy, but before that could happen, she had to beg them to reinstate her to the family. Since they didn't have instant messaging, or even phones for that matter, her mother wrote a letter, groveling to her sister in Spain, and handed it to Isabella, who was to turn it over when she arrived there days later. In the letter, her mother detailed the circumstances surrounding Isabella, asked to be reinstated into the family, and also asked her sister to take Isabella in. In return, Bella's aunt and the rest of the Romani clan would have access to the future fortunes Bella's marriage would bring the family.

"Bella was oblivious to any of this. The first time she learned of the rift between her mother and that side of the family was when her aunt told her about it after reading the letter. Like you, Bella never knew who the Romani were either, but in her defense, unlike you, she was only fourteen and never went to college. I have no idea what your excuse for such ignorance is.

"As you might imagine, under normal circumstances, her shunning family would have told Isabella to hit the road, but Romani recognize an opportunity when they see it, especially the prospect of having a hand in a couple thousand acres of fertile, valuable Italian farmland, so they accepted the proposition.

"Once Isabella's father dumped her at the train depot, she was headed for Spain, which was neutral during the war and turned out to be a safe haven for her and her son. Unfortunately, even after the war ended in 1918, she had to wait a couple years to return home because of the outbreak of the Spanish flu pandemic which killed five percent of the world's human inhabitants, Bella's parents included! She made it back to Valmontone, and even though she discovered her parents were gone, she fulfilled their wishes and manipulated her betrothed into fulfilling his obligation and marrying her, and she and her Romani relatives converted those farms into an international business concern, but that's a much longer and more complicated story."

"Wouldn't her pregnancy have nullified the marriage contract?"

"Hmmm. Good point. You've been paying attention, except her husband had no idea she had been pregnant."

"Didn't the presence of a toddler sort of inspire curiosity?"

"She anticipated that and left her son behind in Spain to be raised by her aunt. It was incredibly difficult for Isabella to walk away from the child she'd raised since giving him life five years earlier, but she did what needed to be done for the greater good."

"Look," he concluded. "A lot has happened between 1914 and now, and I'll tell you all about it sometime, but for now, I have work to do, and you need to get some sleep. Go downstairs and make yourself at home. I'd tell you to unpack, but since we threw all your clothes and everything else you own in a dumpster, you'll have less to do before you go to bed. You're welcome."

GRAVITY

My bedroom was in the basement. That may sound terrible, with no windows to let in natural light and no views of the outside world, but the views in South Philly aren't really all that breathtaking since they're usually of parallel parked cars and houses directly across the street, so I wasn't missing out on much there and natural light streaming into my room wakes me up. Those of us who go to bed late and sleep until noon love the prospect of a subterranean bedroom that can be rendered pitch black. And in this house, sub-street level did not mean sub-par. To the contrary, this level was outfitted beautifully.

None of this mattered, of course, because between my *very* full tummy and my distinct lack of sleep, which now weighed on me like an anvil glued to my forehead, I landed on the guest room bed and was asleep before my face hit the pillow.

Sometime later, I woke up. My face was still where it had landed earlier, as were my chest, legs, and arms. I hadn't moved since I landed in bed, and although I probably should have felt stiff after being still for so long, I was actually oddly refreshed. I had no idea how long I'd been asleep because there was no light or darkness outside to use as a frame of reference. Windowless basement bedrooms don't tend to provide many outdoor clues.

I figured I had probably made it to my room sometime in the late afternoon, but I was so catatonic for so long, it could be tomorrow already. I really had no idea.

What I did know was I was no longer tired, and after rolling over and staring at the ceiling for a half-hour, trying to force myself back to sleep, I decided to get up, leave my ideal sleeping quarters, and go exploring.

There was a glow coming from the kitchen doorway upstairs, so I figured someone was awake. Maybe Guido was burning the midnight oil, or Enrico could make me another hoagie. Since I'm like a hyperactive toddler on crack when I'm finally awake, I bounded up the steps and started asking questions before even knowing if anyone was upstairs.

"So what's the story behind this crib…*G?*"

I should have waited until I was in the room before I spoke. In fact, I shouldn't have spoken at all. I should have walked through the doorway, read the room, turned around, and left in silence. In fact, I shouldn't have gone upstairs at all. I should've just stayed in my room where I was, because I was intruding!

Guido was sitting at the kitchen table, staring down at the floor, like he was Superman surveying the basement through the kitchen floor boards. He was seated in a wooden chair like he was about to compete in an Olympic Seated Long Jump competition, which didn't actually exist, but if it did, Guido had the starting position perfected.

His feet were flat on the floor, set outside the front legs of the chair. His knees were thrust forward. His butt was only halfway on the edge of the seat and he was leaning forward as always, his shoulders directly above his knees. Imagine the profile of a human lightning bolt from shoulder to ankle, and you'd not only understand how Guido sat, but also the spirit of his posture.

His hands were usually clasped between his knees, or set on the table in front of him. His head would be upright, meaning there was no slouching, and he'd be boring imaginary holes into the wall directly in front of him with his intense, laser-focused stare.

This time, though, his posture was noticeably different. He wasn't about to lunge like a beast watching his prey. He was soft and sullen. He was seated like a lightning bolt, sure, but his hands weren't clasped together between his thighs. Instead, his elbows were on his thighs, and his palms were cupping his face, which hung below his rounded shoulders. This was the most vulnerable I had ever seen him, especially because his shoulders were shaking and he was quietly sobbing.

He sat up quickly when he heard me walk in. He threw his shoulders back and his head up to assume his usual posture, because Guido didn't want to be caught being human. Unfortunately, more than his posture belied his emotions. His cheeks were wet with tears and his eyes were red and wet. His gaze wasn't intense. It was soft and sad. If a facial expression could be described as heartbroken, this would be it.

For the first time in my life, I noticed how old Guido was. He usually looked twenty years younger than his age. In this moment, he was wearing every single day of his eighty years, maybe even more.

Even his attire was that of a tired old man. Guido was always disheveled, but never casual. Here, in his hard, wooden chair, he sat in his stocking feet. His sleeves were rolled up. His tie was on the table, with his balled-up sport jacket. His entire look sighed exhaustion. He looked tired, the kind of tired that comes from his soul, the kind of tired brought on by emotional fatigue and surrender.

The gravity in the room seemed to double. Even the air was heavy, somber. Guido's sadness was palpable, like there was a hole in his chest where his heart should be, and he was making no effort to restore it. Instead of springing to his feet as he would normally, Guido merely stayed in his chair and turned toward me, like he was waist-deep in quicksand with cement bags in his pockets. At least in that moment, in the privacy of his home, he appeared beaten and had succumbed to a stronger force—loss of a loved one.

"Sorry, kid. You were saying?" His tone was somewhere between exasperation and fatigue. He was winded.

"It wasn't important, Uncle Guido. I'll leave you alone."

He looked me in the eye and said almost apologetically, "Please don't."

"Are you sure?"

He nodded and gestured with his left hand for me to sit at the table and join him, which I did.

"I'm sorry about Joe," I said. "I really liked him." That sounded even more stupid when I heard it than it did before I said it, but I couldn't think of anything better to say.

"Good, because he was your family. He was a good man, but he was also a great man who accomplished so much, touched so many lives, did so much good, and never sacrificed his character, even when he knew too damned well maintaining his character would cost him dearly. He was so smart, and so knowledgeable, and he *never* hurt *anyone*. Even his adversaries liked and respected him, and whenever he spoke, people stopped and listened, not because he was the most powerful man in the room, but because what he said was usually thoughtful and correct. He was also my best friend, and the loneliest man I'd ever met. I guess with him gone, that title is mine."

"You're never alone, Unc. You have your crew. You have me, and Mom and Pop and Angela."

"Lonely isn't the same as alone, son. I love you all, but Joe and I shared a deeper connection. We had been through so much together over a half-dozen decades—we had become one person in many ways. Sometimes, when we were talking to one another, it felt like we were actually talking to ourselves. He was both my counsel and therapist. At this point in my life, the runway's too short to replace someone like that, even if such a thing could be possible in the first place, which it isn't.

"I remember last week, the first night you stayed in his place, he and I were sitting in his parlor and he told me what a good team he and I were, and wondered what would happen when one of us died. I told him when one of us died, I'd be sure to pick up the pieces and move on, obviously telling him he'd go first. We both laughed at that, not realizing he'd be leaving me in a matter of days not years. Now I realize there are no pieces to pick up. His loss is intangible. It's vapor, a void of the space he used to occupy. I know it's all still fresh, but I'm having a hell of a time coming to terms with it, especially since I'm sitting here, and he's laying on a steel shelf in a fucking freezer in the morgue. I guess I should be grateful for the sixty or so years we had together, but that actually does nothing to ease the pain, especially because sixty years passed by like this," and he snapped his fingers.

"What do you mean he's my family," I asked. "Aside from being our lawyer, how does Joe fit into all this? For that matter, how do *you* fit into it?"

Guido looked at me. A tired, resolute smile eased across his face, like he was being unburdened, and he nodded.

"Kid, this is one *hell* of a weird story, and now that Joe's gone, I guess I should share it with you, because if I don't and something happens to me, Joe's *story* will die, and that can't happen. I couldn't protect Joe, but I'll be damned if I won't at least protect his story. If you don't mind, why don't you make us a pot of coffee and when you come back, I'll tell you something not even your father knows."

Then he paused, furrowed his brow, and sighed. He stared forward into the abyss, at absolutely nothing and said very solemnly, "I'm the only one left." He let that hang in front of him like he was reading it and couldn't make sense of it.

Several minutes went by, much of which was spent trying to figure out where he stored the stuff to make coffee, but I finally set a mug of coffee in front of him. He started up exactly where he left off.

"...so I'm gonna have to burden you with it, kid," he said lightly, with a weak, easy smile.

"With what?"

"Joe's story," he replied, acting as if I'd forgotten why we were there.

"Your family's story really only began when Fredo landed in Philly. Prior to that, it was just him. If you looked for ancestors in Italy, you'd never find any."

"Because they were all killed by the vendetta?" I asked.

"No," G replied. "It's because his family never existed, not really at least. I mean sure, everyone has parents, but Al had no idea who his were. He was a 'Foundling.' Unwanted infants would be placed by their mothers on something called a 'Foundling Wheel'—a sort of 'lazy Susan' built into the side of convents and orphanages. The child's mother would spin the wheel from the outside of the convent, and the baby would appear on the inside. A bell would ring, the mother would disappear into the anonymous ether outside, and the nuns would have a new orphan to raise. They'd name them, too. In Al's case, he was named "Elfo Mantelli," which loosely meant an elf wrapped in a cloak. Al wasn't too thrilled with the name Elfo, so he unofficially changed it to Alfredo when he was a little older, because it sounded similar, and that was the name he inscribed on his emigration documents. So you see, there really are no 'Mantellis.' That name was just as made-up as Valmonti."

All I could do was blink. "Are you fucking kidding me, Unc? I don't even know how to process that. You're telling me I basically have no legitimate last name. You're right. No wonder no one told my pop! It's one hell of a story, but how does Joe fit into this?"

"Oh, that's not the story, kid. That doesn't even scratch the *surface* of the story. The story is a really doozy. The grandfather you knew had one *hell* of a past before you met him. Hang on to your seat, because things are about to get a whole lot crazier.

"What if I told you Joe Acchione is your pop's half-brother? Unlike me, he's your *real* uncle. It all started when Al first hit the U.S. shores in 1914."

Vaudeville and Fredo

An old married couple lay in bed in the dark, basking in the post-coital glow. The husband stared at the ceiling and said, "No matter how much I earn, how much I have, how far I've gone, nor how high I've flown, I will never feel satisfied." Without missing a beat, the old woman said, "Laying here under you all these years, I completely understand."

"Nice," he replied. "That's a good one. Remind me to write that down in the morning. I'll use it in my act," and that's exactly what the old vaudevillian did. That joke became a staple of his quickly recited repertoire, delivered every night in the timeslot between the box juggler and the burlesque dancer.

Vaudeville programs went on for hours and included dozens of individual acts—everything from dramatically delivered soliloquies to one-act plays, clowns hurling pies at one another, and anything you can imagine in between. With all those performances came crowds of performers congregating and passing behind the scenes, and stage-hands rushing to transition from one act's set to the next. Backstage mid-performance was like Grand Central Station at peak travel time, except no one ever left!

The sphere of space surrounding the stage was three-dimensional chaos.

Dozens of ropes hung from pulleys above the stage, and each served a different purpose when pulled or released. Curtains were drawn. Painted backdrops came down from above and went back up again when the act concluded. Bags of sand provided counterweights, and calloused hands tugged and tied ropes below. There were stagehands scrambling over head as well, traversing the stage fifteen feet in the air across catwalks, sitting in suspended buckets dropping stage props, like confetti for a wedding, or soap flakes for a snowstorm as the scenes required, or sometimes they'd even make repairs on-the-fly when something broke mid-act, and something *always* broke mid-act.

The noisy stage of wide, worn wooden planks and trapdoors echoed the performers' footsteps like they were wearing horseshoes. The space below the stage was hollow because, you guessed it, performers crawled around under there to disappear or reappear through trapdoors in the stage floor. Stagehands were down there too to facilitate performer movement, or assist with costume changes, or pop up from below between sets to bring up props and quickly scoot through the openings and pull the lids closed when the curtain rose, so the audience was never the wiser.

The entire sub-stage area was gridded with scaffolding to hold up the stage. To get through that structure, performers and crew had to crawl and navigate idle props and one another. It was a lesson in contortion and wandering in pitch darkness. It was *not* unusual to hear a clunk on a stage board from below in the middle of a performance, followed by an angry expletive from someone whose head was growing a welt from a misstep below. That was often greeted with bursts of laughter from the audience and stage performers alike, especially when the on-stage performance was some melodramatic scene intended to jerk tears.

What passed for theater was less like Shakespeare and more like various drunken college fraternities putting on skits.

The stage was flanked on either side by tall curtains so thickly coated in dust, it camouflaged the original fabric so completely, its original color could only be inferred. The same fabric formed the backdrop behind the solo performers, but at least that prop went up and down frequently enough, making room for sets and scenery backdrops, to shake off most of its own dust layers.

A couple dozen bright, high-wattage light bulbs lined the stage between the performers and the audience, and they were shielded on the side facing the audience so paying customers wouldn't be blinded. It was better for the performers to be blind and stumble their way off the stage, because "talent" was inexpensive and easily replaced. Audiences were irreplaceable.

The comic didn't need to see, and the burlesque dancer welcomed the light-induced blindness to deceive herself into ignoring the thousands of lustful eyes gawking at her as she covered and uncovered herself in choreographed graceful swings of large fans, concealing her private bits from the audience. To the seated crowd, her nudity was only insinuated, but since none of that fan movement shielded her aging rear end from all those crew members backstage and in the wings, her show was enjoyed by them most of all.

Those blinding lights presented a real problem for the juggler and the knife thrower and anyone else who relied on dexterity and sight to perform, however. One glance into the lights would quickly result in a mishap and the failed performer would consequently be shifted down the program into a less popular slot.

Like playing professional baseball, vaudeville was all about survival, which was equal parts relevance, luck, and popularity.

As a ballplayer's batting average slipped, he'd slide down the batting order, until he landed on the bench and got shoved off there into the minors when his performance didn't even merit "riding the pine." A couple unfortunate slides in slots down the program in vaudeville and one night there would be no slot left at that theater, so instead of falling lower on the night's bill, performers would slide down to the next lower tier of vaudeville house.

In baseball *and* vaudeville, once you've failed at the lowest level, you were summarily unemployed. Of all the vaudeville stages in the city, this particular one was the last before oblivion, so falling off this program meant falling from a career as a performer into a career as a cook or waitress, but only if the performer was lucky enough to find work at all!

This was serious business, even if the performances were little more than juvenile, or tawdry, or eye-catchingly acrobatic. The audiences were always packed into the house to capacity. If the theater *sat* five hundred guests, the crowd would often easily exceed a thousand, and the bigger the audience, the rowdier it became. This particular theater was predominately comprised of boisterous, drunken dock workers who were more enthusiastic about conducting mayhem and throwing fruit at the performers than actually watching the performances themselves. The same exhausted crew who ran the show behind the scenes was responsible for cleaning the mess left once the crowds departed, and thank goodness, they did depart, though not necessarily for home, because the next stop on the drunken tour was usually to refuel at local drinking halls within stumbling distance of the theater.

Throughout the evening's festivities, the cloud of cigarette smoke hanging in the air stagnated and expanded like storm clouds ready to explode, and every surface, from the chair cushions, to the carpet, to the fabric on the walls, to the fabric framing the stage, to the clothes of the performers, to the performers themselves wreaked of Chesterfields. The entire theater was like a lung cancer snow globe.

Five cents bought an evening's entertainment, and the theater owner never turned away a paying customer, at least not until after payment was received, then the lout could be tossed on the street for misbehaving. Fredo splurged one night every week to attend an evening's performances, but he wasn't a drunken hooligan. He loved the performances and craved entertainment.

Fredo was surprisingly handsome for a scrawny, malnourished scarecrow. He had thick jet-black hair, a strong jawline, and an elegant Roman nose, but he also had pencil-thin arms and legs, and a belt with extra holes punched into it to make it tight enough to hold up his pants. His English was extremely limited, and even then, he could really only understand small words spoken slowly, so he barely understood any piece of the machine-gun-paced punch-line delivery of the comic who drew roars of laughter from the stage when he finished his act with the one about his wife never being satisfied.

Fredo didn't need to translate live action, though, and he was captivated by the acrobats. He would become so entranced by their performances, he would pantomime the performers' motions right there in his seat, moving his arms and hands like he was juggling, or holding his hands out for balance like he himself was balancing on the wire strung a few feet above the stage. When the burlesque dancer paraded onto the stage, he blushed, but never broke sight of her. Most of all, though, he was enthralled by the magician, or more specifically, the magician's assistant.

She was a paradox, a dark-haired beauty who was thin but shapely, mystifyingly sultry in her black costume, with long legs, heels, bow tie, and top hat, but also somehow gentle with eyes conveying innocence and vulnerability. He shrieked every time she disappeared in the magician's cabinet and clapped like a captivated child every time she reappeared. He watched the same performance, week in and week out, and was equally enthralled the twentieth time as he had been the first. He was smitten by a girl he'd never met, whose name he didn't know, and who had no idea he existed.

Fredo was a shy young man of twenty. He had immigrated into Philadelphia when his ship docked in its harbor five years earlier, and although that's not a long time by ordinary standards, he was considered a seasoned veteran by his immigrant peers. Fredo had overcome a neophyte's struggles, learning some basic phrases in his new home's language, learning local customs, understanding the currency, familiarizing himself with the lay of the land, and knowing where *not* to go.

That last part was particularly relevant. Italians were the scourge du jour in this country back then and were universally loathed by all who preceded them. Generally speaking, in the United States at that time, Italians were human garbage. In fact, between 1870 and 1940, Italians were the nation's second most popular lynching target. Only black people were lynched more often. Quite the dubious distinction for all parties involved.

As shy as he was, Fredo had collected quite a few friends over his time on these shores. Basically, everyone who met Fredo liked him, and once people got to know him, they liked him even more. He was kind, gentle, funny, and always happy to hoist an Americano (Campari, vermouth, and soda) when the occasion called for it.

Even though he had been in his new country five years, Fredo rarely ventured more than a few blocks from the port where he first stepped off the boat from home. A friend who had arrived a year earlier sponsored Fredo for entry into the country and invited him to share a room with him until Fredo got on his feet. They had survived the same orphanage together in Valmontone until the Sisters cast them out onto the street at fourteen. The nuns couldn't keep them forever. They needed to make room for the never-ending influx of abandoned orphans coming in via the Wheel.

Fredo and his friend hustled enough money on the Valmontone streets to buy his friend's passage to America, plus ten dollars, because every immigrant had to have money in their pocket upon entry into the U.S., or the customs agents would send them back. After a year in Philly, Fredo's buddy raised enough money to buy Fredo's passage, and he sent the same ten-dollar bill back too so the customs agents wouldn't send Fredo home when he got here. With two of them in the country, they could afford to bring their orphan friends over twice as quickly, then three times as quickly when there were three of them in this country, etcetera. That same ten-dollar bill made the trip a dozen times, until all the orphan friends were together in the States, sharing a room.

From the outset, Fredo struggled to find even the most menial employment, but he gradually strung together enough consecutive wage-earning days to afford his own room in the same dilapidated rooming house as his friends, and that's where he stayed.

Many immigrants were melancholy, pining for their former homes and dreaming of returning one day, but not Fredo. He loved his adopted land and couldn't wait to assimilate. His rare nights as a bar customer with friends were gradually replaced by him as a full-time bar employee when one night, after being his naturally helpful self, assisting the bartender during a hectic shift, he was asked to fill in for a dishwasher who never showed up for his shift that night or thereafter. That fill-in role turned into a nightly affair, and Fredo's daily quest for work went from desperation (without it he'd starve) to supplemental (picking up extra jobs here and there for extra cash).

He'd work all night washing dishes at the bar as scheduled, and then wake up in the morning and rush to the docks to be selected to remove imported products from incoming ships or load outgoing stock onto ships heading to sea. Whatever the task, Fredo accepted it willingly, doing whatever he could do to accumulate savings so he could one day open his *own* bar and host his friends and compatriots. He saved miserly, except for his weekly nickel indulgence at the local vaudeville theater, and the occasional drink with friends.

In the middle of a row of ramshackle, architectural disasters stood the surprisingly ornate, albeit grimy and many years beyond its prime, theater. Every night it opened its doors to all comers who had a nickel to spare and an appetite for spectacle and laughter. The street outside was cobblestones compressed into dirt by a century of pressure. Grooves had been carved into the stones over time by product-laden wagons being dragged from the docks into the city and beyond by the most miserable excuses for horses imaginable. The areas around the docks made skid row look like high society. Poverty was amplified exponentially. Children barely beyond the age of learning to walk unassisted toiled on the docks with adults instead of attending school, because their families relied on every penny each family member could contribute just to pay night-by-night for the privilege of living in an over-crowded communal dormitory.

Entire families would be summarily evicted if a single night's rent was missed, and landlords ruled with unfettered control. There may have been laws in place, but no one enforced them in this part of town. Human beings exploited those weaker than themselves, and the weakest in this neighborhood gradually disappeared, and were immediately forgotten and back-filled by the next wave of bright-eyed immigrants.

Morality was reserved for the gentry. In the neighborhood surrounding the docks, everyone did what they had to do to stay alive. Prostitution, mugging, and confidence schemes were as common as respectable employment, and everyone understood the lay of the land and navigated it accordingly.

Between the dirt and dust stirred up by all the activity on the streets and docks, and the smoke belched from the river-based mills and factories, every surface of every building, lamppost, door handle, window, or street vendor's display was coated with a layer of filth. Clothes were laundered, but never seemed clean, and baths were a luxury.

The personal hygiene, sterile surfaces, and privacy we enjoy today were earned through the sacrifices of people like Fredo who scrimped and saved to one day invest in a dream and provide for a family he hadn't even begun to produce. It was all part of the plans of people like him whose generation saw the glimmer of the American dream on the distant horizon and wanted nothing more than to carve out their own slivers of it.

One night, Fredo was given a reprieve from his dishwashing station to fill in for the barback, basically a bartending apprentice. The barback does all the shitwork so the bartender can focus on slinging drinks and making money. A good barback invisibly ensures the bartender never reaches for anything that's empty, missing, or misplaced. The kegs are swapped and tapped. Ice is filled. Glasses are cleaned and returned to the queue, empty bottles are replaced with new ones, and all the while the bar is wiped, ashtrays are emptied, and drained glasses are collected.

If a barback fails at any of those tasks, it causes the entire machine to grind to a halt. Any faltering behind the bar impedes the bartender from keeping up with demand, and that equates to a loss of revenue. It was not uncommon for new barbacks to barely last a single night. Conversely, Fredo was a barbacking savant, and after completing only his first couple shifts, bartenders relied on him.

Operating a bar can be easy, except when it's busy with patrons two or three deep holding up their hands and calling out drink orders. In those moments, the operation resembles a maelstrom of carefully choreographed confusion—a ballet of apron-clad dancers who know their roles and perform them seamlessly, or the entire thing resembles a spinning bicycle wheel with a broom handle shoved between its spokes. The barback is a cross between a ballet dancer and an Olympic track star who dashes nonstop between the bar, the stock room, through the patrons to clear and clean tables and back again. When he isn't running, he's slipping and sliding on the beer and whiskey-soaked floor, ducking flailing arms and hands and occasionally dodging an errant punch between drunks.

One night, in the midst of this pandemonium, the bartender called out and teased Fredo.

"Fredo, la tua ragazza e qui," which was Italian for "your girlfriend's here."

Fredo didn't have a girlfriend, but he *was* in love with the magician's assistant. The moment he saw her in the bar, it was like the world stopped and went silent for a moment. In his eyes, she radiated light like the brightest star in the night sky, and his heart pounded the instant he noticed her glow. By this point, she had traded her sultry costume for a conservative dress and high-buttoned shoes. Her face had been wiped clean of theater makeup and her hair was pulled up in a hat. She was younger than she appeared on stage and she wasn't in the bar for reverie, like one of the working girls hustling dances and hoping to provide better-paying services in the alley out back. She was accompanying her father the magician who stopped in for a quick whiskey with the local boys, who treated him like a celebrity and often paid for his drinks. The locals were all broke, but inebriated. He knew the latter made them generous, which is why it was no accident he stopped in every night after his performance. He knew he'd drink for free and had been stopping in since the days when his wife was his assistant and his daughter was in a crib, stage-left.

By now, she was used to the routine. She stood there stoically, patiently waiting for her father who got progressively more drunk, as "just one drink" turned into a night-long mission. Her role was to chaperone him, then guide him home safely after the bar closed. Alcohol never touched her lips. In fact, nothing in the bar did. Although there were no rules restricting her father, his rules for *her* behavior were very strict, and included nothing more than lingering by her father's side until he finally decided to leave.

In Fredo's eyes, she was an angel, a very, very bored and disinterested angel. He couldn't raise the nerve to address her, nor did he have a moment to do so even if the nerve was there, but he noticed her, and in that instant, his entire existence seemed ten pounds lighter. He was no longer running or sliding across the sloppy floor. He was floating over it.

It wasn't long before Fredo had made his transition from dishwasher to barback a permanent one, and in that role he was privileged to gaze upon the magician's daughter every night after her performance concluded. She was even more mystifying a few feet away in the bar than she ever was a hundred feet away on stage disappearing within a cabinet, or being sawed in half in a casket, or standing still with her back against a wooden panel, having knives hurled around her head and frame.

Fredo's life wasn't easy, but it was simple. Mornings began with him rushing to join the queue at the docks in hopes of being selected for day work. More often than not, Fredo would be selected. He worked hard, nonstop, and the foremen liked that.

After a long, arduous, and exhausting shift on the dock, he'd return to his room, drop his day's wages into a bowl on his bureau, change into a white shirt and black trousers, and report to the bar a few minutes before his shift so he could get the bar filled and ready for the night's surge. When his shift ended, he'd return to his room, drop his evening's wages into the bowl and sleep, only to repeat the circuit again the next day, and the day after, and the day after that. Winter, spring, summer, and fall days melted into one another, differentiated only by the weather, and in time, Fredo's savings began to grow.

Although he worked every day shift he could get, one night every week, Fredo had a night off and he spent it at the vaudeville theater.

His life was hard. His callouses had callouses. He could have consumed ten thousand calories a day and never gained an ounce, because he burned twenty thousand laboring, but he was busy and he was in

America, so he was happy. He was progressing toward achieving his goal of opening a bar. He had friends and he was in love, even though the object of his affection still had no idea he existed.

FREDO FALLS FOR SOPHIA

Sophia was the only child of a magician named "Acchione the Great" and his wife, Marguerite, who never referred to herself as "Mrs. Great." The fact was Acchione the Great's act was growing continually more stale on stage and at home. His drinking had gone from convivial to chronic to troublesome. He no longer sought new tricks for his act because he was typically hungover when he should have been honing his craft, and even the tricks he'd mastered in the past began to slip as his drinking schedule crept ever earlier, from *after* his performance to *during* and frequently even *before* it.

Most of his act was rote and harmless with trap doors in the stage and spinning panels in standing cabinets. Drunken errors during those parts of his performance were greeted with eruptive laughter from the audience at his expense. Knife throwing required skill, training, and focus, though, and the one night he nicked his daughter's ear with a blade was the night the stage crew intervened and threatened him with physical harm if he ever drank again before or during a performance.

The crew all remembered Sophia as an infant. She had grown up on and around that stage, and the stagehands there were her adopted family. They watched out for her in the theater and on the street, and their threats against her father worked, at least for a time. Eventually,

Acchione the Great's greatest trick became making alcohol disappear, and one night, on the way to the theater, already in a drunken stupor from an afternoon of indulgence, he tripped over a cobblestone in the street and landed on his face. He was too inebriated to stretch out his hands to absorb the landing, so his head broke his fall instead. He suffered a severe head trauma and died quickly in the street from the injury three feet from the sidewalk in front of the theater where he was scheduled to perform that evening. A passed-out drunk lying in the street was a depressingly common sight, so the audience never took note of him lying there as they rushed into the theater, stepping over or around his prone body in the process. His body was finally discovered when an usher ran outside to look for him when he didn't show up for his scheduled stage appearance.

After years of nightly performances, his finale was far from grand, and just like that, Sophia and Marguerite's fortunes took a fateful turn. With the Great gone, they were left relying upon the support of friends and family until they could pay their own way, and they scrambled to win the footrace between gainful employment and eviction.

Marguerite had been the Great's assistant in the very beginning, even before they were married. After they wed, she was still the one who was disappearing from boxes and having knives thrown at her while her daughter was being watched by the stagehands. She practiced with the Great, and ultimately knew his routine as well as him, possibly better, but performing was a man's game. Women in Vaudeville were typically relegated to supporting roles if they were clothed, or burlesque roles if they weren't, but the theater owner had a slot to fill in the evening program, and the marquee was already painted with "The Great Acchione appearing nightly," so to save money on changing signs, and to avoid finding someone else to use the magician's props, the old man who owned the theater agreed to permit Marguerite and Sophia to perform the Great's act.

The theater owner had nothing to lose. If they succeeded, his problem was solved, and if they failed, they'd bridge the gap he'd need to find a new act. At this end of the vaudeville ladder, there were no rungs beneath him. No one waited in the wings to ascend to openings on his stage. The only acts finding their way to his stage were the ones tumbling down from better theaters above his, and every act did everything in their power to avoid that disgraceful, pitiful fate.

Rarely did a vacancy occur in his program as a result of one of his performers being good enough to ascend and fill a slot in a better house. It always seemed a hole was created when a performer failed out, and the hole was typically filled by someone on a similar path from the house a rung higher.

No one expected the mother/daughter ensemble to become an immediate and rousing success, but that's what happened, and in due time, other theaters began to take note of the crowds the women drew.

Just as Fredo worked days on the dock and nights at the bar, Marguerite and Sophia worked their way up the vaudeville ladder until they were listed on the prime marquees in center city along Chestnut and Walnut streets during the day, even though they never forfeited their evening slot at the old South Philly dock theater where they got their start. It was an exhausting schedule, but they were making more and more money, and were suddenly secure and living comfortably, *very* comfortably.

The original Acchione the Great's curtain call that afternoon on the cobblestones in front of the Dock Street theater was the greatest performance of his career, because it opened a slot in the program for his wife and daughter, and they never looked back. The running joke in town was Marguerite had become Acchione the Great*er*.

Unfortunately, what was great for the Acchione women was less than wonderful for Fredo. Without her father's nightly visits to the bar, Sophia disappeared from Fredo's life, except for when she appeared on stage with her mother. He still caught her shows every week, enthralled as always, but it seemed the climax of their relationship may have come and gone before they ever met.

As the fortunes of the Acchione women improved, they became less and less dependent on their time on the Dock Street theater stage. The rigors of performing day and night were wearing on them too, and they ultimately considered resigning their slot in south Philly to focus on the more prestigious and better-paying gigs in center city. The Dock Street theater's owner was shrewd enough to recognize the impact the loss of the Greater Acchione would have on his enterprise, and he made an offer to Marguerite to share the gate every night she and Sophia performed there.

Marguerite agreed to the split, but in lieu of a contract, the theater owner offered to marry the magical widow instead. Marguerite, possibly recognizing the potential stability such a union could provide, or maybe simply out of loneliness, accepted his terms. In a strange turn of serendipity, the theater crew who had been Sophia's pseudo family since birth were to become her legitimate family through marriage, because the cheap-ass theater owner had only ever hired family to operate the theater.

The newly minted couple and Sophia would move into the theater owner's very large and grand stone home, which would remain in the family for the next hundred years, or more. He was notoriously frugal and must have saved every penny of profit he ever generated, because his home was magnificent and situated in an affluent neighborhood reserved for bankers and lawyers and physicians and commercial overlords. No one knew what the man did for a living, and he did everything within his power to maintain that mystery.

He was in his sixties but seemed older. He chain-smoked cigars and always wore a banker's suit with a vest and pocket watch. He wore a gentleman's hat made locally in the Stetson factory, and his shoes were always polished to such a high gloss, they practically glowed amid the soot- and filth-covered cobblestones outside his theater.

Unlike the anemic neighborhood residents who struggled to find their next meal, he was paunchy, fed on the finest meats in the best restaurants in town. He lived a double life as a landed blueblood, hobnobbing with the Philadelphia aristocracy, while secretly supporting himself with the scornful lucre from the lowest theater, in the lowest cast of the theatrical hierarchy in the city. Vaudeville was not fit for the top hat and tails set who spent their entertainment currency at the Academy of Music on Broad Street, enjoying the ballet or philharmonic. Vaudeville was for rabble, and although Philadelphia's vaudeville scene produced many recognizable stars like W.C. Fields and Pearl Bailey, the Dock Street site was the last vaudeville stop before falling and drowning in the Delaware River.

BELLS RING FOR FREDO

The wedding of Acchione the Greater and the old man was not a big affair.

A big affair would require the theater to close for a day to accommodate the work schedules of the guests (all of whom worked at the Dock Street theater), and for Acchione the Greater to cancel performances all over town. Marriage may be life-altering, but business is business.

The theater needed to operate every day, meaning the crew all had work to do, and Acchione the Greater's shows (plural) had to go on at the Dock Street Theater as well as at those venues in center city.

They couldn't marry before Marguerite and Sophia completed their late-morning and early-afternoon shows, but they couldn't delay too long either, because the crew had to be backstage at the Dock theater in time to prepare for the evening's performances. The result was a simple mid-afternoon ceremony at the Italian church near the docks, followed by a quiet, small, and private luncheon on the theater's stage to celebrate the nuptials.

To some it may seem romantic to host a reception on the stage owned by the groom, and performed upon by the bride, but the simple facts were it was convenient for the crew to attend the reception and then scurry off to attend their duties a few feet away from the party; the stage provided an ample open space for seating and serving, and most importantly, it was the least expensive venue, period. As mentioned, the old man was notoriously cheap.

Neighborhood merchants provided the food and flowers, at a discount, of course, out of respect for the theater driving so much business through their respective doors, and Fredo's employer provided the shots and beers. Of course, whether within the confines of the bar itself, or elsewhere on the road, every bar needed a barback, and Fredo's work ethic assured him the post, providing him a means to triple-dip that day with income from the docks, from the wedding, and later from the bar. It was a financial bonanza for him!

As diligent as he was, performing all assigned tasks in syncopated rhythm with the bartender, Fredo indulged his eyes now and again to gaze momentarily upon Sophia, dressed elegantly for the event and doted upon by her new family. Unlike the demeanor Fredo had always witnessed at the bar, here she was light and gay. She laughed loudly and deeply, her mouth wide open, teeth on full display, and tears of joy streaming from her eyes. She never sat down, twirling on the dance floor with stagehand after stagehand, and even once with her stepfather. She hugged and kissed her mother and exhibited a personality she'd repressed all those occasions she'd visited the bar with her father.

Fredo was more smitten that day than he had ever been, and he finally realized, although he could never be so brazen to interrupt her during such a personal celebration, especially while he was working, he was going to find a moment in the future to finally meet her.

What he didn't realize was that moment was imminent, *really* imminent, and it was *not* going to go as he would have planned.

Marguerite was stunning in her off-white wedding gown, the hue denoting she was not a virginal bride, and the old man resembled a board game character with black tails, bow tie, and top hat. His thick white mustache, turned up at the ends, only made him seem even more like the caricature of a well-heeled gent.

They were a handsome couple, and although their union was ostensibly a professional one, there was an energy between them to inspire an optimistic inference there may be more lurking beneath the surface. Although he worked diligently to maintain an air of reserved elegance and station, his crew goaded him into joining the crowd on the dance floor, and making a turn or two of his own, first with his wife and then with his new daughter. Unfortunately, during one turn on the floor, the old man spun his daughter and she crashed into Fredo, who was carrying a large tray of glasses filled in varying degrees with leftover booze, melted ice, and dozens of extinguished cigarettes.

The tray tipped suddenly to the right, and in an effort to correct it, Fredo made a drastic adjustment to the left, which made matters far worse. First one glass fell to its side on the tray and then its weight tipped another, and those two tipped four, and those four tipped a dozen, and before he could breathe, the tray was perpendicular to the floor and its contents—glasses, leftover beverages, and saturated cigarette butts—slid and splashed directly off the chest and torso of a shocked Sophia.

The world stopped.

Everyone was frozen in time.

Sophia's hands were up, directly in front of her, like she was about to receive a basketball pass. Her eyes bulged. Her mouth was open in shock and she stood perfectly still as the ice-cold, tainted liquid reached her skin and began to drip down inside the front of her dress, and farther down inside her undergarments.

It felt wet and disgusting.

Fredo was the first to react with a facial expression of outright horror, and eyes as big as silver dollars. He had just poured a tray of wet filth down the front of the woman of his dreams. He threw his hands in the air apologetically, grabbed his bar towel, which had fallen to the floor and was saturated with the residual alcohol and tobacco bits, and instinctively leaned forward and tried frantically to dry Sophia's torso, without touching anything inappropriately. His efforts weren't helping. The rag was making Sophia's dress wetter and dirtier.

The crew rose to their feet in silent fury, about to tear the young man to shreds.

The old man looked like a furious pressure cooker under maximum strain, about to release steam through his ears, and all the bartender could do from across the room was clench his eyes closed and cover his face with his hands, awaiting the annihilation of his favorite barback.

But from out of the blue, almost instantly, Sophia burst into the loudest belly laugh of the day, then she apologetically grabbed the towel from Fredo's hand and turned it on him, trying to dab the same mess from his white shirt he had tried to clean from her dress.

"I think that's the first time I've ever seen you drop anything. I was starting to believe you weren't capable of it," she said to Fredo, as everyone expelled their breath in relief, and started laughing at the comedy.

"We'll have to hire you as an acrobat, boy. You were this close to saving that tray," the old man said to Fredo, making a pinching gesture with his right thumb and forefinger to illustrate the margin of error and slapping him on the back with his left palm.

Fredo could not believe how this situation had completely turned. He exhaled deeply and smiled for the first time in what seemed like weeks. She was his magic elixir, his muse, and *she* noticed *him*.

"You *know* me?" he asked.

"Of course. I watched you every night at the bar for hours when my father would stop in and proceed to get pie-eyed. What else was I supposed to do? Watch the hookers dance with their johns?" And she laughed.

"You know me," he repeated, only this time he didn't ask a question; he confirmed it out loud, as though to prove he wasn't imagining it.

"You know *me*?" she asked.

Fredo was not prepared to have a conversation in English. "Yes. Yes. Of course. I uh…" He pointed at his eyes. "See? *See* you *here*," and he extended his hands out to his sides with his palms up. He tried to gesture that "here" meant the theater. "*Every* Friday for a *year*," he said, "and of course, I know you every night at the bar with your *father*." He turned to the old man and said, "Pardon me. Her *other* father. I mean, um, Acchione the *Great*…the *first* one," and he waved and nodded apologetically to Marguerite for implying she had stepped foot in a bar.

Poor Fredo couldn't speak decent English on a good day. Combine that with his shyness and nervousness and he was hopelessly out of his depths addressing this crowd, and he quickly began to panic and hyperventilate. The old man smacked Fredo on the back again and said, "Boy, today's my big day and nothing can spoil it, not even my clumsy stepdaughter. You come back here every Friday this month and there will be a free pass waiting for you at the door."

Fredo tried to thank him but hyperventilated even harder. The old man roared with laughter and Sophia grabbed Fredo by the arm and guided him to exit the stage. "I'm going to escort this poor man outside for a breath of fresh air, and maybe a cigarette if I can roll some spare tobacco off my dress."

The theater is a superstitious house, and left is luckier, so if Sophia wanted Fredo to get better, she'd favor that side of the stage. She exited stage left.

Everyone but Fredo laughed as his knees buckled and he focused intently on not passing out. They stepped out into the daylight, beyond the brass-handled front doors of the theater, and Sophia leaned Fredo back against the wall to prevent him from collapsing like a jellyfish on the sidewalk.

"Are you always this suave?" she asked sarcastically. "Be honest, this isn't the first time you poured a tray of secondhand booze on a girl to meet her, is it?"

Fredo's wits were still not with him, and he shook his head vehemently as he took her questions literally. "No no no no no. I would *never* do such a thing," he blurted out in the best English he'd spoken in weeks.

"Sweet man," and she patted his cheek with her hand. "I am teasing. It was an accident, and all is well. I was never going to wear this dress again anyway. It was just for the wedding. And by the way, you said that last sentence very well. Perhaps panic is all you need to master your new language. How long have you been in this country?"

"Six years—1914."

"Well, you sound fine for having been here for such a brief time. Perhaps I can teach you a few phrases. I'll bet we can get you to sound like a local in no time. How about it? When don't you work? We can start right away."

She was so out-going and confident, *nothing* like Fredo. The more she spoke to him, the more captivated he became, even though he only understood about half of what she said.

Fredo worked all the time. His every waking moment was spent either working, or walking to or from working, or sleeping. He stammered. He wanted to spend every moment with her, of course, but he needed to work. He couldn't afford not to work. His indecisiveness was making him panic, because he was taking too long to answer her questions.

"Oh," she said a bit dejectedly. Sophia misread his lack of response as rejection. "If you're not interested, that's fine. I was just…"

"NO! My…no. No! I am ummm *very?* Yes. Ummm VERY *interested*," he said, trying to repeat her words, but in his own special affected version of Engtalian, a mashed-up version of both languages so brutalized, neither one of them could be translated. "I'm a just… ummm…work. I'm a *no* free. I wanna *very much* talk…*you*."

She smiled wryly and gave him a light kiss on the cheek. "I'll tell you what. To apologize for knocking over your tray and nearly giving you a heart attack, I will meet you at your bar every night after it closes and I'll teach you to speak English, but I can't come inside. Without a proper chaperone accompanying me, it would be improper for me to come inside alone."

Fredo was out of words. He opened his eyes wide and nodded his head spastically, hoping he understood her correctly.

"Tonight?" was the only word he could find, and she nodded and said, "Yes."

Sophia smiled. "Now, if you're breathing better, let's get inside so you can finish your work, and I can change out of this soaking wet dress. I'm drenched clean-through and I'm *freezing*," and she laughed again with what Fredo believed was the most perfect, delightful laugh ever laughed in the history of laughter.

Life Can Be Sweet

Over the ensuing months, Sophia visited Fredo every night when the bar closed. She'd wait outside under a streetlight, and he would rush out after his shift to join her. They would find a public place and focus on Fredo's studies. They didn't start out planning to fall in love, but it happened anyway. Well, he was in love before this began, but surprisingly, in time, she met him halfway.

The task at hand was simply to help Fredo speak passable English, but funny things can happen when you sit closely to one another, focusing intently on what one another says and does. Intimacy becomes an entirely natural byproduct of such close quarters, and if one's not careful, that intimacy can easily slide into strong feelings, and those feelings can easily become affection, and that affection can evolve into touching, entirely innocent touching, but passionate nonetheless.

At times during conversations, Sophia's fingertips would land and rest on the top of Fredo's hand and linger there, like a butterfly tamely pausing before fluttering off. Other times, she would grasp his hand tightly in hers when his efforts paid off and he responded correctly to a question, but then she would hold onto it a few seconds longer than necessary, making the touch seem like something more. When she wanted to make a specific point, she would look directly into his eyes, place her palm on his cheek, and speak slowly, but she wouldn't pull her palm away when she finished speaking and he'd close his eyes in comfort and tilt his head. Squeezing her hand between his face and shoulder. Neither of them would pull away.

Sophia had Fredo wrapped in her spell from the first moment he saw her. She could have had him hopping naked down Broad Street like a frog if she'd asked, but somehow, she was actually falling victim to his charm as well. Because beneath that scrawny exterior of his, there was a soft, sweet, and gentle heart, and it didn't take Sophia long to find it and cherish it.

Within the year, Sophia was no longer teaching Fredo English. He commanded it just fine. She was meeting him at the bar at night to walk with him, or sit under the stars at the dock in silence, gazing at the water and its shimmering reflection of lights from the opposite shore. They shared a connection. It didn't require slick conversations, or passionate embraces. They only needed to be near one another, and when they were, their souls bonded. They became one. Anyone who saw them together would see it.

Fredo worked at the bar at night, and the docks every day, until one evening when he walked Sophia home and her stepfather, the old man who owned the theater, offered him nightly shifts in the theater lobby—not as a barback but as a full-fledged bartender. Fredo's nights at the bar in the neighborhood had come to an end. As it turned out, Marguerite didn't like the idea of Sophia being out on those streets that late, but she knew as long as Fredo closed the bar every night, Sophia would be out there waiting for him, so she persuaded her husband to offer Fredo something with better hours, closer to Sophia.

Working in the theater was unlike anything Fredo had ever experienced.

Of course, he was the interloper again, the neophyte, just as he'd been when he landed on the docks six years earlier, but this time was different. This time he felt like he was setting down roots, like he was building on a relationship with the rest of the crew.

The stagehands were all related—brothers, sisters, cousins, uncles, and fathers. He was the outsider, for sure, but because of his relationship with Sophia, who was their family through marriage, he was tenuously connected to them, and only more so as his and Sophia's relationship intensified.

Of course the crew was protective of their Sophia at first, and were aloof toward Fredo, but after a while, Fredo became more welcome in the ballet backstage, and in turn asked the crew to join him at the lobby bar during intermission to teach them his trade so they could earn some tips along the way.

Even though Fredo worked tirelessly at three jobs to finance his dream, he cared very little about money. He would as quickly donate his wages to a family in need as he would put that money into his own pocket. He'd eschew hoarding tips that were rightfully his in favor of sharing them with friends. That was Fredo. He was a sweet, generous man with strong friendships, who was adored by those within his circle. No one ever had a bad word to say about Fredo. Everyone liked him.

One afternoon, while the crew was beginning to prepare the theater for the evening's performances, Fredo quietly ascended the steps from the theater's lobby and visited the old man's office. He knocked on the door, and after a moment he was invited in. The old man greeted Fredo and spoke to him for a moment, but Fredo heard absolutely nothing the old man was saying. Fredo was fixated on his single task, and was so nervous, a bomb could have gone off in the middle of the old man's office and Fredo wouldn't have noticed.

The office was located directly above the theater's main lobby with only a single window facing the street. One might assume from that description the office was dark, but descriptions can be deceiving, because in this case, that single window spanned the length of the room, and was the top half of a circle whose arc peaked near the ceiling. The window was enormous, at least twenty feet long and twenty feet tall. The entire street below was visible panoramically from the docks on the left to the bustling intersection two blocks on the right. In the afternoon, the office was bathed in the sun's golden rays, but at night, more light passed from the office out than from the outside in.

Unlike the rest of the theater, which was dingy and threadbare and smelled of a combination of laborer's sweat, stale cigarettes, and old socks, the office was opulent and rivaled any executive boardroom in the city's preeminent buildings. The walls were lined with silk, and the ceiling was decorated with ornate plaster friezes. The silk Oriental rug on the floor was imported and massive. The guest chairs facing the desk were high-backed velvet and the old man's desk itself looked like it was straight out of Versailles, and actually may have been. The walls were adorned with original artwork. Statues stood on pillars around the room, and a Tiffany decanter was the centerpiece of a twenty-carat gold tray on a table near the window. Two leather club chairs flanked the table, and the old man gestured to Fredo to join him there to gaze out across the city. Then he broke the ice.

"So to what do I owe this pleasure, son?"

The old man filled two small, delicate, etched crystal glasses with Port and handed one to Fredo. The two men sat down, and Fredo nervously consumed the wine in a single gulp.

The old man smirked and asked if he could guess the nature of the call. Fredo held the glass in both hands down in his lap. His eyes stared at it, and then he nodded his head vigorously without making eye contact with his host. He had been trying to get up the nerve to make this visit to the old man's office for weeks, and this was the farthest he'd gotten so far. He had no idea what to do next.

The old man knew the score. It was very clear by the contents of his office, he was a man of the world and not some flop-house rube as his theater's edifice would imply. He was very successful, mingled with the city's elite, and knew how to read a room. He smiled at Fredo, crossed his leg toward the young man, set his crystal glass on the table, stacked his hands on his knee, and turned to look Fredo in the eye, but the younger man wouldn't meet his gaze.

"Fredo Mantelli, I like you. You're a good man. You're responsible. You work hard and you seem very driven to succeed. My entire family likes and respects you, and I foresee a great deal of success in your future. I also see healthy, beautiful children, but they won't get their beauty from you. They'll get it from Sophia."

Fredo's posture improved immediately, and he jerked his head to face the old man and he finally met his gaze for the first time since he entered the room. An unerasable smile appeared on his face and his eyes actually twinkled. In so many words, the old man gave him permission to marry Sophia.

"Beyond all those fine attributes of yours is how you treat Sophia. A father dreams of his daughter being appreciated by her husband, but you worship Sophia. You both light up in one another's presence, and I can think of no one else I would rather call my son than you. So let's cut to the chase, shall we? I'll give you my daughter's hand in marriage, but if anyone asks, you have to say you begged for it before I gave it to you. Do we have a deal?"

Fredo jumped from his chair and shook the old man's hand so vigorously, a diamond cufflink dislodged from the old man's right wrist and flew five feet toward the window.

"Thank you. Thank you. Thank you. I love your daughter, and I will do everything for her. I will always place her ahead of me and I will protect her with my life."

"Good, because her life is worth more than ten of yours," said the old man with a wink. "And once you're married, we will need to discuss your future. My daughter will not be married to a dock worker, or a bartender. She'll marry a businessman, and I will train you to run my operation. Someday, this will be yours, and your son's after you."

THE BEST OF DAYS

Fredo and Sophia's married life was blissful. They were offered accommodations in Marguerite and the old man's massive residence, but they chose to live near the theater and Fredo's friends in one of the new small but private row homes popping up all over the area. They could walk to the theater, and visit Fredo's friends, and it was only a few blocks to visit the old man and Marguerite (Acchione the Greater).

Sophia continued to perform with her mother, and Fredo was gleaning business knowledge by the handful from the old man. The young couple's lives were idyllic. They had friends. They had Sophia's mother and stepfather. They had their extended family behind the scenes in the theater, and they had each other. Only a child was missing, and try as they did, they could not add a member to their family.

Sophia became despondent over her failure to conceive, but Fredo consoled her. He would have welcomed a child, but he didn't need one. Sophia exceeded his dreams. He assured her they merely needed to be patient.

That patience paid off. After two years of trying, Sophia became pregnant. You can imagine the excess to which the old man and "The Greater" went to lavish Sophia with gifts during her term. After all, the old man never had children of his own, and Sophia was Marguerite's only one, and after so much anticipation, this baby was going to be spoiled to excess!

Meanwhile, backstage, the stagehands embraced Fredo as one of their own. The soon-to-be father smoked so many free cigars in nine months, he was practically Cuban by the time the baby arrived, and arrive it did.

Giuseppe (Joseph) Alfredo Mantelli was born at 1 a.m. on Saint Joseph's Day (hence the child's first name), March 19, 1925. He weighed a whopping ten pounds, thirteen ounces, and nearly split his mother in two in delivery. Considering the family business, no one referred to him as Gio, or Joseph or Joey. He was simple referred to as "Greatest" in deference to his grandmother being the Greater.

Greatest and Sophia and Fredo were ecstatic together. As predicted by the old man, the child was healthy and beautiful and bore a fortunate and striking resemblance to his mother. His first year was as eventful as any infant's, with family charting his every milestone and fussing over every smile and burble and bowel movement. As his name implied, his family held him up as the Greatest, and smothered him with love and joy accordingly.

Sophia took a leave of absence from her mother/daughter troupe to recuperate, but after a couple months, she was stir-crazy and ready to get back on stage, but only at night in the family theater, not uptown in the fancier houses. Sophia's priority was her son, and those other theaters would have frowned upon him crying in the wings. Not so on Dock Street.

While Fredo toiled with the old man in the administrative office on the theater's second floor every night, Marguerite and Sophia performed on stage, and the stagehands watched over the baby as they had watched over his mama decades earlier, bouncing him on a shoulder, and patting him on the back to keep him quiet. This same scene played out every night, and when the last patron left for the night, and the doors were closed and secured, Fredo would come down to the theater and join his family and get the report on the night's performances. He was interested in them all, of course, but he was most interested in the greatest performance of all, the mother/daughter magic act. Some nights he would come down and mingle with the rowdies and watch the program play out, but most nights he was too busy managing the operation upstairs to come down and watch the show.

One night, after the front doors were secured, Fredo came down as he always did. Stagehands scurried about on stage and behind it, as well among the seats where every form of vile mess imaginable had been left behind by the local horde for them to clean. There was a particularly nasty mess on the steps stage-left, so Fredo hopped up the stage-right steps two at a time to get to his beautiful wife. Bad luck be damned!

Fredo and Sophia embraced on stage, while the stage manager stood near the magician's props at the back of the stage, holding the baby and pointing at the young couple and making jokes about them to their child.

Entirely unnoticed, a handsome young man in his twenties, dressed in a very well-tailored suit, was suddenly seated in the front row, applauding. Everyone stopped what they were doing and the house went silent, until the only sound was the smack of the man's hands slowly striking one another.

"So this is your life now, Mantelli? A big shot theater operator with a wife who performs for *animals* in the audience. You've come so far."

"Do I know you, sir?" Fredo responded as he instinctively ushered Sophia behind him so he could shield her from the stranger.

"No, and I don't know you, but I know *of* you. You're Fredo Mantelli from Valmontone, Italy, yes?"

Fredo hesitated a bit but responded, "I *am*."

"Good. Then I am in the right place." With that, the man pulled a large-caliber revolver from inside his suit jacket and pointed it at Fredo.

He held up his other hand and moved it slightly from left to right, to quiet the sudden din in the room and assure everyone it would be best to stay calm, or things would go badly everyone, not just Fredo.

The visible stagehands stood still, but those out of sight mobilized quickly. Although there had never been a need, the old man made sure his crew was trained to defend his business against rowdy customers who may get out of hand, or who become a threat. There were rifles stashed in the rafters above the stage, and the crew on the catwalk maneuvered quickly and quietly toward the stash so they could dispatch the threat, before harm came to anyone.

Two more gunmen, presumably in cahoots with the well-dressed man in the front row, appeared at the east and west doors, which led from the theater to the lobby. They were dressed in suits as well, and stood silently by the doors, focusing Tommy guns at the stagehands scattered in plain sight.

"Who are you?" inquired Fredo, in an effort to buy time, and hoping to diffuse what was obviously some sort of terrible mistake.

"You wouldn't recognize my name, but you *would* recognize my cousin's name: Isabella Conchetti."

"Isabella? *Bella?*" Fredo was shocked to hear a name he hadn't heard in years, and frankly never expected to hear again. "Is she all right?"

"She is fine, no thanks to you."

Sophia spoke up from behind Fredo. "Who is Isabella Conchetti?"

"She's a childhood friend from my hometown," Fredo responded, but he was quickly interrupted by the young man with the revolver.

"But she's a *little* more than just a *friend*, Mantelli. Isn't she? *Wasn't* she?"

"A *dear* friend, of course. We were inseparable as children."

"Perhaps you should have been a little *more* separable, though, street rat."

"I don't understand."

"What does he mean, Fredo?" Sophia asked.

"Yes, Fredo," said the man waving the gun. "Why don't you explain it to your lovely wife?"

"Because I have no idea what you mean. Bella and I were friends. We grew up together. The last time I saw her I let her know I'd booked passage on a ship to America, and she cried and ran away."

"Well, perhaps that was because you were abandoning her when she was pregnant with your child."

Sophia and Fredo both shouted in unison "What?"

"That's not possible," Fredo continued, and he instinctively turned his attention away from the gunman and spoke directly to Sophia. "We were *never* intimate. The most we ever did was hold hands and daydream under the fig tree on her father's property. A child? It's not mine!"

Almost on cue, Fredo's actual child let out a coo from backstage. In a silent theater, it was impossible to ignore.

"Aaaahh, that's right. I heard you have a second child now, right? Congratulations. Let me see him."

But the stage manager knew better, and instead of exhibiting the child, he hid him in the disappearing cabinet prop and spun the back panel so the child couldn't be detected, in case one of the gunmen made it to the stage and opened the prop's door.

By this point, the well-dressed young man who resembled an Italian banker raised his weapon above his head, and in one motion smoothly leveled it at Fredo fifty feet away.

"My family does not take kindly to men who rape our women, let alone abandon them, Mantelli. You are *garbage*, and my family has vowed a vendetta against you and yours. We intend to destroy your line before it can continue. I will execute that promise tonight, right here, by executing you, your whore wife, and your bastard child."

The two stagehands above the stage had returned to their perches and had lined up their targets. There were three co-conspirators, the two with machine guns and the man in the audience with the pistol. Pistols were notoriously difficult to aim from such a distance, and prone to misfiring. The crew decided their first targets would be the two men in the back because their machine guns were far more dangerous than a simple revolver, especially since the man with the revolver would likely only have time to fire one shot, and would likely miss his target from that distance, with that cumbersome cannon. They were sure, before he could fire a second time, one of the two crewmembers with rifles would drop him. They surmised Fredo would get grazed, at worst.

In an instant, four shots were fired.

The two gunmen in the back of the theater were killed instantly. The handsome, well-dressed man did indeed get off one, but *only* one shot before one of the riflemen dispatched him as well. Unfortunately, one shot was enough.

Fredo dropped to the floor in agony, bleeding profusely from his left side. It was a perilous injury, but not a lethal one, and as he battled to remain conscious, he kept calling out Sophia's name, reaching his hand behind him, searching for some sign she was okay.

Sophia lay on the stage behind him. If the large-caliber shell had nicked one of Fredo's ribs and deflected, or had been an inch lower or further to the left as it passed through Fredo, she'd have been fine. Instead, the bullet passed through the most narrow of gaps between Fredo's ribs, and directly through Sophia's heart behind him.

She was dead before she hit the floor.

Fredo's calls turned to sobs when she didn't respond. Once he realized she was gone, he howled. The air was shattered with Fredo's repeated screams until the trauma of his injury, the loss of blood, and his emotional shock conspired to shut him down.

With Fredo unconscious, the house fell silent. In moments, the old man burst through the door behind one of the gunmen, stage-right, looked down, and stopped in his tracks to assess the situation.

Marguerite burst from her dressing room, unaware of the drama preceding the shots, and raced out front at the first sound of gunfire. She saw her unconscious son-in-law bleeding on the stage, and she saw her child, her beautiful daughter, on the same stage where she'd performed thousands of times. Her motionless body leaked life from her heart and Marguerite's heart turned to stone in that instant.

The newly orphaned baby cried from inside the magician's cabinet.

The stage manager retrieved him and held him, rocking him through his own sobs and patting him on the back, shushing him and assuring him everything would be fine, even though he knew nothing would ever be fine again.

The three assailants were removed from the premises and unceremoniously dumped into the river before the police arrived. The scripted story among the witnesses was a lone gunman had burst in and shot the Mantellis, killing them both. When the police asked where the husband and wife's bodies were, they were told they were taken by ambulance to a hospital, but no one knew which one it was. The police were told the gunman left on foot and was seen running north toward center city.

The victims and perpetrators were swarthy Italians, so the police didn't care. They jotted down some notes from witnesses so they could complete their requisite paperwork and never return to the scene.

The truth was Fredo was secreted away to a local physician's private residence and was attended to there. Although he had lost a great deal of blood, the bullet had passed through him and the wounds would be sutured in the front and the back. His recovery would be slow and painful, but it would be a complete one nonetheless.

Sophia was taken to the funeral home of a family friend. Her body was cared for, and two caskets were buried in a family plot following a very private funeral mass and memorial service three days later. Fredo didn't attend, although onlookers would have sworn otherwise, because one of the caskets was his.

After two weeks in a room in the old man's physician's home, Fredo, though still weak, recovered enough to be released. The old man had visited Fredo every day since the shooting, held his hand, and encouraged him to fight.

For the past few years, the two had developed a father/son relationship, working in close quarters in the theater's second-floor office. During the weeks since the incident, the old man visibly aged several years. He no longer looked sixty. He looked to be a hundred. The skin on his face hung from his cheeks. His eyes were sunken and expressed the deepest sadness. He had lost twenty pounds because he stopped eating and his once-perfectly tailored suits now hung on him like oversized overcoats on a scarecrow. His shoes hadn't been polished. He didn't bother wearing any of his jewelry, and his hat hung in his hand by his hip like it weighed a hundred pounds. His shoulders were slumped forward, and he seemed to always be on the verge of tears. He had been robust and on top of the world, but in an instant, with a single gunshot, his perfect little family had been shattered in the cruelest instant, and the depth of his devastation was immeasurable.

"My son," the old man said almost apologetically, "my heart is broken. For sixty years I had no family, and for the last four I had a wife, a daughter, and then a son and a grandchild. These have been the best years of my life, and I owe you an unpayable debt of gratitude for bringing so much joy to us. But now, I'm afraid, we need to say farewell. You *must* go far away."

Fredo was shocked. His only source of strength during recovery had been his remaining family. He lost his wife—his love! Surely the old man can't take his son, too. Joseph was all that mattered to him now. He couldn't lose him too! He pleaded with the old man to reconsider.

"Please, sir. I didn't do those things that bastard said I did. I never would have done those things to Isabella, or anyone else. You *know* me better than that. I could no more force myself on a woman and abandon her than I could lift a house! Please don't cast me away. *Please!* You and Marguerite and Joseph are all I have left. You are my family, my *life*."

The old man broke down and sobbed. This wasn't what he wanted either and it had been tearing him apart since that fateful night, but he knew of no other way. He struggled to regain a modicum of composure, choked down his tears, and assured Fredo he and Marguerite both knew the truth, and knew Fredo would never have done the things of which he had been accused. They knew Fredo, and they knew his character. He also assured Fredo he wasn't being sent away in anger, but because leaving forever was the only way to protect young Joseph.

"If those animals know you're alive, they will come for you again and again until they finish the job. What if Joseph is caught in the cross-fire like Sophia was," and with those words, the old man had to stop and regain his composure. Fredo burst into sobs.

"You need to disappear and stay safe, Fredo, for all our sakes. You'll return one day. You *will*, but for now, you *must* leave!"

The old man handed Fredo a satchel and opened it to expose a passport, and a birth certificate for a man Fredo's exact age but named Al Valmonti. Also in the bag was $10,000. The old man, the most miserly creature to ever choke a nickel out of a penny, was handing Fredo enough money to buy and stock his own bar anywhere he desired. "We've gathered your things and placed them in this trunk. A train ticket has been purchased to take you to New York City. A colleague of mine will greet you there and help you find lodgings and work, but you can't return to the theater business. The community is too small, and you'll be found. My advice is to return to your roots and tend bar. Be among people. There is plenty of money in that satchel for you to one day open your own place, or do anything you want. If you ever need more, you only need to ask and it's yours."

Al looked at the old man, begging him with his eyes to let him stay, but finally dipped his chin to his chest in futility. His shoulders slumped as he realized the old man was right. Lingering here would put his worthless life at risk, sure, but it would also put his son's life at risk, as well as the lives of Marguerite and the old man. As long as that portion of his family survived, Al had hope.

As a foundling in Valmontone, Fredo never had a family. Sophia, his beautiful wife, gave him a family, but she was stolen from him by an assassin, and now the family she gave him was being taken as well.

"What about my sweet boy?" he asked, his voice cracking as he did. "I'll never hold him again? I'll never hear his first words, or see him walk? I'll never hold my beautiful son's hand, or watch him sleep, or hold him when he cries?"

The old man closed his eyes, drawing upon every ounce of fortitude he could find within himself and replied, "We will raise him as our own. He will want for nothing. He will go to the best schools and know the best people. He will be surrounded by family and we will tell him the most glorious stories about his beautiful, loving mother and his courageous, brilliant father."

"Can I visit him?"

"The closer you get to him, the more at risk you place him, but you and I can meet in New York, every month if you'd like. I will bring photos and tell you all about his life. You can come to school performances, or athletic events, or graduations, or anything you want to see. I am just pleading with you to maintain a wide distance so no one links you two together."

And that was that. All those years building a life, all those days toiling on the docks and barbacking and bartending to save pennies in hopes of one day opening his own business, and now he held a bag full of money, more than he could have saved in ten lifetimes. His dream of a business was within his grasp, but it no longer held any allure to him, because he had already achieved his greatest dream of love and family and that was all gone. He had had it *all*, and then it was taken from him in a flash when two gunmen above the stage chose to prioritize the men with machine guns in the distance over the man in the foreground with the revolver.

"This letter arrived for you at your home while you were her recuperating. The crew found it while they were cleaning your place. It seemed important. It's addressed to you from Valmontone."

Al was handed an envelope with blue and red stripes around its edges. Those stripes were a telltale indicator of correspondence from Europe. It was addressed to him, or at least his former self, Fredo Mantelli. He didn't care enough about anything contained in it to open it cautiously, so he ripped the envelope open and found a multi-paged letter inside. It was from Bella, and it described the lie she'd created out of desperation more than a decade earlier, and how she never imagined that lie would inspire a vendetta, let alone inspire anyone to act on it. As it turned out, the handsome and well-dressed young man was her cousin who was present when her son was born, and who vowed vengeance. Bella had pleaded with him to leave Al alone, but hubris superseded compassion.

Bella went on to caution Al and told him she would forbid anyone else from trying to enforce the ridiculous vendetta ever again. She mentioned how ashamed she was of what had happened, and how it was all her fault because of that one moment of weakness when she lied. She wished she could do or say something to ease Al's pain, or to bring back his beloved wife, but to Al, it was nothing but words. All she had to do was confess to the lie years ago and bring an end to all of it, but she chose her reputation over honesty, and it had cost him his family.

He folded the letter back up and replaced it in the envelope. He handed it to the old man and asked him to read it and share the story with the crew, and Al's friends, and Marguerite, and Joey when he was old enough to understand. At this point, all Al had left was his reputation, and at the very least, this letter restored it.

Al left for 30th Street Station straight away and boarded the train for New York. He met the old man's friend when his train arrived at Penn Station, and he took up residence in New York's version of Little Italy. He spent most of his days speaking Italian again, and working as a bartender and occasionally as a cook in local restaurants and tap rooms. Old habits are difficult to break, which is why he worked multiple jobs day and night, as he had done in the past, except for one glaring difference.

Years ago, he worked tirelessly to save enough money to pay for his dreams. Today, he worked tirelessly to *forget* his dreams. Work kept him busy, and the busier he was, the less time he had to spend in his own mind. Memories of his losses resided in his mind, and he wasn't strong enough for the idle time when he'd have to face them.

In 1930, a year after Wall Street's Black Friday plunged the planet into the Great Depression, the once wealthy and powerful old man no longer owned the Dock Street theater. That asset and nearly all others had been sold to support Marguerite and Joe. The old man was left clinging to his home as his final possession, and the day he'd sell it for pennies on the dollar seemed to be looming imminently on the horizon.

One day, the old man's friend in New York, the one who helped Al transition to life there, was drinking at the bar Al tended, and during casual conversation shared the news of the Old man and his dire financial straits. The conversation immediately changed for Al from casual to dire. The old man's circumstances meant Joseph was at risk.

Al left the bar immediately, returned to his apartment to collect his few possessions and boarded a train out of Penn Station, destined for Philly. He arrived at 30th Street Station a couple hours later with the same trunk and satchel he had when he left five years earlier. He had come full circle and headed to the old man's neighborhood, standing on the sidewalk in front of the old man's home, paying a boy to deliver a cryptic message to the man of the house, asking him to meet an old friend in center city.

An hour later, and several blocks from his home, the old man approached Al at the old brass eagle in John Wannamaker's massive center city department store. Seeing Al, the old man smiled from ear to ear, secretly thankful the "old friend" from the note turned out to be his surrogate son. This would be the highpoint of what had been a very low year.

What felt like a five-minute reunion was actually an hour standing at the department store's main lobby, catching up on everything from the catastrophic economy, to Marguerite, to Joey and everything in between.

Although the old man was five years older, he looked older still. His once stylish and tailored suit was dated and fraying. His gold chains and bejeweled cuff links had been sold off and replaced by cheap fabric knots, and his always-polished shoes were worn at the heel, and hadn't been shined in a long time, because the nickel he saved not getting them cleaned-up was needed in about a thousand different and more important places.

As tattered and weathered as he was, the old man still considered himself blessed to have Marguerite and Joseph in his life, and he profusely thanked Al.

Al's heart broke every time the old man thanked him. Even though he knew living in that grand home with a mother and a father was better than any life Al could have given him, his heart ached to be with Joseph.

The visit concluded by Al letting the old man know of his intent to remain in Philly, but also of Al's assurance he would maintain a safe distance from the old man, Marguerite and Joe. He also shared his plan to spy on his boy whenever he could, just to see him and dream of what could have been. Finally, Al handed the satchel to the old man. The bag itself was scuffed a bit since the old man gave it to Al years earlier, but the contents were still intact—$10,000.

Al never knew what to do with so much money in the first place, nor did he ever feel right about taking it. It always felt to him like pity, even though the old man never intended it that way. Al knew the old man desperately needed the money to support his family, Al's family, and that was more important than Al keeping the Satchel under his bed forever. Besides, money never mattered to Al. He had started with nothing before, and he was pretty sure he could do it again, which he did.

The shocking sight of the money buckled the old man's knees. It was enough money to rescue him and assure his family of their home and a comfortable life until he could get everything back on track. The old man was down, but with capital, he would be back on top quickly. He was still financially shrewd and knew what needed to be done. He knew how to make massive sums in a down market, but those moves required capital and until now, he had none. All he needed was an infusion of cash to get started and the seed money Al handed him would grow exponentially and in short order. He embraced Al, kissed him on the cheek, and then embraced him again.

Al kissed the old man in return and choked back tears as he headed south on Broad Street toward the river which had first delivered him to America sixteen years earlier. And although he would never believe it if someone told him, the 32-year-old immigrant still had forty-four years ahead of him, and they were going to be amazing, but no matter how wonderful those years would be, they would never include being in the company of the old man ever again. Their paths intersected for the last time at the Bronze Eagle at Wanamaker's.

When the old man returned home, he called his Marguerite and Joe down to the foyer and there, amid the rich paneling and the leaded glass of their elegant residence, he opened the satchel and everyone laughed and sighed relief. A five-year-old Joseph, like his father, cared little about the money and instead reached into the bag and pulled out a cape, a flattened top hat and a small wand, asking what those things were.

Marguerite gasped and put her hand to her mouth. She hadn't expected to find such a present from Al for Joe, and it instantly brought her back to the days when she would teach her magic act to Sophia when she was Joseph's age. She grabbed the flattened hat and gave it a quick tap to make it pop open. She placed the top hat on the boy's head, handed him the wand, and wrapped the cape around his shoulders. Once it was unfurled, Marguerite began to cry. Across the back of the cape, inscribed in marquee style letters were the words "Acchione the Greatest."

PURGE

"Damn, Unc. I don't even … I mean … where do I …? That's a lot to process."

"Look kid, I didn't tell you all this to upset you, or tell you who you're *not* – Mantelli, Valmonti, whatever. It was to tell you who you *are*, the product of Al, and Joe and your Pop. *They're* your legacy, not Sonny's or some arbitrary family name. Al never had a name, not really. He was thrown onto the streets at fourteen and could've easily died there. Foundlings usually did. They were loathed by everyone, except each other.

"That tough bastard didn't care. He dreamt of better things and figured out a way to come to America, but he wasn't satisfied with saving himself. He busted his ass working 'round the clock in bars and at the docks just so every one of his fellow Foundlings could join him. He built a life here, and pursued a woman he had no business winning, but he persevered and worked hard and earned her love and the love of her family, and just when he was on top of the world, enjoying the fruits of his labor, at a time when other men would have settled back and lived off their good fortune, his beautiful life was stolen from him. You know what? He didn't break. He didn't give up. Even when his family was taken from him and everything he had was gone, he re-invented himself. He persevered.

"He took on a new name but was still the same man. You understand what I'm saying?

"He started *another* family. He started a new business. He created a new legacy and lineage, things he didn't have when he was dumped at that convent. Al passed that strength on to Joe, your uncle. He passed it on to your father, John senior, and all of them passed it on to you.

"Your name doesn't matter, kid. The height and width of your family tree doesn't matter. Al, and Joe and your own Pop *are* your tree. That's what matters. They are proof you come from hardy stock. Like them, you have the blood of a grinder coursing through you.

"Those three men are as good, and honest, and strong as any man you'll ever meet. They withstood torment and anguish. Lesser men would have crumbled under such adversity, but you know what? Those three guys *always* stood up taller the tougher things got. That's your legacy, kid.

"You have a rare privilege to pick your last name, John. It can be Mantelli, or Valmonti or Acchione, or anything else you want. It doesn't matter, because it's all bull shit. All that matters is whose blood is flowin' through your veins, and your blood line started with the tough little 'elf in a cape' who rode the Foundling Wheel in Valmontone more than a century ago."

I could almost feel the weight lift off Guido when he concluded the story, like he had somehow been holding his breath for decades and finally released it. He settled back into his chair—the first time I'd ever seen him do that in my life—leaned his head back, closed his eyes, and sighed. "Joe Acchione wasn't Joe Acchione, kid. He was Joe Mantelli. Both of those names were made up. Do you want to keep one of them, or invent one of your own?"

"And you mean to tell me, not even my Pop knows this story?"

"Nope."

"He doesn't know the story *of his own father*?"

"Did I stutter?"

"I mean, how is that possible?"

"Rose never knew either."

"My *grandmother*, never knew my *grandfather* had a son?"

"… or that he was married, or *anything* about Isabella. He wanted a clean slate with Rose, because he didn't think it would be fair to burden her with his past, and years later, he couldn't exactly tell your father his story, because then Rose would find out, and since Al died before Rose, well, he never had a chance to tell your dad. I'm the only one he ever told.

"In fact, here's the *really* crazy part. I knew before Joe. Even after Marguerite died, Al kept his distance from Joe. He didn't want to put him at risk. It wasn't until Al needed Joe's help running Sonny's, when your dad went into the Army and Al introduced me to Joe as some sort of value proposition, that I insisted he come clean. As you might suspect, Joe was *pissed* when he found out, but after a while, he cooled off and understood why Al never came forward. Al wasn't an absentee father trying to ignore his responsibilities. He *desperately* wanted contact, but only remained as close to Joe as he dared.

"It's tough to be mad at a guy who forfeited everything after his wife was murdered, just to protect his son, and the fact he's the one who gave the old man all his money to keep going during the Depression proved he wasn't a deadbeat dad. Once Joe realized the poor guy had done and given everything for his kid and was heartbroken in the process, he realized Al was a saint. He also agreed to keep the secret."

"That's insane. How did you *not* tell my dad all this time?"

"There were thousands of times I wanted to tell him, but I think your dad would've been hurt if he knew his father told me instead of him."

"Yeah, but then he could have had an older brother."

"There are always two sides to a coin, kid. Your dad is a great guy, and I love him dearly, but he's a pig-headed son-of-a-bitch, and if he took the news the wrong way and realized me and Joe knew all along, he might've shut us both out permanently. You've seen him do it."

"Yeah, I have. Once he's done with something or someone, he's done. Period."

"Exactly, and above all else, my job is to protect him, not be his buddy, so I couldn't risk him putting up any barriers. Trust me. Joe and I discussed this topic on many occasions. Joe was your dad's brother. He *craved* that relationship. Secretly, he always looked out for John, and remained tight with him and Toni, and tried to be close to you and your annoying sister, but it never really worked. In the end, Joe was an island and really wasn't good with families. It's why he never had one."

"Woulda-coulda-shoulda," I said, a little sadly.

And just like that, Guido smirked, harrumphed, nodded and drifted off to sleep with a look of relief on his face. I walked over to the sofa, grabbed the blanket there, and placed it on Guido, tucked under his chin. Then I grabbed a few sofa pillows, piled them under my head, and reclined on his sofa. I didn't figure leaving him alone was the best call, so I stayed behind and fell asleep again in a second.

In what seemed like a minute later, Guido was lightly shaking my shoulder. "C'mon, kid. It's a new day and we gotta get rollin'."

Bleary-eyed, I slowly focused and saw Guido, fresh and clean-shaven in a pressed suit, ready to pounce on the day.

"C'mon!" He yelled and pointed at the kitchen door leading to the basement. "Get your ass down there, get a shower, and get dressed. There's new clothes on the bed for you. When you're done, come to the kitchen. Breakfast'll be ready. How do you like your eggs, dippy? I'll make 'em dippy. Hurry up!"

"What time is it?"

"Six a.m. We got a lot to do today and sleeping late doesn't get it done."

"Unc, I'm a restaurant worker. We work late. We *go* to sleep at 6 a.m. We rarely get up before noon."

"Oh, I'm sorry. Did you close a kitchen last night? No? Then don't give me that shit. Get up and get moving. *C'mon!*"

I sat up and rotated around on the sofa, blinking very slowly in an attempt to moisten my bone-dry eyes. I could almost hear my eyelids scrape over my eyeballs, like sandpaper rubbing over Velcro. I couldn't focus, and my eyelids barely hung at half-mast. My head lolled around on my shoulders like my neck needed a dose of Viagra just to keep that damned orb floating above my shoulders. My tongue was stuck to the back of my teeth, because the only thing drier than my eyes was my mouth, and when my mouth opened, the odor it expelled was like smelling salts under my nose. My breath smelled like ass, and if I thought about it, that was the flavor my dry tongue was detecting, too. If I didn't know better, I'd swear Guido's little rat of a dog had taken a shit in my mouth while I was sleeping.

My first attempt at standing failed, and I fell back into the sofa where I started. I grabbed the armrest a little tighter the second time and got to my feet, but I was reeling like Muhammad Ali had just landed a solid uppercut to my jaw. I leaned my head to the right and my body followed. The momentum carried me toward the door, and if I didn't hit anything along the way, I'd be able to propel myself down the steps to my room. There was every chance in the world I would flop onto my bed when I reached it, but at Guido's urging, I would do my damnedest to make it to my bathroom and shower, which I ultimately did.

I turned on the shower, stripped, and climbed in under the water. I placed both palms on the wall in front of me and let the shower work its magic, pouring a steady stream of hot water over my head in hopes it would revive me. This shower was much better at resuscitating me than the shower in that shit-hole Pittsburgh hotel had been.

I was shocked out of my stupor when I heard Guido's pinky ring tapping against the glass shower stall door.

"Here," he said as he handed me a mug of black coffee. "Drink this. You'll feel better."

"Jesus! A *little* privacy would be nice."

"You want the coffee or not?"

"Obviously yes, but still."

"Stop your whining. I've seen everything you got, except in adult sizes. Hurry up. Breakfast will get cold."

I finished and stepped out of the shower, dried myself, and found everything I needed to prepare for the day—toothbrush, toothpaste, comb, hair dryer, deodorant, toilet paper. I put on the clothes laid out for me on the bed, which weren't mine, since those had been tossed into the Melrose dumpster yesterday, but the new stuff still fit me well enough. Within a few minutes I found my way to the kitchen, where breakfast was set for me, and Guido was waiting, reading the morning *Inquirer*.

"You waited for me to eat?"

"Of course, I always wait for my sleepover guests before I start eating."

"You have many sleepover guests, Big G?"

"Well, you're the first *guy* but yeah, a few. You like your scrapple thin or thick? I got both."

"Thin."

"Ketchup?"

"No…never…on *anything*. Damn."

"Your choice. I like it on my scrapple."

I should probably take a moment here and tell you what scrapple is. I have no idea where this concoction started, probably with the

Pennsylvania Dutch, but scrapple is exactly what its name suggests. It's a combination of cornmeal, spices, and meat scraps from the butcher. I think it's pig, but I honestly don't know. It could be cow, or goat, or horse, or dog, or elephant. We all know better than to ask.

When someone wants to know what's in a hot dog, the standard response is "everything but the oink." Well, my friends, scrapple's the oink. Basically, it's whatever isn't fit to be put into a hot dog, if such things actually exist.

It is sold raw as a gray semi-firm loaf at the meat counter, and the preparation method is to slice it down and fry it in a pan on both sides. The goal is for the outside to be crispy, while the middle is soft, like an undercooked meatball.

Anyone else from anywhere else on the planet would refrain from trying this, and rightfully so. It sounds positively disgusting. It's one of those local foods that you'd never touch if you weren't raised on it, like Vegemite, or guinea pig, or that weird fermented canned fish they eat in Norway—or Sweden or Finland or someplace like that. But you know what? If you don't think about what's in it, you might find you like it.

Personally, I love scrapple, especially in a hoagie roll with a couple fried eggs and melted American cheese on it. On the other side of the Delaware River, in New Jersey, they love pork roll, but over here in Philly? We're scrapple people.

I read somewhere that eating a hot dog takes thirty-six hours off your life. If it cost double that to consume a slice of scrapple, it would be worth every delicious morsel.

Unfortunately, cretins like Guido ruin a perfectly good slice of scrapple with ketchup, or sometimes vinegar; maple syrup too. We purists call them heathens, but I'm trying to refrain from disparaging my uncle too aggressively in his own home, him grieving and all.

"*JEEEEsus*, Unc. The ketchup isn't bad enough? You have to put Tabasco on your eggs, too?"

"What? It's delicious. You ever tried it?"

"Unfortunately, that shit is so overwhelmingly pungent, just unscrewing the cap is enough to waft its flavor everywhere in the room. I can't *help* but try it. Seriously, can you close that bottle?"

"You know, none of my other overnight guests ever complain like this."

"Probably because you pay them to be here."

"Cute. Can I butter my bread, or do you have some sort of purity issue with that, too?"

"You using butter or margarine?"

"Butter."

"Good. Proceed with god, and then pass some of that shit over here when you're done. So what's on the agenda today?"

"I have a business to run. We also have to make arrangements for Joe. We need to deal with his estate, and oh, if we have a free second, we need to find Gina and kill her, maybe her grandfather too. The jury's still out on him."

"Who is he, anyway?"

"The grandfather? He's Isabella's youngest son. He's actually about my age—couple years older."

"Seriously? She had a kid in 1915, and another about twenty-five years later?"

"Yeah. Remember, she was only fifteen when she had her first, but no one was supposed to know about that. She and her actual husband started when she was twenty. They had three boys—boom, boom, boom—after they got married. Then a decade or so later, they had produced Gina's grandfather."

"So she was forty? That's pretty old to have a kid."

"You think that's bad, her husband was forty years older than her."

"He was *eighty*? Is that even possible?"

"Watch your ass, kid. Remember how old the guy you're talkin' to is. You're goddamn right it's possible. It happens more frequently than you'd believe, too. There was this guy in Hollywood—TVs and movies—he played a tidy roommate in a TV show. Anyway, he *started* his family in his late seventies. Just because we're old doesn't mean our swimmers need floaties—know what I'm sayin'?"

"No offense intended, G. I wasn't questioning if it's biologically possible. I'm questioning the sanity of anyone that age who would *want* to make a kid."

"Oh. Yeah. That part's fucked up. And for the record, the sloppy guy in that TV show was from Philly."

"Did he have kids in his late seventies?"

"No. He's from Philly. We're smarter than that," and Guido winked at me and smiled.

"So Gina's grandfather is your age, and Gina is my age. How the hell is he old enough to be her grandfather? The math doesn't work."

"Sure it does. Gina's mother was his oldest. Gina's uncle, the guy you killed, was his youngest."

"Seriously? Damn. You Romani are like *rabbits*."

"And you Italian Catholics aren't? You know how many of these South Philly rowhomes are filled with two parents and a dozen or more offspring … and *one bathroom*?"

Before I could answer, Guido interrupted. "You eating that slice of toast?" And he grabbed it right off my plate. "I ran outta toast before I ran outta yolk and I don't feel like makin' another slice."

"And if I said I wasn't done with it?"

Guido pointed to the kitchen counter and, with a mouthful of food, told me where to go to find bread and a toaster to make myself another slice. Thank god this man never had children. They'd have murdered him by now. I had spent one night in his place, and I was already plotting it.

...Meanwhile

After coming up empty at the Melrose, the old man directed his driver to return him to the Ritz-Carlton, where he could shower off the nightmarish past several hours, change his clothes, and decide what to do next. No one else spoke for the rest of the ride until the car pulled up to the marble steps leading from the sidewalk into the Ritz. The doorman reached down to open the rear door of the limo, but as he did, Gina lowered the window from the inside and held up a single digit to him, asking him to give them a moment. Then she raised the window for privacy.

"So what do we do now, Grandfather? He's out there, so we need to find him, right?"

"And what do you propose we do, child? He's gone to ground. You are the one who killed the old lawyer. Had you not done anything, as I *instructed*, no one in that family would be on alert. We could have easily knocked on your boyfriend's door, had a civil conversation, identified fair reparations for all parties, and put this entire sordid business behind us. Instead, you killed a harmless old man, and ignited a fire under the Mantellis all over again. If you had put your gun away in the hotel room as I *instructed*, John would not have had access to it, and we would not have been rendered naked together on his bed while he sped off into the night. What else would *you* propose we do?"

Gina tried to look contrite, but her face betrayed her. She was eager to get things moving again. Every second John was alive, there was a risk he'd tell her grandfather the truth, how the whole thing was her idea. All of it. She hadn't worried when her uncle bragged about her role to John in Sonny's. She actually liked the idea of John finding out *she* was the puppeteer, the reason his family was falling apart and about to die, but John was supposed to die after that, and he didn't. Once he escaped, he became a loose end, which was even more reason to kill him.

She inhaled to begin a reply but was interrupted by her grandfather, who leaned past her, opening the door from the inside and gestured for her to step outside with him. Once on the sidewalk, the old man instructed the limo driver to leave, asked the doorman to call Gina a cab, and handed her a twenty-dollar bill, suggesting that should be plenty to get her home.

Her indignity was quite a sight—barefoot in November in center city during a workday when the sidewalks were filled with business people and tourists. She was wearing only an oversized man's dress shirt and nothing else—no bra, no underwear, nothing. Her clothes had all been saturated in a hotel tub in Pittsburgh and were still sopping wet in the trunk of the limo which had just pulled away. Her grandfather, having made his point, walked up the steps without her, leaving her to fend for herself as some sort of childish punishment.

She was incredulous as she watched the car drive off down Broad Street, and her grandfather walk up the marble steps away from her. This wasn't a whim on his part. He had obviously planned this. He wanted to teach her a lesson, possibly in humility, possibly to illustrate who was in charge, or possibly to illustrate what happens when she deviates from his script. Regardless, she was being humiliated by a man with authority over her, again, for what seemed like the millionth time, and she was fucking sick of it.

The doorman tried to speak and she simply turned to him and hollered "CAB!" She turned her attention away from him and brooded, arms crossed across her, chin pressed into her chest, lips pressed together so tightly they were turning white from a lack of blood circulation, and eyes glaring out from below her turned-down eyebrows. If this was a cartoon, there would be steam releasing through her ears to the wail of a fire alarm. The doorman raised an arm and summoned the next cab in the queue, and she climbed in. There was nowhere else for her to go, so she barked out her mother's South Philly address and sat back with her arms still crossed in front of her, furious. Her only hope was Guido didn't have anyone stationed at her home, or she was sunk. She'd have to tell the driver to keep rolling, and she'd be forced to get out at a different curb, practically naked, wandering the streets aimlessly without a dime or prospects for getting out of this hole into which she'd been tossed.

Fortunately, no surveillance was evident when she returned home. She threw the twenty at the driver, exited the cab, and stepped up to her door, only then realizing she didn't have her key. It was with her saturated things in the limo.

She closed her eyes, then inhaled and exhaled deeply, trying to regain what little composure she could muster, and then prayed that her dead mother had been stupid enough to leave a house key outside.

At first, she looked under the front mat, which was nearly as old as her, and was completely thread-bare…no key. Then she stood on her tippy-toes as tall as she could, trying to run the fingers of one hand across the top edge of the door frame to see if a key was there, all the while holding down the back of her shirt with her other hand to avoid flashing her naked ass or other bits at the neighborhood.

Once again, nothing. Before she went to the alley to try and break a window and climb through, an exercise she was sure would end up in some very unpleasant scrapes and cuts, especially in her compromised attire, she decided to open her front storm door and see if there was a key in sight, *anywhere*. For the first time in days, she got lucky.

The storm door was a typical aluminum affair, the top two-thirds comprised of a storm window (replaceable with a screen in the summer) and the bottom a solid aluminum panel. Because South Philadelphians tend to take any opportunity to make something simple look fancy, this particular door had a cursive letter "G" inside a circular appliqué in a contrasting and grossly oxidized vomit green color that contrasted with the natural gray finish of the aluminum door. It was absolutely hideous.

Years ago, a key had been taped in place on the inside of the door, just below the storm window. The tape had long since dried out and failed, but instead of falling to the ground, gravity had wedged the key between the hydraulic door closer and the door. It was an incredibly lucky break, and it had been concealed there for years. Thank god!

She stepped inside and immediately stepped out of her grandfather's shirt before she had even closed the door. She seriously considered wiping her ass with it in spite later but decided she didn't ever want anything of that man to touch her again. She stormed off to the bathroom, the filthy soles of her feet leaving marks on the worn carpet on the stairs along the way. She stopped only long enough to turn on the shower before sitting on the closed toilet seat, grabbing a bath towel, holding it over her own mouth, and screaming into it for nearly a minute.

She was so angry, if she stepped under the freezing cold shower water right away, it would have converted to steam as it hit her. She slammed every door and cabinet she crossed. She threw the shower curtain open so violently, the shower rod was nearly torn off the wall. She. Was. *Livid!*

GINA

Gina had married halfway through high school, according to an arrangement between her Romani parents and another local Romani family. The boy was local and nothing spectacular. He was dull and doughy, about five-and-a-half feet tall, and already balding at sixteen. His father had started an aluminum siding business in the early '60s and had become successful. It was all a scam, of course. He'd go door-to-door, convince homeowners they needed siding to cover the brick on their house to hold-in the warmth, or keep water from leaking in, or just to make the place look better. He'd get half the payment up front so he could order the materials and the other half when the materials were delivered. He'd take the first payment, buy a fraction of the materials he'd need to do the job, have them delivered, collect the second check, and disappear. Sometimes, he'd steal the supplies from previous jobs and just recycle them from sucker to sucker.

It was a shrewd business tactic, if not completely unethical and immoral, and certainly illegal.

Ironically, in Romani culture, it is desirable to be considered honorable (they refer to this as "baxt" where the "x" sounds like an "h"), but in some cases, honor is exhibited through public displays of success. Sometimes being honorable means being generous, but sometimes it means showing off, so even though the wealth may be ill-gotten, it can still be considered honorable. Gina's in-laws weren't very generous, nor honorable by any common definition, but they were very good at showing off. They drove nice cars. They wore designer clothes. Their home was filled with fancy furniture and light fixtures and TVs and stereos.

Bluebloods, the upper-crust, old-money Philadelphians from Rittenhouse Square in the city, or from the western suburbs along the Main Line (where wealthy people live who can trace their families in this country back to Plymouth Rock, or at least the signing of the Declaration of Independence, and started buying land and building estate homes in the 1800s) would walk into such a Romani home and vomit from the garish display. Homes like Gina's in-laws' epitomized nouveau riche, but they didn't care what the country club set thought, because those elitists were often broke and struggling to maintain facades, while these Romani were flush with money, and everything they did was cash. They never paid taxes.

Although Gina's parents were related to Isabella, none of the family's old-world money made it to Philly. Gina's father received a dowry when he married Gina's mother, but those few coins were long gone by the early '80s, and her father was hopelessly unmotivated to make anything of himself. Instead of climbing, he wanted others to pull him, so he was thrilled to marry into his daughter's new family. He was given a meager sales job by Gina's father-in-law, selling siding as well as other home improvement projects that were never performed, and he successfully did the absolute minimum to get by until he died.

Gina's mother came from hardier stock. Isabella's blood ran through her veins, and she was shrewd. Once her husband died in the '90s, she kept her head above water by assuming his role in the business. Essentially, she took over his job and ended up doing it better than he ever did.

Meanwhile, Gina and her new husband moved in with her in-laws on her wedding night and she immediately became a baby factory. Living with her in-laws was degrading. The family considered her to be little more than a domestic servant. She cleaned their house. She cooked their meals. She did everyone's laundry, and at night, she had the privilege of lying under her blob of a husband, and if she was lucky, she'd get pregnant again. She got pregnant almost immediately, like Isabella, and then she proceeded to have four kids in three years. The last two were born during the same calendar year, but one was in January and the last in December. It may sound strange, but fortunately for her, she had complications with the last one and had to have an emergency hysterectomy. If it wasn't for that, she'd have probably produced twenty kids.

Of course, having children didn't mean she was relieved of any of her other domestic duties. They just complicated her job because she had to raise her offspring single-handedly while everyone else in the house sat back and waited for her to wait on them, even her husband's siblings. His younger brothers and sisters would command her to take care of their needs—clean their clothes, run their errands, do *their* chores—and one of her brothers-in-law actually forced himself on her. Of course she never told anyone, and to this day she doesn't know if her third kid is her husband's or his brother's.

Unfortunately, when her family paid her in-laws a dowry, meager pittance that it was, they literally paid the in-laws to take her. She could never ask her parents to intercede on her behalf. They couldn't do anything for her, and quite frankly, even if they could, they *wouldn't* do anything for her, because they didn't want her back: No need welcoming another mouth (or five if her kids came with her) to feed. Their work with her had ended, and she was someone else's problem. She had become chattel.

And all of this was unfortunate on many levels. First and foremost, although she had no idea at the time, she was a descendant of Isabella, who had diligently created a Romani empire. Gina was practically Romani royalty, but no one in South Philly knew that, nor cared.

She was also remarkably beautiful. She resembled her great-grandmother. She was diminutive, at something less than five feet tall, but she was beautifully proportioned and her face was angelic, framed by long, thick, black, wavy hair. She was the sort of girl people, men *and* women, would stop in their tracks to watch. How she ended up combining her genes with those of a drab, forgettable lump of a marshmallow was almost criminal. She was far and away out of his league, yet somehow, *she* became *his* (and his *family's*) slave.

The seed of her contempt for misogyny had been planted in her fertile mind, and it was thriving with every indignity her in-laws thrust upon her.

Gina was also shrewd, like her great-grandmother. She was an abysmal school student. Leaving high school without a diploma was hardly a loss for her, because she was never going to do anything in life requiring a formal education anyway, but school is not a measure of intelligence. School is theoretical. Gina was a doer. Just as learning about dance doesn't make one a dancer, learning theory in school assures no one of success in real life.

After a few years, Gina's husband was sent away to expand the family enterprise in another market, and she dutifully accompanied him, four toddlers in tow. She found a home, furnished it, maintained it, raised and managed the children, and otherwise resembled a whirling dervish for two decades, until one day, her youngest daughter was finally married off and Gina and her husband were alone.

The years had done him no favors. The pudgy teen grew into a corpulent flesh-sphere of an adult, but unlike similarly sized and shaped planets, his gravitational pull didn't hold moons in orbit. It attracted pastries and cheeseburgers and hookers. In her wildest dreams, she never believed it could be possible, but as disgusted as she was by him when they married, her husband actually became *more* repugnant over time. Like the Big Bang, Gina and her husband spun away from one another into entropy.

Of course, socially, his extramarital activity was not only acceptable, it was encouraged. After all, married men often joke with one another about how little sex they get from their wives, and he considered himself a desirable and virile specimen of a man. How could he possibly allow such a noble husk to wither from a lack of use? She, on the other hand, would have been rolled in honey and dropped on a red ant hill if she so much as flirted with the bag boy at the supermarket. She could only occupy herself with watching her grandchildren when she could, and otherwise sitting around waiting to die.

With neither sun nor water, this gorgeous orchid of a girl was drying up.

Then something happened.

About two years ago, Gina's mother died. She was born in the old country in 1953, which doesn't seem so long ago, especially for people born in 1953. One of the benefits of having children young is you don't tend to be too old when they're grown and gone. In her mother's case, though, she was lucky to nearly make it into her mid-sixties. She had not led the healthiest lifestyle, and between alcoholism and a life of chain-smoking, it was nearly a miracle she made it as far as she did.

Gina's husband granted her permission to return home to Philly and tend to her mother's estate, and while she rummaged through her mother's possessions—old magazines, worthless mass-produced figurines, kitchen appliances that were garbage when they were new fifty years ago, and mismatched hand-me-down plates and flatware—she got a glimpse of her own future.

Her mother didn't start her life as a worn-out hag. She wasn't always devoid of optimism. She must've hoped for more, yet here was Gina, knee-deep in what her mother left behind, all of which was crap, and she realized this would be her fate if she didn't do something to stem the tide.

Although her mother was only fifteen when she gave birth to Gina, in true Romani fashion, she had delivered another child a year later, also a daughter. Gina and her younger sister were friendly enough growing up, but Gina was married off when her sister was only thirteen, and once Gina married, she became estranged from the family.

Gina literally had no idea where her sister had ended up. She could be living within three blocks of the empty South Philly row home Gina was clearing out, or she could be living thousands of miles away, or she could be not living at all. Who knew? This meant Gina, as the oldest, was left holding the bag, obligated to sift through her parents' life by herself, arranging for a dumpster, and ultimately selling the row home, subsequently handing any proceeds over to her husband in the process.

One afternoon, while sifting through her mother's belongings, deep in the bottom of her parents' bedroom dresser, mixed in with her mother's marriage certificate and a few photos from childhood in Italy, Gina found a trove of old correspondence from the family she never knew. The letters and envelopes were all yellowed from time, and everything was handwritten. Hardly any were in English. Some were in Italian, while others were written in a Romani language she'd learned from birth. Gina may not have been good at school, but she was fluent in all three languages, because they were all spoken in her home while she grew up.

With only the slightest kernel of curiosity, she began. She read the salutation on one letter, flipped to the end to see who it was from, and then read the body of the letter. Hours later, she hadn't moved. She was seated on the threadbare rug in front of the dresser, leaning against her parents' bed, reading every word of every letter there. She read some multiple times as she subconsciously started placing them all in piles when she finished reading them.

There was a pile from her Romani relatives in Spain and Italy. There were others from family located elsewhere in the world as they dispersed. Those two piles were interesting enough, but were general, friendly correspondence between cousins and siblings and aunts and uncles. Much of it focused on who was living where, who was dead, who had a baby, or other sloppy, sappy family gossip, but then there was the pile from her mother's father—Gina's grandfather.

These letters changed Gina's life, right there on the floor of her parents' bedroom. In those letters, she rediscovered her optimism and found purpose. By the time she had finished reading them, she figured out what she would do with her life, and how she would get there.

All her life, she believed the Gianettis just landed in South Philly, as if god himself dropped them from the sky into some lackluster rowhouse. Her lazy father sat around the house every day while her mother did all the work. Once Gina was married, her father finally took a job, but he was dead from a heart attack before he was fifty. Her mother remained where she was, though, even though she lost contact with her daughters, and her husband was gone. She was alone. Neither she nor her husband ever had any friends. There was no other family. They even stayed clear of the neighbors. Her mother was an island, which is how she remained until the sea of alcohol and nicotine swallowed her up in death.

As Gina learned, that façade was a very thin veil over her family's actual purpose in this country. Her grandfather had sent his daughter to Philadelphia to spy on their sworn enemy.

In one letter, her grandfather provided details about the vendetta their family had against the Mantellis. Gina had no idea who the Mantellis were, but the letter detailed chapter and verse of how Fredo had raped her great-grandmother and left her to fend for herself. Having been raped by her own brother-in-law, Gina felt a connection with Isabella, and an instantaneous loathing for Fredo.

Her thoughts moved from the written word to the stories developing in her mind. Perhaps the parallels with Isabella were more than simply coincidence. Perhaps Isabella had been reborn in Gina, or more specifically, when Isabella died, which she surely must have done by now, her spirit found a home in Gina. Perhaps Gina is Isabella's vessel to right the wrongs committed against her a century ago. Gina felt an instant connection with Bella in these letters. There *must* be more here. Why else would she find these letters? Why else would Gina's mother have kept them all these years?

She learned of her family's shame, "ladz" to Romani (pronounced like "badge" with an "L"), and how they would hold the Mantellis accountable. She learned of Isabella's father creating the vendetta that still burned, unsatisfied to this day, decades upon decades later. She learned of the day when someone from their village sent a letter home from America, announcing Fredo had been discovered. She learned of the failed attempt on his life, and how he survived and changed his name to Valmonti, believing a ruse of his death would conclude the vendetta against him.

That letter's content hit Gina like a lightning bolt. She sat up, her eyes as big as saucers, and stared at the wall in front of her. It was an epiphany. She had lived her entire childhood next to her family's nemeses. On the other side of the wall, the subject of her family's vendetta still lived. Al Valmonti was, in reality, Fredo Mantelli!

Holy. Shit.

Her great-grandmother's rapist and his family were right next door, *for her entire life.* She no longer assumed a connection between herself and Isabella. Now she *knew* her purpose was to enforce the vendetta and free Isabella's spirit, bringing it peace.

She read on and learned Joe Acchione was Fredo's son, and that her friend growing up, John, the boy upon whom she had a crush since grade school, had been marked for death before birth.

She learned her mother was sent there, not to act on the vendetta, but to keep an eye on the family and report back to the old country what transpired. After the attempt on Fredo's life, her great-grandmother had forbidden anyone from pursuing the vendetta further. Her children, Gina's grandfather and his siblings, agreed to honor their mother's wishes, but secretly agreed to do so only until Bella died. After that, they would restore the vendetta and act!

Gina had found her purpose. Surely her great-grandmother was gone by now. She would be 120 years old. She had no idea if her grandfather, or any of his siblings, were alive, but hopefully *someone* was. Gina decided to assume the role her mother vacated and watch the Valmontis for her family, and ultimately, *she* would be the one to exact justice when called upon to do so. A part of her mind she never realized existed had suddenly become animated. She was formulating scenarios to end the Valmontis and find favor within the ranks of her own family. Her mind had gone from spark to forest fire in an instant.

Finally, after decades, she knew who she was and what she must do!

Then she found the letter…*the* letter. It was from her grandfather. It informed Gina's mother of his ascension to the role of patriarch, because his mother had passed away. The year was 1976. Gina's mother had been in the US a little more than a decade, first with only her husband, but then with her two daughters.

Upon news of Isabella's demise, Gina's mother expected to be deployed to execute the vendetta and return home, but instead, her father informed her the vendetta was a ruse. His mother had lied all along. Fredo had never done anything to her, and the Mantellis actually meant absolutely nothing to their family. Gina's grandfather was heartbroken. His cousin had attempted to murder an innocent man. He had *succeeded* in killing Fredo's wife. He murdered the wife of an innocent man, all because of his cowardly mother's lie.

The vendetta was being called off. Gina's family was to remain in

Philadelphia to keep an eye on the Valmontis, but instead of destroying them, they were expected to quietly atone for what Gina's family had done to them. They were to watch over the Valmontis, reporting home if there were any problems or threats against them.

Still seated on the floor, Gina went limp. Her hands fell to the floor beside her legs, and the letter gently landed in her lap. Her head lolled back against the mattress she had been leaning against, and her eyes vacantly stared at the ceiling. As quickly as she had discovered her life's purpose and her mind had exploded to life, it was all taken away. Her sad, boring life had been restored. She became the same pathetic creature she had been only a few moments ago—the broken, middle-aged mother of four, cleaning out the effects of her destitute, deceased mother. She wasn't going to be her family's champion. She was little more than a used-up hag, daughter of a withered, old drunk, and great-granddaughter of a spineless, lying coward.

Gina's parents, once upon a time strategically placed behind enemy lines and tasked with gaining the enemy's trust before killing them, had been reassigned to being their babysitters. No wonder they became alcoholic saps, Gina thought. Their purpose had been ripped from them, too! For the first time in her life, she didn't hate her parents. She pitied them.

The letters continued to arrive, and Gina read through them all, but her interest waned after she learned the vendetta had been a farce. Her grandfather continued to subsidize her mother's income, but ultimately, his letters stopped, and so did the money.

It was Gina's uncle, her mother's younger brother Stefano, the one born five years before she left for America, the one who remained home and was groomed to assume the role of patriarch of the family when it was his turn, who replied to Gina's mother's letters, telling her to stop reaching out to her father, because no one wanted anything more to do with her.

He ignored the requests to continue the subsidies, and effectively told Gina's mother it was time for her to support herself. The last letter Gina found was from her uncle, indignantly refuting her mother's claim he was blocking her in America so he could become patriarch, even though she had seniority and deserved to assume her great-grandmother's role. He told her her very existence brought Ladz on their family, and she was being shunned.

An hour earlier, Gina's fertile mind was ignited by the vendetta, before she learned it was moot, but that small flame, no matter how brief, proved to her she was a fighter. Maybe there was more to her belief she was Isabella reborn, after all. Isabella may have covered her ass with a lie, but she returned like a phoenix. She took control of a fragmented family and built an empire. Isabella possessed the heart of a warrior, and now Gina believed she did as well.

So what if the vendetta had been called off? Maybe the cause of the vendetta wasn't a lie at all. Maybe the *letter* was the lie. Maybe Isabella didn't even *write* the letter. Maybe there was no letter at all, and her grandfather made the whole story up to maintain the peace. Maybe Isabella's heirs were all *chickenshit* and couldn't bring themselves to pursue the vendetta any further. Maybe *she* was the only one with the intestinal fortitude to see this through! It had been Gina's experience, the only ones in their family with real balls were the women!

Maybe there was a plot against Gina's parents, because they wanted to pursue the vendetta. Maybe it was her conniving uncle who destroyed her parents, and indirectly damned Gina to a life of servitude and abuse at the hands of her pudgy husband and his disgusting family!

Now her mind was reawakened, plotting how to vindicate her mother against her family. She was tired of women being exploited by weak men whose only source of power was having something hang between their legs. She was tired of men assuming the leadership of the family, even though the family would have never been anything without the efforts of a woman, *Isabella—whom Gina believed now existed inside her*. She decided it was time for a woman to regain control, and she plotted her scheme to get there, and the first step was to crawl out from beneath her husband, literally and figuratively.

Gina stomped down the steps from her mother's bedroom to the kitchen, sat at the table where she had daydreamed over her homework as a child, and drafted a letter to her uncle. She explained who she was, and taking a page from her great-grandmother's book, fabricated a tale of physical abuse at the hands of her husband, and how she lived in fear and was hiding in a dingy row home in South Philadelphia until that awful man would ultimately find her.

Her husband's physical abuse against a member of her family should resonate with her uncle and grandfather, she thought. She pleaded for help, now that her parents were gone and she was all alone in the U.S. with no family.

Although she was not book smart, Gina had excellent instincts. In some ways, she *was* like Isabella. She knew one of the best ways to get someone to owe you a favor is to get them to help you. It sounds contradictory, but people feel invested in the people they help, a much stronger connection than any they'd feel for someone who does *them* a favor. Gina never learned that anywhere. It came to her organically. She was much smarter than anyone gave her credit for being, and being underestimated would become her greatest asset in future endeavors. Her innate ability to be a master manipulator was worth more than anything she or anyone else could ever learn in school. Again, she was a doer—screw theory and books!

Gina used the address her uncle had included as a return address on the last letter he sent two decades earlier. He may not be there, but someone who is may know him and be able to get her message to him. She dropped the envelope at the post office, and then returned to the task at hand, clearing out the old row home.

She spent a few more days identifying what to throw away, and what to keep. The former pile was much larger than the latter. Aside from all those letters, and her own baby teeth, there was really nothing worth preserving. Since it really didn't matter how long she lingered there, because her husband certainly wasn't missing her, Gina decided to tidy the place up and stay in town for a few days, maybe longer. She visited her favorite restaurants. She wandered the streets within a few blocks of her mother's home to reacquaint herself with her surroundings, and then sat in her mother's living room, relaxing, basking in the peace and quiet, until the day her cell phone rang. It was her oldest daughter.

Gina's son-in-law had been in an accident. Her daughter was going to spend a lot of time visiting him at the hospital and helping him with rehabilitation, and she needed help raising her children—a six-year-old, a seven-year-old, and a baby.

Gina agreed to care for the kids under one condition: she could bring them back to Philly with her, because they'd be too much of a disruption for her husband if they lived with him. That moment on that call was the one where Gina decided she was never returning home to live with her husband. Like Isabella plucking that lie from the ether in an instant to protect herself from her father's wrath, so now had Gina relied on a fabrication of her own on the fly to protect herself from a life of ennui. It was no longer a matter of *if* her pursuit of power within Isabella's family was going to happen. It was a matter of *how* it was going to happen.

Gina traveled home long enough to collect her grandchildren and some of her own things—clothes and bathroom supplies mostly—and let her husband know she was going to take the kids back to Philly so they wouldn't disrupt his life. He grunted and nodded, and that was the last she ever saw of him.

She was going to be *mostly* independent. She didn't have any source of income, but since she continued to have access to their shared bank accounts, she'd be able to pay her bills with ease. Other than that, she was entirely on her own. Within a month, the two older children were enrolled in the local Catholic school and the baby was home with Gina every day, just the two of them. She had never had such time with any of her own kids, because she was always juggling caring for her husband's family instead of focusing on her own. This was a first, and she loved it.

Weeks passed, and although she spoke with her daughter every day, inquiring about her son-in-law's condition, and sharing the latest stories about the grandchildren, she never heard from anyone else. Then one day her phone rang, and it was the police informing her they had found her husband beaten to death, and would she please come home and identify the body.

She did as asked and returned home. She packed up the kids, since there was no one in Philly to cover for her, booked a flight, and ultimately arrived at the morgue, holding a baby. The other two little kids clutched onto her dress on either side. She began handing children to the protesting officers so she could identify the body, unencumbered. She joined the coroner and stood patiently while the staff pulled together paperwork and slid a drawer open. There, on a cold steel drawer lay her husband, bruised and battered, but immediately recognizable. She nodded her recognition, signed a few forms, collected her grandchildren, and left. It wasn't until she reached the car that she realized how entirely numb she had been to the whole affair. She certainly possessed no remorse, but she also felt no pleasure. She was ambivalent, which when she thought about it, defined her marriage from their wedding night to this moment.

Gina returned to the home she had shared with her husband, inviting her kids to come visit and take anything they wanted. She arranged a funeral service, and between the ride from the church to the cemetery she signed the contract to list her house for sale. The home sold quickly. She sold or donated its contents, took the proceeds and whatever cash remained in their bank account, filed a life insurance claim, and returned to Philly with more money than she'd ever need and three little kids with whom she was becoming increasingly attached.

It was a Monday afternoon around lunchtime. The two older kids were in school—kindergarten and first grade—and the baby was napping. She quietly sat alone in her mother's living room staring at the walls, enjoying the peace, wondering what to do with her life now that she had assumed the role of mother to her grandchildren, when there was a light knock at her front door. There, dressed in an absolutely beautiful, tailored suit was the most handsome man she'd ever seen. He was a few years older than her, but he was *gorgeous*. Unlike her husband who had always been soft and disheveled, dressed in discount suits and cheap shoes, this man was impeccable. Not a single hair in his thick mane was out of place. His skin was tan. His eyes were blue, and every piece of his wardrobe was bespoke; even his shoes appeared to be custom made. She imagined the cows sacrificed themselves willingly so their skins could be privileged enough to be used to encapsulate his perfect feet.

As she opened the door, she heard him exchanging pleasantries with Toni Valmonti, the old lady in the adjacent row home whose own door was mere inches away from Gina's. Toni was returning from her family restaurant and told the handsome gentleman who looked like an Italian banker she was just coming home to check on a few things and was heading back out momentarily. She invited him to the restaurant to enjoy a meal.

Gina said hello to Toni, who was shocked to see her. Gina had kept such a low profile, not even her neighbors knew she was back and living there. They exchanged their own pleasantries, and then Gina turned her attention to her handsome visitor.

"Mrs. Gianetti?" the man asked in a very controlled, almost bored manner.

"Yes?" Gina responded, with butterflies in her stomach, parts of her body coming alive for the first time in decades.

"My name is Stefano Ariano. Your mother was my sister. May I come in?"

Gina welcomed her uncle into her home, albeit dejectedly because she'd been hoping this would lead to something far more intimate than a chat in her living room with a relative.

"May I sit?"

"Anywhere you'd like. Could I get you a coffee or biscotti?"

Stefano surveilled the room and turned up his nose. "Nothing, thank you," as if to say he wouldn't consume anything prepared in such a dump.

He sat down very formally, feet together, and then turned to Gina, almost robotically, crossing his legs and placing his hands above one another atop his knee.

"I received your letter and am sorry to hear about my sister. I would like to extend my condolences to you."

"Thank you, I..."

Stefano held up his hand to stop her. He hadn't finished speaking and didn't want to be interrupted.

"The purpose of my visit is to inform you we addressed your husband's unacceptable behavior toward you, and to offer my apologies for not protecting you from him in the first place. We do not tolerate such treatment of the women in our family, least of all from someone *outside* our family, like your husband."

Stefano stopped speaking. Gina stared back, not wishing to interrupt again. Then he tilted his head and raised his eyebrows as if to nonverbally say, "Well?" Gina responded immediately.

"Oh. Thank you. It is such a relief to be free of his abuse. I no longer fear for my life in my own home. I cannot begin to tell you how hor..."

Again Stefano raised his hand.

"Then that's settled. My concern for you goes beyond your safety and includes your financial security. No member of this family will live in squalor…" He looked around again, "…or worse. That said, I do not favor wantonly remitting stipends to family members. There is no sense of accomplishment, or personal value if one is on the dole. People feel better when they earn their own wages, when they support themselves. Don't you agree?"

Gina inhaled to respond, letting him know she didn't need any money, but Stefano held up his hand again. Apparently, that last question was rhetorical. Gina had no idea how to behave in this conversation, so she simply sat quietly and stared at her uncle.

"Our family has business dealings around the globe. In some locations we are developing massive and complicated real estate projects—resorts, housing communities, office buildings, anything and everything. In others we are financing manufacturing operations and entire companies. No matter how significant our dealings may be in some areas, we still pay homage to what got us to where we are today. We train new personnel in simple confidence schemes, not so much for the money anymore, because it's immaterial, but to help determine who will do what it takes to get ahead in the world. Businesses on both sides of the legal line operate similarly. The only difference is some behavior is sanctioned, and other behavior isn't. Do you understand?"

Gina didn't speak. She just nodded.

"Okay then. These confidence schemes are embarrassingly childish, but they help us determine who has leadership abilities, who can adapt to situations, and who can act without the burden of morality or ethics. There are times when actions like those brought against your husband must occur, and someone needs to do it. Do you understand?"

Again, Gina nodded. She really wasn't sure if she was being offered a job in the family business, or someone was going to walk in and murder her like they did her husband, but she nodded just the same.

"We are going to offer you an opportunity to work in one of our small local operations. The goal is to make money, as much as possible, no matter the means, but always without getting caught, or drawing attention to our family. In this case, you will be visited by a man named Umberto Roselli. Please repeat that name back to me so I know you understood me correctly."

"Umberto Roselli," Gina repeated.

He shook his head and repeated "Um-*ber*-to Ro-*selli*."

This time she mimicked him: "Um-*ber*-to Ro-*selli*."

"Good. Ostensibly, you will be working with Mr. Roselli to sell driveway sealing services to homeowners and businesses. I cannot believe I am lowering myself to discuss such things, but you are my sister's child, and I want to be sure you are afforded every opportunity to succeed. Mr. Roselli's job is to find potential customers and sell them this service. He may call upon you to help him close the sale, meaning you are an attractive woman, and the men to whom he will be selling may be susceptible to your wiles. You understand the word *wiles*, yes?"

Gina nodded again, even though she assumed in context what *wiles* meant. She figured it meant she was to seduce potential customers to get them to sign on the bottom line.

"I mentioned the word *ostensibly* because we never actually provide the service we sell. Profitability is much higher when you're paid full price for a fraction of the job. In the case of driveway sealing, we basically paint the pavement with black water. The surface looks perfect until the first rain, when it washes away completely. By then, we've been paid and have disappeared. This enterprise is entirely illegal. Do you have a problem with that?"

Gina shook her head.

"You may have to perform certain distasteful acts to accomplish a goal. Do you have a problem with *that*?"

Gina leveled a half-smile on her face and again, shook her head. Not only did she not have a problem with it, she was prepared to use her *wiles* to get sales, and to work her way up the ladder within the family. The fire in her heart to channel Isabella, which had temporarily fallen dormant, was once again ignited. Stefano may be family, but Roselli isn't. It wouldn't be long before Stefano recognized her contributions and complete lack of inhibition and promoted her beyond Roselli. She was on the path to avenging her mother, and her target was laying the opportunity at her feet.

Stefano continued, "Roselli will be here tomorrow. I understand you are raising your grandchildren. When is a good time for him to arrive and not be interrupted by them?"

"The baby is usually down for a nap by noon and awake by 2:00; but he can occupy himself in his playpen for a while if necessary. The other two leave for school by 8:00 and return by 3:00. So, I guess any time between noon and 3:00 would be fine."

"Excellent," Stefano responded as he stood up and brushed the air from the room off his hands. "I am personally responsible for all activity in this country, so I am always somewhere on this continent. I will visit this city periodically to make sure you are doing well. In the meantime, do whatever is asked of you by Roselli, *anything*."

And with that, Stefano made his way to the door as the baby began to cry upstairs.

"I will see myself out. In the meantime, please quiet that *thing* (he gestured toward the crying child upstairs). I don't ever want to hear it again. Please be sure it is elsewhere if I ever visit you in the future."

It's Just Business

The next day, the baby had just gone down for his nap at noon and Gina, anticipating Roselli's visit, began to prepare for their first business meeting. She had never had a professional job interview in her life. Her fifty-plus years could be summarized as child, to child bride, to young mother, to empty-nester, to widow, to here.

She possessed so little real-world experience, she felt insecure about the whole thing—feeling more like a fraud than an interviewee. How would she convince Roselli she was qualified for anything besides being a wife and mother? What else was she qualified to do? She realized she'd be at his mercy and hoped he would be kind and tolerant of her naïveté.

Insecurity even found its way into selecting her wardrobe. She ransacked her closet, trying to find the outfit of a professional business-woman, throwing dress after dress after dress on her bed in desperation. She'd hold a dress in front of her, look at herself in the mirror, decide for one reason or another why it was inappropriate, and toss it onto the heap of other discarded options on the bed. One option after another made her look cheap, or slutty, or matronly, or it was too casual, or too formal, or the color or pattern was unprofessional. Finally, she landed on the option she thought would work. She'd wear a black skirt and pressed white cotton blouse, black stockings and heels, a gold necklace, bracelet and earrings. Nothing too flashy or subdued, so she'd look professional, but also like a woman, not a haggard matron or nun.

Her hair was pulled back and held in place with a gold clip. Makeup was lightly applied, and she sat in the living room awaiting her guest, practicing how to say hello, and how to act professional. She wondered if she should reach out to shake his hand, and if so, should she offer a soft, genteel hand, or a firm overhand grip and a single, vigorous shake from the shoulder.

She'd received no confirmation Roselli was even coming, aside from Stefano's passing comment for her to expect him. For all she knew, today may or may not be the day, but she wanted to be prepared for anything nonetheless. She started wondering if today *wasn't* the day, if she would go through this routine every morning until he finally arrived. She thought about that for quite a while until there was a solid bang on her front door.

It *was* the day. Roselli arrived a couple minutes past one o'clock.

She greeted him with the firm grip of a handshake and turned to walk to the living, asking him to come in, but before she could ask about her role, he grabbed her shoulders from behind and tore her blouse down to her waist. He spun her around, pushed down on the top of her head until she was kneeling in front of him, and told her to unzip his pants and get to work. Ten minutes later, he was finished and she was naked, collecting her torn clothes off the floor and sofa. She realized her blouse wasn't good for much else anymore, so she shoved it between her legs and clenched her thighs together to keep what Roselli left there from running down her leg onto the furniture or the floor. Roselli leaned back on the sofa, hands clasped behind his head and elbows pointing outward, still wearing a shirt, but naked from there to where his pants were gathered above his shoes.

"You'll do," he said with a triumphant smirk, and then told her to get a warm towel and clean him up.

She walked off, fighting back tears, not because she was hurt, or offended, but because she was absolutely fucking furious.

Sadly, this was not her first rodeo. Her disgusting husband and brother-in-law had raped her, so she just added this asshole to the list. She got her revenge on her husband. She'd get her brother-in-law too one day, and now she added this piece of shit to her list.

She was so fucking angry about being manhandled—literally—that the rage built like a volcano behind her eyes. She fought back her tears because she didn't want Roselli to misunderstand and believe he had hurt her. He hadn't. She wasn't fragile. He had empowered her. Now, more than ever, she wanted her revenge against men, *all* men!

If she didn't want to kill her uncle before today, she did now. *Earning my stipend instead of being on the dole. BULLSHIT!* she thought. He *knew* this was to be her fate today, and instead of telling her what was happening and giving her a choice, he only let her think she was going to have a real role in the family business so his buddy could force himself on and *in* her. She realized the only time men in this family took offense to someone abusing one of *their* women was when it wasn't one of *their* men doing it!

Once again, she was made to feel like garbage by a man, only this time by her uncle—her *family*…and his disgusting, mouth-breathing crony.

Gina obliged Roselli. She ran the water in the sink over her hand until it was warm and returned with a warm, damp dishtowel to swab up the mess on the man's hairy lap, thighs, and belly. He slapped her ass as she walked away and complimented it in the most degrading manner possible, and she excused herself to get cleaned up and put on other clothes.

He told her not to hurry back, because he was on his way to an appointment, but he'd be back again tomorrow for more. He urged her to be naked tomorrow when he arrived, and to have a warm towel prepared in advance, because he was a busy man and didn't have time to waste waiting for her. He threw some money on the coffee table, pulled up his pants, and left.

She wanted to murder him right there, but she had no idea how she'd do it. Sure, she could plot his horrific, painful, and immediate demise, but she knew she wouldn't do it, at least not yet. She had been treated like chattel since she turned fifteen. She was becoming immune to it, but that didn't mean she liked or accepted it. It took her decades, but she finally landed on a way to deal with her husband. Now she'd find a way to deal with Roselli and Stefano, but it wouldn't take her decades this time. It may take time, but knowing she would have her revenge would help her endure the indignities in her immediate future.

Above all, she held her head up, because now she knew where she came from, and that didn't mean from Philly, or from her parents, or even her grandfather, but from Isabella. Bella had suffered indignity and cruelty and rose above it all to create an empire. In her heart, Gina felt she possessed Bella's spirit. For the first time in her life, she believed she had value.

After that day, it wasn't long before Roselli was pimping her out to potential customers to get them to sign on the bottom line. Sometimes she was prostituted to cover Roselli's debts, too. He made sure she understood her role, and rarely passed up the opportunity to physically violate her, occasionally in public to demean her even further—sometimes with a tap on her ass, or a squeeze of her breasts in front of his cronies. But she didn't care. Using her body as currency wasn't personal to her, not after being raped repeatedly during her marriage. In this case, she rationalized the abuse as a means to achieve her ultimate goal of revenge against Roselli and her uncle, and to ascend her family's ranks.

Gina's elitist uncle had treated Roselli like a subhuman for years, and Gina was Roselli's means to take out his aggressions against her family. She was the embodiment of all he hated in Stefano, and he took his wrath out on her at every opportunity. His misplaced abuse would cost him one day. She'd see to that.

He was a despicable, bottom-feeding jackass who did everything in his power to push Gina's face into the gutter, but with his every shove, her resolve grew stronger. She wasn't Stefano. Roselli was taking his frustration out on the wrong person, a *much* more *dangerous* person. More than ever, she believed she was bred from royalty and would rise up, giving Roselli and especially her uncle their comeuppance.

In time she realized, if this was how she was going to be used, she would be sure to be the one to benefit from her labor, so she began to cultivate her own clients. She started to run her own games behind Roselli's back, and when her uncle visited months later, he met with Roselli and Gina in her living room and asked for a full report on business and opportunities. Roselli quietly shrugged and dropped a bag of cash on the table in front of Stefano. The bag contained just enough to keep Stefano satisfied. The rest stayed in Roselli's pocket or landed in the pockets of his bookies. Her uncle nodded, picking up his bounty, and asked Roselli if Gina was being appropriately obedient. Roselli shrugged and crinkled his nose as if to say she was adequate.

Stefano glanced over at Gina, waiting for her to complain about Roselli or the degrading work. To Stefano and Roselli's shock, she remained silent and produced a bag with three times the amount of cash Roselli had delivered.

Roselli was furious, calling her every derogatory name in the book and asking how she dared defy him and run a business behind his back. She ignored her accuser and instead addressed Stefano, looking him in the eye and letting him know Roselli was wasting her talents and pocketing most of the returns. If Stefano wanted profits above all else, he should put her in charge.

The first time they met, Stefano told her money was the most important goal of her enterprise, and she provided him proof of her ability to generate a lot of it.

He looked at the different-sized bags, smiled, and granted her request, informing Roselli, from that moment forward, *he* was working for *Gina*. Roselli began to protest, but Stefano held up a single finger for the man to stop and informed him his options were to do everything Gina instructed him to do or be fired and dumped in the Delaware River.

Gina had finally won a battle, and it felt good. No. It felt *great*! This single victory lit a fuse within her. She was committed to her grand scheme more than ever. Not only did Roselli get his due, but she manipulated Stefano into being the one to make him pay. Roselli's road to ruin had begun, but she also realized she had the ability to manipulate Stefano.

She would never have to be under Roselli again, in any sense of the word. One day, *no* man would be above her, and when that day arrived things would change for her and all the Bellas in the family. They would become Amazons, and the *men* would be subjugated!

As the two men were leaving, Gina called after Roselli. "I want everything you skimmed by the end of the day because trust me, you can't afford the vig. Oh, and I have a tally of every penny, so don't think you can shortchange *me*."

He never turned around, but instead slumped his head forward and walked out. He understood. Like it or not, he had no options. Gina would now treat him worse than Stefano ever did, and if Roselli balked, Gina would call upon Stefano's resources to deal with him.

The Climb

Each time Stefano came calling, Gina had more money for him as she took the initiative to expand the business in the region. They were still doing low-level scams like seal coating and the home improvement one she learned from her husband, of course, but now she was running confidence scams, getting suckers to send her money, or swapping real currency for counterfeit.

Gina's favorite was setting up a jewelry cleaning booth at a flea market, or street fair. On the surface, she was trying to convince the "marks" to purchase a jewelry cleaner with electrostatic cleaning and miracle solutions, but that was a classic case of misdirection—get the rubes to focus on the machine and decide whether or not it was a rip-off, while committing the actual crime right under their noses without them noticing.

The jewelry cleaners were legitimate, which is the key to any successful con. For a good con to work it has to withstand some test of proof if challenged. Marks would need to be convinced the cleaners were legitimate because they were suspicious about getting scammed. In fact, they *were* getting scammed, but not by the cleaner. In this case, the machines were real, but the jewelry would be swapped through sleight-of-hand.

Gina's agents produced a filthy piece of costume jewelry from a Ziploc bag full of similarly soiled pieces and ran it through the cleaning process. The con artists, or "grifters," would extract the brightly cleaned specimen from the solution in the tank and display it for the marks to examine. Then, to win the marks' confidence, they'd hand the clean jewelry to them for closer scrutiny.

"Now, promise you won't run off with my jewelry," Gina's people would cautiously say, giving the impression the marks were the ones whose integrity was in question. The marks would assure them they would never do such a thing, and they could be trusted, which immediately lowered the mark's guard.

The marks were invited to remove their own dirty jewelry and compare it to the grifter's in the mark's own palm. Getting the mark to remove his or her jewelry was the toughest hurdle to cross. Once the jewelry was loose, the game was on. The marks would see the remarkable difference between their own ruddy jewelry and the con artist's pristine ones, and then they'd be invited to place their own jewelry *themselves* into the cleaner, dropping it into the pool of cleaning solution.

The marks would slyly believe they were getting their jewelry cleaned for free without having to purchase the machine, believing they were getting one over on the grifters.

It's important to note, the grifters sought marks who wore generic jewelry matching the fakes they held in stock for the swaps—a simple diamond solitaire in a gold or platinum setting, a gold wedding band, gold hoop earrings, etc. Once the real stuff was in the cleaner, and the surface started bubbling and clouding, giving the impression the device and solution were working their magic, the con artist would reach in and swap the real setting for the faux ones they had concealed in their hand and give the clean fakes to the marks. The best part was when the marks would be so impressed, they would actually purchase the cleaners, which were marked up a thousand percent and were such crap, they broke after the first couple uses. This scam worked one hundred percent of the time and generated a fortune.

Another favorite along the same vein, but more deviously manipulative, involves exploiting the weaknesses of local, private jewelers who have drug or gambling habits and then offering to forgive the debts for stolen jewels.

Basically, unwitting customers would come in to get a setting repaired, or gems appraised, and the jeweler would switch the stones in the back room. The theft, though egregious, wasn't the genius of the plan. The genius behind this type of grift is controlling loose ends. The more people involved, the more risk there is that any con will blow up in someone's face. Those perpetrating the con must be more invested (and therefore at risk) in the theft than those above them, to ensure greater safety for those at the top. Underlings need to understand dropping a pebble on a boss would result in dropping a boulder on themselves.

Once a leveraged asset (those who wouldn't ordinarily perform such an act, but are now at such a disadvantage—owing debts, needing drugs, fearing perilous information will be leaked, etc.) pulled a single con, he became Gina's slave for life. She informed them they could never stop, or she would send the police an anonymous tip and the jeweler would land in jail and lose everything. Loyalty was invaluable, whether given freely or leveraged through extortion, and Gina was a gifted grifter. She would get the stones they stole, use another of her extorted jewelers to re-set them, and then sell them elsewhere, through another jeweler she had on the hook. No single jeweler was privy to the full process, so they were never aware of the extent or breadth of the operation.

Not only was she making a fortune through her myriad cons, she was also exhibiting creativity and initiative that Stefano rarely saw at this level. Best of all, Gina wasn't some volatile kid, or substance abuser, or over-extended high-roller he had to worry about. She was a mature woman who didn't need the money (a fact she conveyed to Stefano when that knowledge suited her) and had a stable, albeit modest, home. She was a grandmother, for god's sake, and best of all, she was blood. Family was favored above all others, and Gina even resembled the family's original matriarch, whom Stefano grew up knowing.

He also recognized she was a master manipulator—a *natural* grifter, if such a thing exists. He saw her manipulate everyone below her to perform otherwise uncharacteristic or unthinkable acts. He considered himself a genius for unearthing such a rare and valuable jewel. Unfortunately for Stefano, he was either too arrogant or stupid to imagine she could just as easily manipulate him, and was already doing so.

It didn't take long before Gina was conning Stefano. He bought her bullshit hook, line, and sinker. She was delivering profits and was always playing up to his ego—how smart he was, how debonair he was, how shrewd he was, how he was always a couple steps ahead of everyone else, how she would *never* have thought of all the amazing things he suggested. She was always asking him to describe other lines of business in the country, and then acted insipid, asking Stefano to explain things that were too complicated for simple-minded little Gina to understand. It was a variation on the getting people to do her favors theme to win them over. She got him invested in her by explaining things to her, mentoring her, and making him feel superior and smart at the same time. He believed she idolized him, and he also believed she would never be smart enough to outwit him because he was the one teaching her. She made him feel important and valued, so much so he wanted her with him at all times. He trusted her because he desperately needed to believe what she told him. His arrogance made him an easy mark, and she played him to the end.

When it was finally time to get Stefano to act, she exploited his ego, asking why he was *only* running the US. Why wasn't he running *everything* by now? When he explained he would one day, when his father passed away, Gina asked why he should wait so long when the family's business would clearly benefit from his considerable skillset *now*.

It wouldn't take long for Gina to convince Stefano to sabotage the old man, and all it would take would be successfully concluding the vendetta. It wouldn't take long, but it would take some masterful manipulation.

She needed him to believe the vendetta should still be enforced, but to do that, she had to convince him his father and uncles faked Bella's deathbed confession because they were afraid to execute it. She had to convince Stefano, if he executed the vendetta, he would prove he had the guts to do what no one else would *attempt* and the rest of the family would hand him the reins to the empire.

Stefano initially bristled at the suggestion, but Gina anticipated that. She agreed it was too much for a man to believe he could accomplish. His father and uncles may have been cowards, but they were powerful and not to be trifled with. They conspired to make up Isabella's lie to avoid their duty. Maybe she went to her grave wishing someone in her family would finally have the courage to hold the Mantellis accountable. Maybe they even promised they would do it to appease her, but once she was gone, they saw no need to pursue it, or they simply lacked the nerve.

If only someone would show that initiative, he would surely win the respect of the rest of the family, and the brave, smart man would be given the keys to the kingdom, but it was too risky, she'd tell him. It would take a special man of vision and courage to ever accomplish such a plan. Better to wait for the wheels of time to overcome his father in another ten or twenty years, and then Stefano could assume his rightful seat on the throne, assuming he lived long enough.

Gina planted enough seeds and left the fertilization to Stefano's own mind. He would come to conclusions, and Gina would be able to say it was his idea all along.

It didn't take long. She convinced him to buy and then renege on Sonny's, tear it apart, and then lie in wait for the Valmontis to come to him. She would lure them out of the shadows, hand them to him on a platter, and he would eliminate them. He became so committed, he began to dedicate more time and physical resources to the endeavor. He committed personnel. He stepped from behind the curtain and personally visited city officials, something a person of his station would never do for fear of assuming personal risk. He strutted like a peacock, believing he was smarter than everyone else in every room. Other aspects of his national operation moved to the back burner as he focused nearly all his energy on Philadelphia, Sonny's, the Mantellis, and his ultimate seat of power in Italy.

On the day he agreed to meet John in Sonny's, Gina knew she had her uncle in the trap. She reached out to her grandfather once the meeting commenced, introduced herself as a dutiful member of the family, and filled him in on what Stefano was doing that very moment. She let the old man know what Stefano's motive was, and how he had misappropriated hundreds of thousands of dollars to buy Sonny's, how sloppy he was being threatening city officials directly, instead of through go-betweens, how he was recruiting an army to forcibly displace the old man from control, and then how he intended to murder the entire Mantelli family, in direct contradiction to the old man's orders.

She said she tried repeatedly to discourage Stefano, but he would not be deterred. He was on a mission.

The old man thanked Gina for the heads-up. He urgently and repeatedly tried contacting Stefano, but his calls went unanswered, probably because Stefano already believed his father irrelevant, so the old man left for Philadelphia immediately to try to stop the debacle before it happened.

He had begged Gina to keep Stefano from going through with the plan, but that's the opposite of what she wanted. To the contrary, she goaded Stefano on, encouraging him to strike soon before the opportunity passed. She knew Stefano would kill John, and probably wipe out most of the rest of the family before her grandfather arrived, and then all she'd have to do was assassinate Stefano, so he could never tell the old man it was Gina behind the ultimate grift all along. With the old man's trust, Gina would step into Stefano's role, and then she'd only have to bide her time until the old man died and she ran the whole show.

Everything was running perfectly, until John was rescued. On one hand, he did Gina a favor by eliminating Stefano for her, but the result wasn't very different. Whether John or Stefano survived didn't matter, because they were both dangerous. Stefano had told John everything. Either of them could tell the old man the truth, and Gina's elaborate con would fail. The only way her plan could work is if *both* Stefano and John were dead.

She and Roselli, whom she dominated with an iron fist, broke into the old lawyer's house to kill John last night, but he wasn't there. They killed Acchione instead to send a message. Roselli wanted to kill Marilyn too, but Gina would have none of it. She was tired of women being collateral damage, so she left a witness behind. She knew this was a risky decision, but damn it, women have to stand up for one another, even at their own expense. She explained it to her grandfather as retribution for the Valmontis murdering Stefano. She knew that explanation would work. Her grandfather would prioritize family over everything else, and would probably even praise her for doing it. Okay, maybe not praise, but hopefully not excommunicate her.

Everything was coming together all at once. She was scrambling. She was in the home stretch. After months of manipulation and chess playing, she was within days of taking over the US operation. She was rid of Stefano, and if things went to plan, John Valmonti shouldn't be too far behind him in the queue to the Pearly Gates. All she needed to do was kill John, ideally without the old man knowing it was her. Earlier, that would have been tough because she was by his side all the time, riding in his limousine, bouncing back and forth between Philadelphia and Pittsburgh, but now she was alone, and had time to plot her next moves.

REALITY

The combination of showering, being fully dressed, and being alone and safe within her private sanctuary was enough to lower Gina's blood pressure to only slightly above that of an ordinary angry person. She was still massively pissed off, but no longer on the verge of having a stroke.

She sat at her kitchen table and plotted. She didn't make herself a cocktail, or a cup of coffee. She didn't grab a snack. She didn't turn on the TV. She just sat there, unconsciously picking at the curled, delaminated vinyl lip of her table—*click, click, click*. She breathed in and out like a bull snorting as it stared at the brightly clad matador across the ring. She was just as focused, only her matador was vengeance.

She needed to manage her grandfather. She needed to find her grandchildren (who had been kidnapped by Guido the day before as leverage to get Gina to put the meeting at Sonny's together with Stefano). She needed to keep her daughter from coming to town to check on her kids, complicating Gina's life further, and somewhere along the line, she needed to kill John Mantelli…Valmonti, or whatever the fuck his name was now.

Every breath he took put her at risk. Her grandfather wondered why she kept the gun trained on John in the hotel room, even after she was told to put it away. It was simple. If there was even a hint of him mentioning her involvement in reactivating the vendetta, she'd have shot him dead.

Then there was an epiphany. Maybe the one she really needed to kill was her *grandfather*. That would enable her to skip a couple steps and take control of the whole family network in one shot. Indeed. That's where her focus should have been all along once Stefano was out of the way. Her grandfather was the key to everything. With Stefano and his father both gone, no one else would know the vendetta was disavowed. Not only could she gain control of the family, but then she could turn all their resources against John and Guido, both of whom she was growing to hate more with every passing second.

YES!

She needed to stop relying on others to get the job done. She needed to take things into her own hands. That's what a strong woman would do. A strong woman would take charge. *Bella* would take charge!

That old man needed to die, especially after humiliating her the way he did, but the only way she was going to be satisfied is if she was the one to kill him. And she realized she was going to have to be the one to kill John and Guido too. She was practically salivating. She was tired of being put in her place by arrogant, foolish boys. Fuck them all!

Since her cellphone was still in the limo, she stood up and walked across the kitchen to the antique, rotary-dial wall phone her parents had gotten new fifty years ago. Gina kept paying the phone company bill when she returned home because she didn't feel like bothering with canceling service. Sometimes, procrastination pays off, because when she picked up the receiver, there was a dial tone!

She dialed Umberto Roselli.

"I have a job for you."

Now she could have that drink, while she waits for Roselli to show up.

PROBATE

Probate is a weird word. It sounds like one of those made-up names for erectile dysfunction medication: "Would you like to masturbate, but are stuck on the sidelines? Well, get back in the game with *Probate*!"

This is the bizarre shit that goes through my mind three seconds after a lawyer starts talking. No matter what they say, my ears shut off and my mind wanders, even in this case when the lawyer is my sister's husband.

Tom's a great guy. You know the saying "there's a lid for every pot" when trying to explain how two people ended up together? It applies to my sister and brother-in-law. Like my mother, my sister was blessed with amazing natural, physical beauty. Imagine the most beautiful Italian supermodel. Now shrink her down to five-foot-two. That's my younger sister Angela. She's also very smart, educated, and vivaciously outgoing.

On the surface, she is a straight man's dream, and I'm not saying that because I'm her brother, because that would be creepy. I'm saying that because she has literally caused traffic accidents just walking down the street. Guys slam on the brakes to watch her, become mesmerized, and then get rear-ended, or side-swiped, or whatever. Trust me. The older she gets, the more she loves to share those stories. Looks don't last forever, though, so what's underneath tends to be what really matters.

Scrotie is usually a house dog in *Guido's* place, relegated to the kitchen and living room where he and I sat last night, but whenever G comes to Angela's, he likes to bring the dog so it can run around freely in the backyard out here in the country. It's like, in his mind, Scrotie is some sort of prized stallion, born to romp pastures on bucolic farmland. Mind you, Scrotie doesn't run. It doesn't even walk. It just stands in one place and shivers when G places it in the grass, even when it's ninety degrees out and humid. It refuses to move, acting like it has absolutely no clue what to do while it's out there. G coaxes it to frolic or something, but Scrotie just stands there, blinking. After several minutes, G will concede defeat and bring the pathetic creature back inside, which triggers some reflex behavior in Scrotie, who immediately pees on Angela's floor.

I don't know which is more hysterical, the dog not peeing outside and then peeing inside or seeing this big, scary eighty-year-old brute apologetically kneeling in Angela's kitchen with a roll of paper towels, sopping up the thimble-full of urine this dog's bladder held.

Anyway, probate.

Essentially, it's a lawyer term for reading a will. Since Tom is an attorney, and those guys tend to believe one another is supremely qualified to do anything having to do with reading, Joe named him executor, which is like being a traffic cop. I asked if that title came with a fancy hat, white gloves, and a whistle, but was immediately hushed for being silly. I responded appropriately and shut up, even though I still wanted to know about the hat. Regardless, Tom was busy reading aloud various heretofores and recitals and definitions and other things for which lawyers typically get paid a lot of money to draft and which put listeners to sleep, and then he finally got down to business.

Joe had been financially successful, single, and childless for many years, and although I figured purchasing and furnishing that home set him back a rather large fortune, it didn't. He had actually inherited it from his grandmother Marguerite "The Greater" Acchione in the 1950s. She had inherited it from her husband, the old theater owner, and he had purchased it in the early 1900s from the family who had owned it since new. As it turns out, with the exception of his first year of life when he lived in a tiny rowhome near the docks with Al and Sophia, Joe had never lived anywhere else but this mansion in his life. He grew up in that big house, commuted to high school, college, and law school from there, remained there when he was starting his career (too broke to live anywhere else), and then dutifully stayed to watch over his Marguerite after the old man died.

He lived in that same Delancey Street behemoth, just off Philly's ritzy Rittenhouse Square, more than ninety years, and he *never* re-decorated it!

If not on that house, where else could he have possibly spent his money? He didn't dress in the latest fashion. He didn't have a vintage Ferrari parked in his garage (trust me, I checked). He didn't have any original Impressionist paintings adorning his castle walls, and I didn't get the impression he had a string of gold-digging ex-wives with little illegitimate Joes prowling South Philly, either.

As we dug into probate, it became apparent he had barely spent anything, ever. Aside from generous support of the arts, myriad charities, and money he infused into the neighborhood at Guido's behest, he had amassed a rather substantial fortune, no doubt kicked off by Al's ten thousand dollar contribution of seed money to the savvy old man when he was skimming along rock bottom in the 1930s, and compounded through investment, reinvestment, and a steady (and impressive) stream of career revenue. Fortunately, Joe was also savvy and protected his family's assets in a trust.

Tom discovered the trust documents in Joe's will and proceeded to provide an impromptu legal education about trusts, their various types, the benefits of one over the other depending upon circumstances and goals, and then when and how trusts are created. Then he spent a few minutes describing different types of trustees, who could be a trustee, and what various legalities and restrictions apply to trustees.

I'm embarrassed to admit, I was bored and was imagining what goes on in Scrotie's minuscule pea brain while he sat there with his little pink tongue sticking out from the side of his little closed mouth, while the rest of him shivered and stared at me the entire time Tom spoke. I figured his mind was either a volume of empty space except for a single blinking cursor, or a crowded mess of geometric formulas spinning around in a tornado-like fashion while he plotted my sudden, inevitable demise.

I finally realized what had been bothering me about Scrotie. I really hated that dog. That was it. And the moment I had that denouement was when he farted with a squeak. His facial expression never changed.

The takeaway from Tom's version of juris prudence was trusts protect assets from the government, creditors, and future spouses, and I was the trustee. Wait, what?

"You're the trustee," Tom reiterated.

"*You're* the trustee?" Ange asked with a combination of surprise and scorn.

"Oh? You think you're a better candidate?" I asked.

"Well, I *am* a lawyer. That *would* make more sense. What the hell does a nomad spaghetti cook like you need with a seven thousand-square-foot house off Rittenhouse Square?"

"What the hell does the mother of two on a Main Line acre need with a pied-à-terre?"

Angela looked at me and blinked.

I continued, "And yeah! I used *pied-à-terre* in a sentence. *Fuck* you."

Tom responded in a very Tom-like manner, by staring at the document with his hands folded in front of him.

Guido turned to me and said, "Congrats, kid. Joe and I discussed this last week. His will was actually revised then, and I signed it as his witness, in case anyone here was considering contesting." Guido let that hang in the air for a moment, like the thinly veiled threat it was, then continued. "He wanted you to have a place to call home, even if you decided to continue to travel and would only have it as a place to come home *to*. He also really liked you and figured you would respect the place until you bequeathed it to the next person in the family."

Angela, still unreasonably pissed off, shot back, "Yeah, if he doesn't sell it first! It makes no sense. That place and its contents are worth *several* million, and this idiot keeps all his possessions in a *Hefty* bag!"

"Not anymore," I replied defiantly. "That Hefty bag got thrown out in the Melrose *dumpster* last night, so I don't have it *or* my possessions anymore. So *there*! Shows how much *you* know."

Needless to say, as I played that back in my head, it didn't come out as the vindication I had hoped it would be.

"So, now you have *no* possessions?" she replied sarcastically.

God damn it. She saw the hole in my comment too!

I had to think quickly. "No, I have a seven thousand-square-foot house in Philadelphia's most prestigious neighborhood, filled with antiques, most of which were purchased new...bitch."

"How you gonna pay the property taxes and upkeep?" she asked, relentlessly coming after me like a trained litigator, or alligator, or some other nasty, cold-blooded creature.

"...fuck."

That was the only response I could muster. I had absolutely no idea how much that would cost, but I was reasonably confident it was going to exceed my rather meager restaurant cook salary, especially since I was currently unemployed.

Tom finally spoke up. "If I may continue?" And he glanced back and forth and back again between Angela and me.

She sat back and harrumphed with her arms crossed, and looked away from me, toward absolutely nothing on the ceiling. I just dismissively waved my right hand at him and said in a faux dramatic fashion, "You may continue." Guido rolled his eyes and lightly patted Scrotie, who was now seated on his lap, staring at the deer in the backyard.

Then a little *phhssshh* blew at me from Scrotie's ass.

I almost suffocated. "Jesus, Unc. Stop petting that ugly ball sack. I think that makes it fart."

Guido just leaned over and whispered into Scrotie's ear loudly enough so we could all hear him. "Good boy, Zipster."

Tom shook his head in disbelief and continued. This was *not* how things went on the thirtieth floor of his downtown law firm. "The documents provide a mechanism for all future maintenance and operating costs for the residence to be paid from the proceeds of the investment portfolio. The annual annuity income exceeds…" Tom stopped, probably to collect his thoughts. "…five million dollars per annum."

Apparently, when paltry sums like my own pittance of a wage are expressed, they are done so as dollars "per *year*," but when you discuss *real* money, it's "per *annum*."

Angela and I looked at each other from across the table, gobsmacked. She and Tom were both attorneys. I was the one with the bachelor's degree from a private business school (commerce and finance, to be precise), so I spoke up, calling upon my years of study in the fine art of money.

"Holy shit. That's a ton of dough," I said with reasonable certainty.

"Is that your professional opinion there, Mister BS in Business?" she asked.

I continued, "If the annual proceeds are a *few* million, and we assume today's interest rates of around one percent apply, his portfolio's principal must be around *fifty* million dollars!"

Guido tilted his head, looked at my disappointingly, and said, "Move that decimal one more place over, JP Morgan."

"Five *hundred*?" Angela and I spouted in unison.

"Plus a little," Tom responded.

Guido didn't react to any of it. "Sounds about right, he said. Joe was a big swingin' dick for a lotta years. He didn't have many obligations and he was shrewd, plus he inherited a sizable nest egg from his old man. Come to think of it, he must've donated a hell of a lot to charities, because that number should probably be a lot bigger 'n that!"

We all just sat back and let the dust from those numbers settle. Then Angela turned to Tom and said, "You better get your shit together, Counselor. You got a lotta ground to make up before you catch up to Joe Acchione."

Tom replied succinctly, "Yup."

Tom read more of the docs, which essentially provided a lifetime annuity for Marilyn, and Mom and Pop. There was also money set aside for college and graduate school for Angela's kids, and a lump sum to pay off her mortgage, which she, not surprisingly, did not consider to be generous enough.

In the end, Joe Acchione worked a lifetime, was a steward for the family home, and amassed a fortune he barely touched and then left it all to his family. That reality hit me suddenly and a wave of immense sadness came over me. Joe had lived a good and successful life, but I doubt it remotely resembled the life of happiness Al and Sophia had hoped for him. It seemed so hollow, incomplete.

As always, Angela was the first one to pipe up.

"Why did he leave this all to us? Didn't he have any family?"

Guido responded. "Yup. We're all seated around this table."

"I mean blood relatives," she replied.

Guido nodded and said, "In that case, everyone here except me and Tom."

"And Scrotie," I added. "No fuckin' way that fart box is related to us."

"From the smell in my guest room this morning, kid, I'm going to have to say the jury's out on that one."

Angela, being Angela, the one who could never let anything go, and who was born to be a pain-in-the-ass lawyer, asked "How is that possible? None of us are named Acchione," but instead of retelling the story he shared with me the night before, Guido succinctly responded, "He was related to your grandfather."

"Mom's or Pop's?"

"Pop's," I finished.

Guido loved my sister, but she tended to be a pedantic ass, and he had little patience for that. It didn't take him long in her company to run out of tolerance for her. He sure as shit wasn't about to regale her with the fascinating story he'd dropped on me the night before. The more time I spent around him, the more I started to understand where we all fit with one another, and why he was always Angela's "Uncle" but my "Unc."

Tom continued reading the docs and occasionally muttered things out loud if they were pertinent and something we should all hear.

"…Timeshare in Florida…. Timeshare in Hawaii…. Apartment in Italy…. *Funeral* arrangements."

And the rest of us stopped what we were talking about and listened.

Tom murmured a little more and then looked up at us to summarize. "Joe made his own arrangements years ago. The funeral home is listed here," and he said the name.

Guido nodded and interrupted. "They're in the neighborhood. They're fine."

Tom continued, "He would like his services performed privately at the gravesite without a church funeral."

Guido interrupted again. "Yeah, he had drifted away from there several years ago. Long story."

And then Tom added, "But here's the interesting part," and his brow furrowed and his nose scrunched up a little. "He wants to be cremated, which doesn't seem like a big deal, but he only wants a portion of his ashes interred at the cemetery. He wants the remainder scattered into the Schuylkill River at Boathouse Row, preferably at Bachelor's Barge Club, to which he has carved out a sizable donation from his estate."

"That's not all that odd," I interjected. "At the end of the day, that river was about as close to his lifelong love as any human. You could see it in his eyes when he talked about rowing. He accomplished a lot in his life, but his time on the river was probably when he felt most connected."

"Well, Mr. Trustee, it's your call. Would you like to make the arrangements and carry out that request?" Tom asked.

"Don't take this the wrong way, but I think I'd actually like that. It would bring him some closure and possibly bring me closer to him in the process. Who knows? Maybe I'll sign up and learn to row while I'm there."

Boathouse Row is one of the most recognizable locations in Philly. The iconic image of several buildings, side-by-side along the river's edge, is used in every Philadelphia travel brochure and is ubiquitously displayed in nearly every office in the city—law firms, brokerage houses, accounting offices, hospitals, everywhere. It's located along the front edge of Fairmount Park, which is itself a source of pride for the city, what with its huge public art display, rivaling cities like Paris or Rome, and complementing Philly's reputation as the "Mural Capital of the World." Fairmount Park is also the site of the first zoo in the US. That whole part of town is a beautiful environment and the perfect resting place for my Uncle Joe.

"When should we do this?"

Guido cut to the chase, as Guido tends to do. "We gotta retrieve Joe's body from the city first."

Tom offered to "pull some strings and see what I can do," and Guido added his support if needed.

We got up to leave, and Angela, who was still pissed off about me being trustee and keeper of the Acchione mansion, obligingly asked us if we needed anything for the drive home. I asked for a cork for Scrotie's butt, since we'd be stuck in a closed car with him for an hour, but Angela shook her head and declined, noting she was more inclined to feed the thing fast-acting Brussels sprouts, hoping to coax his inner workings a little. I seriously contemplated walking back to South Philly.

We made our farewells. Guido tried to get Scrotie to pee in the front lawn before we left, but nothing happened because he was probably holding it until he could pee in the car. Guido, the dog, and I climbed into the back of the awaiting Cadillac. Rocco held the door open for us and once he shut us in and climbed into the front passenger seat, the driver put the big car in gear and we quietly and smoothly rolled off. Angela waved to us, but the driver didn't return the gesture with a honk from the horn. He was all business, and a farewell toot would set the wrong tone for our ride, even though that's exactly what Scrotie's ass did the moment we were underway.

CONTACT

A few turns from Angela's house, and we were heading south on the Blue Route (the local north/south freeway) to I-95, which would provide us the quickest access to our South Philly home. Once we merged north onto 95, Unc leaned forward to Rocco and asked him to lower his windshield visor and open the flap so Guido could use its mirror. The old man leaned back into his seat, with his left hand acting like Scrotie's personal hammock, and gesturing with his right hand toward Rocco to move the visor left or right and tilt it up or down until he was satisfied.

"Ant?" Ant was short for Anthony, our driver, although where we come from "Anthony" is pronounced "Antnee."

"Yeah, boss?"

"How fast we goin'?"

"'bout seventy, boss. You want I should slow down?"

We were rolling along smoothly in the right lane, not engaging with the rest of the cars, which were frenetically jockeying for position in the lanes to our left. The speed limit on this stretch of the highway is fifty-five, but if you're going to putt along at that pace, you're likely to fall victim to someone's road rage and get run off the road, or worse. Something between seventy and eighty is a comfortable pace, but it's not uncommon to see cars sailing by at double the limit. Meanwhile, the police cruisers sit idly by in predictable speed traps because they're not looking for speeders. They're looking for drug runners. I-95 is the north/south drug transport route from Florida to New England and all points in between. For traffic cops, catching speeders is like catching a half-pound tuna on a deep-sea fishing excursion. Yay! You caught one. Now throw it back because the focus is on bigger fish.

Guido kept his eyes on Rocco's vanity mirror and replied, "No, Ant. I want you to gradually start pushing the speed a little. Move into the left lanes as necessary and get up over a hundred. I'll let you know what to do from there."

The Caddy sat back slightly on its haunches as Ant gradually fed the big V8 some inspiration with his right foot, and we started accelerating very smoothly. The vintage, immaculate Fleetwood Brougham from the early '70s was the epitome of old-school elegance and eased from the slow lane leftward three lanes until settling into the passing lane. I sat up a little and watched the speedometer needle smoothly and effortlessly change its angle as it pointed from 70 to 75 to 80 to 90 to 110 before Guido was satisfied and let Ant know he could ease back to his original cruising speed in the far right lane.

Unlike when Washington crossed the Delaware a little farther north and a couple hundred years ago, we were crossing it at a triple-digit pace on the top deck of Girard Point Bridge—northbound up top, and southbound down below—when Guido spoke up.

"Ant, you see that white Chevy Tahoe behind us? It was parked up the street from Angela's house when we came out of the house earlier. It's been behind us ever since."

"I noticed it when we were parked there, boss. I took the liberty to call Jimmy and Nick back to Angela's house to babysit the place like they did the last couple nights, in case the guys in that rig decided to move in when we left. I had planned to circle the neighborhood if they didn't follow us, to support J & N, but since the Tahoe followed us, I kept drawing them away."

Rocco broke in. "I been textin' Jimmy. No one approached the house, but they're staying there until you call 'em off, boss."

"Good job, boys. Rock, tell them to stay there overnight. The other night's kidnappings are still too fresh to loosen security. Tell 'em to relieve the guys who are there already. Those guys should hustle back to South Philly. We may need 'em."

Ant continued to look forward and navigate ordinary, heavy, but flowing traffic. "I called ahead to two other crews. Once we pull off the Delaware Ave exit, Rocco will let them know we're close and they'll pull in behind the Tahoe when we turn up Washington. We'll take a left to Federal and turn right there. I figured we'd lock it down at 4th and Federal, at Jefferson Park. A few guys on foot from the park will converge on the Tahoe from the right when it's boxed in. Two cars will block the Tahoe in from behind, and two more will block the intersection at 4th as we pull through. Some friends from the row homes on the west side of the street should be able to lock things down good on the left. The Tahoe'll be trapped."

"Good, but change of plans. I don't want to drive off. I wanna know who they are and why they're following us. Pull through the intersection and park, and when we get the 'all-clear,' we can walk back and have a chat."

"Boss," Rocco chimed in anxiously. "No disrespect intended, but are you sure about this? I'd feel a lot better if we got you and Johnny back to the house. You're too exposed out there on the street. We can grab those guys and bring 'em anywhere you want, but they may have other guys following us we don't know about, waitin' for us to let our guard down."

"I'm not safe in my own neighborhood, Rock? Is that what you're sayin'?" Guido was indignant, and a little pissed off.

"If I was gonna hit you, boss, I'd do it where you feel safest. That's all I'm sayin'."

Guido sat there quietly staring at Rocco.

Rocco was about to shit his pants. He *never* had the balls to stand up to Guido, and Guido knew it.

"Unc!"

"What?"

I pointed at Scrotie. In all the excitement, Guido had unconsciously clenched his hands into fists, and his left one was squishing the dog who had been sleeping in it.

"Not that I'll miss it, but you're chokin' out your hairy ball sack of a dog."

"Jesus," and Guido loosened his grip on his dog. Scrotie never moved. He never peeped. He didn't do anything. He just went back to breathing in through his mouth and exhaling through his butt.

"*JEEZUS!*" I echoed, but for an entirely different reason. I instinctively reached for the window switch to evacuate the interior's suddenly befouled air.

"Don't open the window," Rocco and Guido shouted in unison. "It's bulletproof." Then we all choked and gasped. I should have let Guido kill that smelly-assed little fucker.

"Rocco," Guido finally said. "You would have to feel strongly about your opinion to say what you said to me, so I'm trusting your instincts. Let's get home. Grab the guys from the Tahoe and take 'em to Sonny's. We'll meet 'em there. Good job. I'm glad you stood up to me. Never do it again," and he smacked Rocco on the back of the head to show him he was kidding.

Rocco sighed loudly in relief and asked if the crew should tenderize the guys a little before they took them to Sonny's. Guido responded vehemently there was no visible need for that, especially because we had no idea who they were.

"They could be nuns sent to pray for us, for Christ's sake," he said, not realizing the irony of talking about nuns praying and then breaking a Commandment using Christ's name in vain in the process. "Just grab 'em, and make sure they're not armed. Leave their phones in their truck and then bring 'em to Sonny's."

"Yessir," Rocco blurted and then began feverishly texting Guido's guys because we had just turned onto Washington Ave and would be closing the trap in about thirty seconds.

Guido nudged me with his left elbow. "Exciting stuff, huh kid? Since we'll be there anyway, what's cookin' at Sonny's tonight? Got any veal parm on the menu?"

"Damn, I wish, Unc. I have this insatiable urge to get that place back open. Me and Pop need to rattle some pans in that kitchen!"

"Atta boy. I haven't had a good veal parm in months, since your parents sold that damned place. Maybe we can use some of old Joe's dough to fix the place back up and get back in business. He'd *love* that idea."

We kept chatting like that as the Tahoe was boxed in at 4th and Federal and the occupants of the white Chevy lowered their windows and stuck their empty hands outside so everyone could see no one inside was a threat and didn't need to be shot. Unlike Guido's hypothesis, the occupants were *not* nuns sent to pray for us, but four men, possibly sent to prey *upon* us, so as the old man instructed, the four men in the Tahoe were disarmed. Their phones and watches were tossed in the truck and it was parked and left behind on Federal. As long as these guys behaved, they'd be brought back there later and released. If they misbehaved, one of the boys on G's crew just got himself a new white Tahoe...some guns and watches too.

Sonny's Redux

The last time I had been to Sonny's was a day much like this one. The weather was almost identical. The air smelled the same. The cars parked on the street even seemed eerily similar. That wasn't really surprising of course, since all of that happened *two days ago*.

The other day, I stepped across Sonny's threshold around noon and was yanked through the door by a mesomorphic Neanderthal who tossed me around and bounced me off the floor, walls, and bar like the gorilla did to his Samsonite luggage in that old TV commercial. I'm not gonna lie. As Guido and I approached the front door today, I hesitated a little. A combination of PTSD and self-preservation washed over me.

Guido sensed my apprehension and assured me. "It's okay, kid. It's friendly territory again, remember?"

The last time I left the dining room, after shooting Gina's uncle a couple times with a very large-caliber handgun, the entire interior of the space was covered with a combination of blood, grime, and bits of bad guys that had been blown off in a gunfight. Not a single surface—wall, floor, ceiling, bar, tables, lights, nothing—was unaffected. Imagine what an environment would look like if a human being exploded, then increase that by a factor of ten. That was Sonny's when I walked out that afternoon.

Now, miraculously, it looked like Sonny's again, at least sort of...

Granted, what had been broken or dismantled was still broken or dismantled, but everything was clean—not merely tidied, but legitimately clean. The tin tiles on the ceiling glistened. The ancient white and navy mosaic tiles on the floor were scrubbed to a point where the grout gleamed white. I didn't even know that grout *was* white. I always assumed it was supposed to be dark gray or black. The bar was clean, all the way down to the brass foot rails my face had landed on after being tossed across the room the other day.

It was surreal.

I pointed to all the places in the room that were clean, my eyes darting from left to right, and up and down, and finally asked Guido, "Is this the same place where I shot a guy?"

"Yes, and you really have to stop saying things like that out loud," Guido replied.

He was right.

"I keep telling you this neighborhood looks after itself, but you don't believe me."

"I just don't think I understood the extent of it. It's like little elves came down here after they baked cookies in a hollowed-out tree and scrubbed every surface and disposed of unwanted bits of humans and otherwise turned back the hands of time."

"I'll make sure they leave behind some of those cookies with the chocolate stripes on 'em next time for you."

"That would be much appreciated, but I prefer the chocolate sandwich kind." I replied, and then we both looked at the four guys sitting in dining room chairs, facing us, hands in their laps, feet flat on the floor, utterly unmolested, waiting patiently for us to acknowledge them.

Guido is not a rookie when it comes to interviews (calling this an interrogation would be a little premature), and unlike Gina, whose mouth got her in trouble with her grandfather the night before, I was perfectly content watching, listening, and otherwise melting into the background shadows.

The old man looked at the foursome, turned his palms upward, leaned his shoulders forward, and shrugged as if to ask "Well?" without uttering a word.

Although there was no clear leader when they sat there in front of Guido, when the one guy second from the left addressed us, it became immediately obvious he was in charge. He was early thirties, but unlike the wrestling team Gina's uncle surrounded himself with the night before, he and his companions were non-threatening. No sane person would walk up to any of them and pick a fight or anything, mind you. They all looked perfectly capable of defending themselves, but they weren't foot-soldier muscleheads—no offense to my buddy Rocco. These guys appeared to be management. Not bosses, mind you, but not front-liners either. If this was a department store chain, they could be store managers, but not regional managers.

The leader of this crew probably *was* a regional manager because he appeared to be a little more equal than the others. He was tan with jet black hair, slicked back with a lot of product. He had one of those overtly handsome male-model faces with chiseled jaw and cheekbones and deep-set, naturally sincere-looking eyes, and they were light blue. His nose was both distinctive and handsome—slender, straight, and masculine. He had the kind of face plastic surgeons would photograph and offer to mimic for their ugly clients.

It would not have taken much for me to hate this guy.

Although he didn't wear a fancy, custom suit, his casual attire came from Gucci. His appearance and mannerisms screamed "money." He was very confident and at ease, even in this situation where the chances of his pretty face getting rearranged were pretty goddamned good. Even if this guy was only notched slightly above the others now, the gap was likely going to be widening quickly and soon. He only appeared to be stopping here to pad his resume, because nepotism was going to pull him up through the ranks at a quick pace. He bore a striking resemblance to Gina's grandfather and the guy I perforated the other day in this very restaurant, only instead of looking like a banker, he looked like a nightclub owner.

"Thank you for inviting us to meet with you," handsome guy said so calmly I was tempted to take his drink order. He waved his hand from left to right and turned his head in a gesture like he was taking in the entire room. "I like what you've done with the place. From what I've heard, it looked quite a bit different recently," and he chuckled, but it wasn't an ignorant or pompous chuckle. It was like he was acknowledging what was done was done and everyone had moved forward.

This was the sort of guy who always came in the next day, after the dirty work was done, and got down to business. Apparently, we were having an unscheduled "get down to business" meeting.

"My name is Giovanni, like yours," and he looked at me and nonchalantly gestured again with his hand. "I'm also a junior, but instead of being called 'Johnny,' I'm 'Gio.'"

Now, a less experienced guy in his position would have stood up and extended his hand in an effort to shake my or Guido's hand, but this guy knew that was premature. If he did that, and we left him hanging, it would have been awkward for him in front of his crew, and he knew we weren't at the shaking-hands part of the meeting yet. At this point, we were at the "Am I going to shoot you, or let you go?" part of the meeting. Regardless of the formal handshakes, he kept addressing us as if we were friends, even though no one on our side had made such an overture.

"My grandfather asked me to make contact with you, but I was to do so covertly, without anyone on our side being aware," and he raised his eyebrow to us to be sure we knew exactly who was being excluded from that "need to know" group: Gina. "One can never place one hundred percent trust in anyone, especially when that person is only a recent acquaintance, family or not, so Grandfather called upon me to represent him this afternoon. He has known me since my birth and has watched me grow up in his home. He knows me, and there is very little about him I don't know as well. May I continue?" and he shrugged with a tilted head and a light smile.

Guido didn't feel a need to begin speaking, so he waved him along with his hand and kept listening.

"You know Grandfather," he said directly to Guido, "and although you are not friends, you certainly understand one another. And I would hope you also share a degree of respect, if not for one another personally, at least for your respective positions."

I didn't get a warm vibe from Guido when Gio tossed that one out there. He may have overshot a little, but he was still doing fine and he continued.

"He and I would like to sit with you, privately, the four of us…" He gestured to both me and Guido. "…at a location of your choosing, to discuss our histories, the regrettable actions of the past several months which your family has endured at our hands, and also the disturbing murder of our uncles—yours *and* mine, John," which he said making eye contact with me. "If I may have a piece of paper and a pencil, I will give you my phone number. Please discuss this offer between yourselves and call me with your decision. Hopefully we can come together soon, as one family, Guido, and resolve this silly comedy of errors we share. We would like to move forward without looking backward over our shoulders for one another for the rest of our lives, and the lives of those who will follow us."

Guido finally spoke. "You don't need paper and pencil." It was like he considered the guy a risk if he had a pencil in his hand, and he could have been correct. "Say the number out loud and John will save it on his phone."

Before Gio spoke, I interrupted.

"Um, I don't have a phone. Gio's uncle took mine from me and smashed it to bits on this very floor the other day…and then you told me to toss my replacement out the window on my way home from Pittsburgh, and I haven't really had a chance to replace it yet." I looked around the room at our guys and asked if I could borrow anyone's phone.

Guido shut his eyes in a sort of resigned frustration, dropped his shoulders, and said, "Somebody give John a phone, please."

Rocco handed me his. "Here you go, John. Use mine."

"Thanks, Rock! I appreciate it."

Guido turned to both of us, opened his eyes wide now, turned his palms up, shrugged, and said, "Are we finished?"

He turned his attention back to Gio and shook his head as he asked him to proceed.

Gio recited his number. I repeated it back to be sure I got it right. Guido looked back at me like he couldn't believe something this inane was turning into something so elaborately complicated, and then gestured for me to leave with him. On his way out the door, without turning around, he told Rocco, "Take them back to their car and be sure they leave no worse for wear!"

When we reached the sidewalk I told Guido I knew I shouldn't feel this way, but I actually liked that guy.

Guido responded, "He's actually always been a good kid. I don't trust him, but I think he's sincere. I can't say the same for his grandfather."

"What's the story between you two?"

"I'll tell you over dinner. Let's check in with Tom to see how we're doing with getting Joe's body released. I'd like to get the funeral gears turning today. I can't relax until Joe's at peace."

A Proper Italian Meal

A few hours after our "down to business" meeting with Gio, Guido and I were seated at another neighborhood favorite of ours. He spent the afternoon taking care of business, and I lounged around his place, avoiding Scrotie and otherwise relaxing. After days of beatings and unnecessary driving, I needed the downtime. It also gave me a chance to start plotting how to spend the lottery winnings from the morning's probate meeting.

Like most of the joints around here, the fare was southern Italian and Guido didn't even have to order. Everything arrived at the table just the way he wanted, because they knew him so well. He'd been eating dinner every night here since Sonny's closed, and now that *I've* eaten here, I'm not sure how we're going to win him back.

Traditional Italian meals are paced differently from meals in this country. Italian meals don't start with salad, followed by the main course and then dessert, and they never simply include an entrée and a check. There is a rhythm. Just as a play has a succession of acts, so does a meal.

It's food theater.

Meals begin with a first course, usually something small, like a bruschetta, or a cheese and meat board. Then there's a pasta course, which isn't intended to be a meal in and of itself, but rather something to whet your appetite for the meat course, which is essentially the climax. That's *followed* by salad, then something to cleanse the palette, and finally dessert and coffee. The meal may begin with a cocktail, but dinner is complemented with house wine, and it *never* concludes with cappuccino. That's a breakfast drink. Those who can sleep through an atomic holocaust may opt for espresso, but most diners finish up with a simple café or a digestif, like brandy or port to help the stomach break down that big meal. And don't believe those lies about Americans eating over-sized portions, and Italians eating smaller ones in the old country. That's crap. We come by our penchant for excess honestly in this country. Italians will feed you until you burst and are only truly satisfied when you do so.

The afternoon had gone well. Tom's phone calls had reaped dividends. The coroner had completed the study of Joe and was agreeable to working through the process to release the man to the funeral home so the right thing could be done for him. Joe had a lot of contacts in the city, even still after all these years. None of them liked Joe spending one second more than necessary in the morgue. It was a black eye for everyone. Once he was assured the whole ugly affair was in process, Guido was able to relax and enjoy a meal.

The salami and cheese first course had come and gone, and we were already plowing into the pasta course, which, tonight, was a lovely Pappardelle and braised short rib in a light tomato and olive oil sauce with shaved Parmigiano Reggiano layered over top—shaved in strips, not grated like grains of sand. Much to Guido's satisfaction the meat course was a largely apportioned veal parmigiana.

This was no chain restaurant dropping prefabbed, breaded veal patties on a dish, smothering them with mozzarella, and drowning them in gravy. This place's kitchen was an art studio.

The veal wasn't pounded into submission, because the chef wanted to preserve the natural air pockets in the meat. There's a difference between flattening and bludgeoning, and this chef knew it. Those air pockets provide little flavor explosions and need to be preserved. Remember that. It's why big pockets of air in bread and even ice cream are to be cherished.

The breading was fresh and so was the oil for frying. Fresh oil is important, because it's only there to facilitate frying. It's not for flavor. When oil is re-used it leaves a sour, burnt taste behind. And don't use olive oil for this. It has to be vegetable oil.

The frying was quick, so not too much oil reached the meat, and nothing burned. Blackened breading tastes terrible and is unforgivable. The breading should also be freshly prepared for each cutlet, and as I mentioned, fresh vegetable (not olive) oil should be used for frying, to keep the breading light.

Are you getting all this down? Because you should. This is all very important stuff and is what differentiates a good Italian restaurant from those lazy, corporate places. Go get paper and pencil. I'll wait.

…you back? Good.

The ultimate goal is to plate a meal where the primary flavor is the veal, and everything else—the breading, the frying, the gravy, the cheese—are all the supporting cast. And the meat should be slightly undercooked in the kitchen because meat continues cooking after its removed from the heat. The desire is for the meat to be perfectly cooked when it arrives at the table, not when it leaves the stove. If it's done perfectly in the kitchen, it'll be overdone when it reaches the table. Remember that too.

Finally, only rookies smother these delicate masterpieces in mozzarella cheese. In my humble opinion, mozzarella cheese is for pizza. Leave it where it belongs. A well-plated veal parm is fried light brown, a quarter to a third of an inch thick and tender. It is lightly drizzled with a thin ragu, which has been cut with a little olive oil to make it thinner than what would be poured over pasta, and finally, *finely* grated

Parmigiano Reggiano cheese is liberally added on top of the filet at the table. In a pinch, Locatelli cheese can absolutely be substituted (I actually prefer it).

That is how a veal parm should be done, and that's how it was done here. When our platters arrived, we both commented how one serving was enough for two, but when the salad course arrived, both our entrée plates could bypass the dishwasher and be returned to the cupboard they were so clean. The salad course was a perfect complement to a generously sized meat course. It was a small plate of house salad—a simple handful of fresh greens, onion, bell pepper, seasoning, and a light vinaigrette. The entire meal was accompanied by Cascia's rolls, which are crusty on the outside but somehow both dense and airy inside. Again with the flavor-bursting air bubbles.

Unlike Sarcone's, which have sesame seeds on top, Cascia's rolls are smooth and more crusty. Because both versions are perfect in their own right, very few will say one is better than the other. If either version lands in a basket at your table, consider yourself blessed, and *mangia*!

Like any good Italian restaurant, we were assured the tiramisu we were about to enjoy was the best in the world, and it stood tall against the hype, and the Lavazza espresso was the perfect finale.

We barely spoke during the meal, because one does not speak in church, and once the food onslaught concluded, we toasted one another with the remains of our wine glasses, and sighed, wondering how we were going to get our fat asses and over-stuffed bellies out of our chairs, and out to the street to walk home.

The walk home was a couple blocks and the air was chilly. It felt great and refreshing after the cozy heat of the small dining room where we'd just consumed enough calories to sustain an adult male for several days. Of course, Guido is never alone, especially not when he's walking through the neighborhood. Various members of his crew were positioned strategically along our path, and two of his guys kept pace with us, but from a half-block behind. Another pair were keeping pace a half-block ahead. It never felt like we were being crowded, but if not visible, the presence of the security detail was always reassuringly felt.

We got in the door and Guido told me we'd be back at it tomorrow. I adjourned to my windowless, basement apartment, where I changed into shorts and a t-shirt, but had an epiphany while I was brushing my teeth. I spit out the toothpaste, wiped my mouth and ran up the steps hoping to catch Guido before he went to bed.

It turns out, the guy is a vampire, and a hungry one at that. Although my dinner was still sitting like a bag of wet cement in my belly, when I reached the kitchen, I noticed the only light on the first floor was coming from the open refrigerator. Guido's right hand was holding the door open while he leaned over, inspecting the box's contents for a lost prize.

GUIDO

"You *can't* be hungry," I said. Although you'd think my sudden presence in the kitchen would have surprised him a bit, his focus on the refrigerator's contents never wavered.

"I'm lookin' for the meatballs Enrico had saved for me in here. They were in a little plastic container about yay-big," and he turned to me and gestured with his hands, like he was holding a small invisible box.

"Yeah. You're not gonna find those. I ate 'em."

"Are you fuckin' kidding me? Is nothing of mine sacred here? Those were mine! Son of a *bitch*!" And he slammed the appliance door closed so hard, Enrico probably heard it in the house next door.

"Forget about the meatballs, which were delicious by the way. I have a question for you. If Joe was worth a half-a-billion dollars, and you guys have been working together for decades, you've gotta be worth just as much, right?" I swung my hands outward, like I was including the entire contents of the room into my question. "What the hell are you *doing* with it?"

"That's a personal fucking question, you meatball thief. What makes you think I'd tell you *shit*? For all I know, you'd steal my fortune the same way you stole my goddamned meatballs."

"Well, for the record, that container didn't have your name on it."

Guido interrupted, "*It's my fucking fridge!*"

I ignored him. "Secondly, as you know, I now have my *own* fortune, and don't *need* yours."

Guido, now walking from kitchen cabinet to kitchen cabinet, and opening doors in search of something else to sate his inexplicable hunger, replied without looking at me.

"I never made as much as Joe. Joe was raised by the old man who taught him how to turn *some* money into a *lot* of money. Very few people have an innate ability to build and *keep* a fortune. Oh sure. Some people earn a lot of money, but few know how to keep it. Joe learned, and tried to help me.

"He taught me money is nothing more than a tool, and how much you need really depends on your goal. His favorite phrase was 'you don't need a sledge hammer to tap in a penny-nail.' Basically, you don't need to be a millionaire to buy a Happy Meal."

"That makes sense, but what's that have to do with you?"

"Well, it helped me figure out how much money I needed, and with a better-defined goal, I was able to work toward it. Without goals, we wander aimlessly."

"What was your goal?"

Guido wryly smiled at me and said "Make a *shit* ton of money," and then laughed.

He continued more seriously. "My primary goal was always to protect Al and his family, and I realized providing a safe environment would improve my odds of success, so in order to keep Al safe, I needed to keep this neighborhood safe. To do that, I needed control, and to gain control, I needed to own as much of the neighborhood as possible. That way, I would decide who stays and who goes.

"Joe not only helped me buy real estate, but he helped me manage it. He wrote the leases I used. He found people to help me qualify tenants and maintain the places and pay the bills. Over the years, I bought a lotta goddamned real estate around here, and I filled it all with allies—residents, merchants, my crew, people who needed help and people who can lend some help.

"Remember that place we used the other day to watch the Melrose? Well, I own that house, and several other dozen like it. That nurse was a young girl from the neighborhood who found herself pregnant and unable to pay her bills. I helped her with a place to live and put her through nursing school. Now she's married and she and her husband have another kid and they support themselves. I feel good about that. I'm taking care of my neighborhood. That was my goal."

"How'd you get the money? I mean, Joe was loaded, and I don't mean to get too personal, but you run an expensive operation and don't seem to be struggling financially either."

"It's a perfectly reasonable question, and before you start believing I run some big illegal enterprise, I'd like to help you understand the truth. Kid, we see everything before it happens. Imagine getting tomorrow's lottery numbers today. That happened to us every day, except instead of lottery numbers, we learned of real estate deals on the verge of happening, or we were brought in on the ground floor of a business about to 'go public,' or we'd get a piece of deals we facilitated. Not every deal worked, of course, but when you consider the volume of deals we were in, you can imagine how many really good deals we saw, and it was all legal. Our partners were *thrilled* to share their good fortune with us, because without us, there'd have been no good fortune. Follow me?"

I just nodded. "It all sounds too simple though. How is *everyone* not doing this?"

Guido laughed and shook his head. "Human nature, kid. Everyone looks for a get-rich scheme, but they're looking at the wrong goal. Their goal is money. That's a stupid fucking goal. Joe and I never did this for the money. We did it to help people, because that in and of itself is really rewarding. Seeing the people with influence relieved by having their problems solved made us feel good. Helping artisans earn a living doing what they loved doing, all while successfully navigating a world they really didn't understand was *beyond* satisfying. Believe it or not, Joe and I were just trying to help people, and we ended up being rewarded in many different ways, financial being one of them.

"Plus, to do what we do, you have to assert yourself, recognizing and sometimes creating situations where you can help. That takes guts, because people can be defensive when you ask them personal shit. Even when you're trying to offer help, if the person doesn't realize he needs help, helping becomes a giant sales job, and you get a ton of people telling you no. Fortunately, sometimes they say yes, and that's just the beginning. After you sell someone on the idea you can do something, you have to actually do it. That takes elbow grease. It's hard work, and not many people are willing to put in the work these days. They want shit to just happen, and the only things that ever seem to just happen are *bad* things. It all comes down to the same bottom line. You wanna get paid? You gotta put in the effort."

"Isn't knowing stuff before anyone else illegal? Like, insider trading?"

"Apparently not. According to my lawyer, Joe Acchione, anyone could have invested in these fledgling companies, but they chose not to do so. Sometimes the investments failed. The businesses just simply couldn't get off the ground, but the vast majority of the time, Joe made *bank*. That's why I was surprised he *only* had a half-billion dollars. He probably could have had multiples of that, but he was generous to a fault. Sometimes he actually returned the investments to his clients because he didn't feel he'd earned as much wealth as that ownership was generating."

"I'm not so sure I'd have done the same," I muttered.

To my surprise, Guido looked me in the eye and said "I know you would have. Any guy who keeps all his belongings in a Hefty bag probably doesn't give a shit about money. You get that trait from your grandfather, uncle and father, too," and he smiled.

I looked back at him, my lips pressed tightly together, nodding agreement and then finally saying, "Fuck. Now I'm hungry too. Is it too early to wake Enrico up so he can make us hoagies?"

Guido pressed himself up from the table, mentioned something about not really needing all those calories before going to bed anyway, and wished me luck rousting Enrico who's not only Guido's personal strength trainer, but also a black belt in about a dozen different martial arts. I agreed my stomach could wait until breakfast, and returned to the dungeon.

ENOUGH

I laid in bed for hours, trying to convince myself I wasn't hungry, but with its constant rumbling, it was only a matter of time before my stomach convinced my brain otherwise. Laying on my back, I slapped my mattress with both hands, yelled *"Fine!"* at the ceiling I'd been staring at since I assumed that position, climbed out of bed and trudged my way upstairs to the kitchen, defeated.

Since I invaded his fridge hours earlier and stole his leftover meatballs, I knew there wasn't much left in there to eat, but I'm a cook, for fuck's sake, this can't be that difficult.

Twenty minutes later, a fried egg and cheese sandwich was in my belly, quieting things down in there; the fry pan was cleaned and restored to its original home in the cabinet under the stove, and I was making my way back to bed.

Down to Business

I finally fell asleep around 7 a.m., which was perfect because by 9 a.m. Guido was holding a plate of freshly cooked bacon under my nose like smelling salts.

"C'mon kid. This little piggy went to market wrapped in cellophane, just for your breakfast pleasure. It would be disrespectful to let him go cold."

I groaned and blinked repeatedly, trying to determine if I was alive or dead, and hoping for the latter. I asked if I had time to bathe. He told me I did, as long as I didn't want any bacon because there was no way he possessed the restraint to hold off eating it until I arrived in the kitchen. He pushed a slice of bacon between my teeth and told me to "get crackin'," which I did.

We ate a hearty breakfast. He stole my toast for the second day in a row and I finally excused myself to get cleaned up and dressed. The next time I saw him, he hadn't moved from the table and didn't look up from the morning *Inquirer*. He told me we were meeting Gio and the grandfather in an attorney's office in the suburbs at noon to discuss a few things and hopefully put the vendetta to rest once and for all.

September 11, 2001, changed our world in many ways, and one of those is the tightened security in downtown office buildings. Prior to that, a visitor off the street could enter any building in Philly, walk through the main lobby, climb into an elevator, and go to any office on any floor, one hundred percent unimpeded. Office tenants kept their doors unlocked, often propped open, welcoming guests. This was all true for the smallest office buildings, the tallest ones, and everything in between. Mind you, the prestigious buildings had security desks, but the staff functioned more as concierges than security.

After those events in 2001, every building, large or small, stationed security guards in the lobby, and access to the elevators would only be granted once a visitor was signed in and approved by the tenant whom they were visiting. Guests would stand for a photo and wear a temporary badge (peel-and-stick strip of paper with a bar code and an indiscernible photo of the visitor) they were instructed to wear at all times while on site. Then the guest would pass through an electronic turnstile between the lobby and the elevators before they could ascend through the building. Once they reached their desired floor, they'd have to knock on the tenant's door so the doors could be unlocked electronically and remotely from the receptionist's desk.

No one came and went freely in the city anymore, let alone anonymously or unnoticed.

In the suburbs, most buildings still believed it was the 1990s. Doors from the parking lot into the lobby were left unlocked. Access to elevators was unimpeded, and office suites were accessed freely from lobby corridors. That sort of free access and anonymity was exactly what the four of us sought for our meeting. We didn't want anyone to know we were there, because for the record, until we figured out what would happen going forward, none of us was officially there, because neither of our respective camps would have received the news of our meeting very well.

Because we were trying to be discrete, arriving via chauffeur didn't really seem like such a great idea. I offered to drive us in my Challenger, which was parked at Joe's, but Guido reiterated the word "discrete" to me very slowly—"dis…cr…ete"—and we went to a garage he rented down the street and climbed into his BMW instead.

I think our definitions of discrete differed wildly. This was not a low-end model, nor an SUV. It was one of their sleek six-figure, high-performance coupes with a ton of horsepower, seats that grabbed you around the ribs like a Venus flytrap when the car turned and exhaust so loud it rendered the stereo completely superfluous. The only thing discrete about this car was its color, black with heavily tinted windows. It was a modern-day Batmobile, and no matter how much I begged him to let me drive, without speaking a word, Guido pointed me to the passenger door like I was Robin and then he climbed behind the wheel. I begrudgingly conceded the point and buckled in, shotgun.

As one might suspect of a man who was always poised and ready to pounce, Guido drove like a madman. On our way down I-95, I nonchalantly leaned back to gaze at the speedometer, but before I could read it, Guido said, very matter-of-factly, "130" and kept going. Most passengers would probably be anxious and frantic, possibly yelling at him or at the very least begging him to slow down, but I was not that guy. I simply replied to his comment with "pussy" and he smiled and sped up.

We were heading to Valley Forge. Although Washington and his troops had wintered there in hardship during the Revolution, these days it's home to affluent neighborhoods, one of the world's largest and swankiest shopping malls, the intersection of the region's largest highways, a robust high-end office market, and about six zillion white-tail deer. If you've never hit a deer around here in your car, it's either because you don't drive or you hit one in someone else's car.

Our destination was situated in a large, parklike cluster of office buildings intertwined within a large planned community of townhouse clusters and walking paths on the edge of the area where Washington slept. Everything around here looks colonial, even stuff built yesterday. And there's brick. When future archaeologists excavate to find this part of Philly, they'll wonder if the area was infested with packs of big bad wolves, because everything's built with bricks. No one was blowin' this shit down!

The subject building is forty years old, and modernish, with multiple decks and long expanses of windows, but the whole thing is still clad in brick.

Guido and Grandfather

As he slowed the BMW to nearly a complete halt, he sighed with disappointment, realizing his fun behind the wheel had quickly and abruptly ceased. We'd caught up to a bottle neck of traffic approaching the northbound Blue Route, and had been absorbed into a slowly-slithering snake of hundreds of cars heading to the same place. Worst of all, we were at least a dozen miles away from our turn-off. We were trapped for at least the next twenty-to-thirty minutes, and suddenly the vacuum created by our lack of conversation became palpable. I seized the opportunity to ask the question I desperately wanted answered.

"So, Unc, since you've diabolically kidnapped me, and are whisking me away to meet some horrible fate in Valley Forge, why don't you take this time, like any rational evil genius, and monologue about your history with Gina's grandfather?"

Guido sighed again, this time in resignation to his own fate of having to tell a story he really didn't want to share.

"Fine. I got nothin' else to do while I'm stuck behind these *ASSHOLES*," he screamed loudly.

I nearly pissed my pants from his sudden yelling. As my heart tried to return to its usual pace, I asked him if yelling made him feel better, and he told me to go fuck myself. Then he continued.

"I came here in 1957 as a seventeen-year-old kid, and really didn't know my ass from a hole in the ground. I didn't know the town. I didn't have any contacts. I didn't even speak the language. I was a raw resource full of energy and promise, though, and that's why Bella herself sent me here. Since she was the old lady running the show, I felt honored to accept her offer. Of course, she was really only in her fifties then, not really old, but to a seventeen-year-old, she seemed ancient.

"What's really scary is Gina is a dead-ringer for her. Physically, that is. That's where the similarities end, though. Bella made mistakes and learned from them. Gina is a fucking psychopath.

"Bella was still beautiful and full of life in '57. By that point, she was running a sprawling empire, and it wasn't because she was a dictator, even though she could be tough and demanded respect and deference. And it wasn't because she was so widely loved, although she was by many. She could be all those things and much more, but above all, she was an effective leader because she was shrewd. She understood the long-term goal for the family enterprise and could put the right people in the right roles with the right resources, so they could be successful, and then she very clearly guided them, detailing what was expected, what would not be tolerated, and how to get the job done.

"That was the case with me," Guido continued. "She knew what she wanted done, and I was the right tool for the job, so she clearly defined the overall goal, provided me with the necessary resources to make it happen, and sent me off to the States to accomplish my task, even though the task required me to invest the remaining years of my life.

"Bella was devastated when news of the attempted murder of Fredo reached her. She was relieved to hear her friend had survived but was inconsolable to learn his innocent wife had been taken from him and their child. She reflected on the days in Spain with the cousin who went to America to kill Fredo and his family. He was the one who spent all the time during her pregnancy holding her hand and assuring her he would make this right. All she ever had to do was tell him about the lie, and how the vendetta was fake, but instead she hid behind it. Her cousin killed Fredo's wife, and died in the process, and he did it for Bella, to bring her justice, and to win her favor.

"She was disgusted with herself for what she had done.

"Her silence had compounded her lie. She knew she had to atone for the lives of her cousin and Sophia, because their deaths were her fault. Her lie began its life in 1913, but by 1920, once she learned her parents had died, there was no longer any reason for the lie, or the vendetta it created. She could've proclaimed her dishonesty—the innocent fib of a desperate young girl—and disavowed the vendetta because it was without basis, but perhaps she believed the vendetta was what inspired her extended family to push the boundaries of the family's business. More likely, she was merely being a coward, knowing such a lie would undermine everyone's confidence in her. She had five years to recant the lie and save Sophia's and her cousin's lives, but she let the vendetta keep going. They both died in 1925 for no reason, and Bella never forgave herself for that, and rightfully so.

"She enjoyed playing the role of the victim, gaining the respect of others by promoting the story of her pulling herself up against the odds. She didn't favor trading that esteem for the potential scorn of getting pregnant outside of marriage and then deceiving her parents. She also didn't want her husband to learn of her illegitimate son. The family maintained secrecy to ensure the union between Bella and her wealthy husband remained intact, but if she lost favor with her family and the truth leaked out, her marriage could be put in jeopardy as well, and her entire empire could fall as dominoes began to tilt.

"Ironically, it was her shrewdness and her ability to get people to do what she wanted them to do that got results, not some bullshit, contrived battle cry of the vendetta, but she wasn't brave enough to put that to the test.

"Whatever her reason for doing so, she compounded the lie every day by not renouncing it, and that irresponsibility cost a woman her life, Al a wife and Joe his parents. It also cost her aunt, the woman who took her in, the life of her son.

"From that day until she died, Bella was haunted by what had happened. It took her lie only ten years to destroy the lives of so many innocent people—her parents, her cousin, her aunt, Al, Sophia, Joe, the old theater owner, Marguerite, and all those who cared about them. She lived with that pain for the next fifty, but even then, her sorrow didn't balance the scales.

"She sent Al a letter immediately, apologizing and telling him she'd do anything to earn his forgiveness, but it was too late for that. Her letter wasn't penance. It was a plea for forgiveness, which she frankly didn't deserve and never received. Al passed the letter along to his father-in-law and ignored it, which was more than the letter deserved.

"Back home, although she didn't admit to the lie, she renounced the vendetta, forbidding anyone from ever acting against Fredo again. That may have stemmed the tide, avoiding future damage, but it did nothing to atone for what had already been done. Furthermore, Al, the old man, and Marguerite had no reason to believe they were safe, so Al was sent into hiding, and had to give up his infant son. Had Bella just mentioned in her letter to Al her plan to protect him forever, he could have at least lived with his remaining family and been a part of Joe's life, but again, she fucked up. For a brilliant, shrewd, savvy woman, she kept unwittingly ruining poor Al's life.

"Thirty years later, she finally did something right. She sent me to America to keep an eye on Al and protect his family. Somehow, she realized the hiatus on the vendetta would probably only last until she was gone. After that, she didn't trust her family to honor her wishes and stay away from the Valmontis. Vendettas, even mistaken ones, can be very powerful, because they are rooted in evil, vengeance, jealousy, and pride. Men who crave power can be easily persuaded to chase their dreams through a vendetta. That's how Gina got her Uncle Stefano to defy her grandfather."

I interrupted Guido's story. "Why you, though? Why didn't she send one of her own sons?"

"Well, there are a couple answers for that. First, her sons were all doing important things, and were being groomed to run various aspects of the family empire. Second, no one knew me, so they wouldn't miss me when I was gone."

"You weren't a stranger to everyone though, right? The grandfather guy knew you. Otherwise there wouldn't be any bad blood between you."

"Yeah, him. Before I get to him, I should back up a little. In 1913, Bella was sent away from her home in Valmontone to Spain to live with her aunt, who was Bella's mother's sister. Bella gave birth to a boy in 1914 and raised him until she returned to Valmontone in 1920."

"Wait," I said. "I thought her return home was delayed by World War 1. That ended in 1918. Why did it take her two more years to get there?"

"Because no one was going anywhere after the war. The Spanish Flu was arguably more dangerous than war. It killed nearly five percent of the world's population. A half-million Italians were claimed, Bella's parents included. There was no way she was traveling anywhere until it was safe, and that wasn't until late in 1920. So by the time she left for Italy, her son was six years old. No one in Valmontone knew she had a kid, but everyone in Spain who knew her knew the kid was hers. For the boy's sake, they tried to convince him his mother's aunt was his mother, but that ruse didn't work at all. I doubt even Bella believed it worked. Regardless, when she returned home, her son was left behind.

"Remember, the whole idea of returning was to marry the guy she was betrothed to and expand her family's holdings. If he knew she wasn't a virgin, let alone she was actually a mother, the marriage would have been called off.

"Her son was named Roberto, after the piece of shit who knocked her up and who then ran away to get shot in the war. Bella didn't realize he'd abandoned her when she was cast away and actually felt remorse for abandoning *him*! She learned the truth years later, but by then, her son couldn't really be renamed.

"Of course, part of the deal for the aunt in Spain to take Bella in was for her parents to accept and welcome Romani into their lives, which they did. Bella was also being trained in their ways. She had no idea of the family connection initially but was a quick study and ultimately relied on the Romani when she began running things in Valmontone and elsewhere. Her aunt held up her end of the bargain and raised Roberto. He, himself, was soon betrothed to a young girl named Lavinia, whose family promised a sizable dowry and whose own land would be absorbed into his family's network."

Guido added, "The young girl's name was Lavinia. Most people called her Vinnie. I preferred calling her Mom."

And he left that one hanging, to see if I was paying attention, which I obviously was. "Excuse me? Mom? So Roberto is your father? And Isabella is your *grandmother*? So you're as related to Bella as Grandfather. Which one of you is older, because you might actually be the guy who should be in charge?"

"Slow down, kid. First of all, he's older than me, only by a few weeks actually, but still, and even if I was older, he'd still have priority as the family elder. He's her son. I'm her illegitimate grandson."

Guido and Bella

By the 1950s, Bella—Isabella (Conchetti) Ariano—only wore black, in deference to the widow tradition. Her husband had survived to his nineties but no further, and although theirs had been a contractual union, they had become dear friends over the years—confidantes, business partners, and on *very* rare occasions, lovers, at least to produce heirs. She had proven herself remarkably fertile at thirteen when she became pregnant in that single instant when she lost her virginity, and she maintained her success rate of one hundred percent, having intercourse with her husband precisely four times in twenty years. Three times in their first three years of marriage, and again seventeen years later when she literally begged her husband for contact.

She always assumed her penance for her adolescent moment of indiscretion was to spend a life of near-chastity, living with a husband who preferred men to women. She accepted her fate and lived a life of faithfulness for the sake of her family and its business enterprises. Several years after he passed, she decided it was time to hang up her black dress and dress to possibly attract a new partner, before it was too late and she withered away entirely. She wasn't actively pursuing callers, but for the first time in decades, she no longer intended to spurn advances. Of course, as a woman in power, not many suitors had the nerve to approach her, so even though she'd have welcomed an advance, *damned* few were immediately forthcoming.

One day, while shopping in the local street market, years after the town had been ravaged by the Second World War and had only recently finally become livable, Bella noticed a tall, handsome, muscular young man watching her move from booth to booth. She rarely left her home and the tall walls surrounding it, and on this occasion in public, she chose to wear a bright red dress, and her long, wavy, dark hair cascaded over her shoulders. She felt pretty. She *wanted* to feel pretty, and for the first time in what seemed like a lifetime, she felt a twinge, the slightest spark of attraction when she noticed the young man who was noticing her.

He matched her pace through the market, moving only when she moved, maintaining a couple peddler booths and a few dozen feet between them. He acted like he was shopping, picking up and inspecting merchandise from booth to booth, but he always met her gaze when she looked his way. He'd smile and tilt his head, acknowledging her, and never appearing to be a threat. To the contrary, his posture and smile and eyes conveyed nothing more than a simple, innocent flirtation, and as emotionally vulnerable as she may have been, Bella was never without her wits, and was always on her guard.

She finished purchasing produce and meats and cheeses and handed the bag to her companion, her cook's assistant, and as they left the market, she looked back to find her mysterious observer, but he was gone. She smiled at the thought of her flirtatious little game with a man a third her age, and began the half-mile walk home.

A block or so into her return, the young suitor stepped from the shadows of a building to her right and stood before her. Bella stepped back in surprise, but she didn't feel threatened, and that was at least in small part because she knew she was surrounded by her security detail from the moment she left the walls surrounding her home until she returned. Consequently, as quickly as the young man stepped in front of Bella, her escorts stepped out from their own shadows and stood between them.

The young man confidently looked her in the eyes and calmly asked Bella for a moment of her time. In that instant, the youngest member of the security detail stepped forward and shoved the interloper, but he never had the opportunity to follow that with a verbal threat because he was immediately reduced to kneeling on the ground hyperventilating. The young man from the market was very quick, and very deft at physical conflict, and never hesitated. When others may think before they respond to aggression, this young man never did.

That was the first time Guido met Gina's grandfather, and the score was 1-0 in favor of Guido.

The other escorts grabbed Guido and held him, but before the young man on the ground could get up to take his free shot, Bella yelled for them all to stop. While he was still being constrained, Bella asked Guido why he wished to speak with her and he replied with one word: Roberto.

Bella's eyes widened and she was instantly whisked back in time forty years. Roberto was her son's name, but her son was named after her lover. She immediately recognized the desire she felt in the market as the desire she'd felt for Roberto Sr. forty years earlier. This young man bore a striking physical resemblance to her lover, but he possessed a fire Roberto never did. He was obviously far too young to be her *own* son, so perhaps he was her lover's son from a subsequent liaison.

She waved everyone off, including her security entourage, told them to remain several dozen feet behind her, out of earshot, so she could speak privately with Guido.

Once they were far enough ahead of the others and could speak openly, she asked, "How do you know Roberto?"

"I'm his son."

This confirmed her assumption. After all, her lover all those years ago was only a couple years older than her at the time. Her own youngest son, who was still catching his breath several feet in her wake, was about this young man's age, and her husband was proof men much older than Roberto could be virile in their later years. This young man could easily be her lover's son. Had Roberto sent his son to her to make contact, to gauge if the flames from decades ago were smoldering and could be rekindled? *Were they?* she wondered. *Could they be?*

"How *is* your father? Where has he been all these years?"

"He's in Spain, exactly where you left him when you returned to Italy. He was left consoling your aunt when her oldest son who held your hand in your moment of need died in defense of your honor," Guido spewed back, finding it difficult to contain his contempt for her.

They had been strolling together, side-by-side when Isabella stopped dead in her tracks and reached out with her right hand, grabbing Guido by his left sleeve. She reached for him for stability. If he had moved aside, she'd have collapsed in a heap on the ground. She never anticipated that response.

The young man was not her lover's son. He was *her grandson.*

Her entourage stopped quickly to maintain the distance they were directed to keep, puffs of dust kicking up from their feet on the loose gravel street. Well, everyone stopped but her son, who quickly ran to his mother's aid, pulled her hand from Guido's shirt, and put his other hand on Guido's shoulder.

Apparently, being dropped to the ground with a punch to the gut moments earlier taught her son nothing, because the moment he placed his hand on Guido, his knees buckled and he fell backward with a bloody face and a broken nose. The rest of the escorts rushed forward and Bella stood between them and Guido, once again ordering everyone to stop.

Guido two, dumbass, still zero.

"All of you go home and take my son with you. Get him cleaned up and have someone look at his nose. I am fine here with…," and she looked at Guido and shrugged.

"Guido," he replied.

"…Guido," she finished.

None of her people were pleased with her decision, but they knew better than to defy her, so they begrudgingly continued along the path out of sight.

"You're my grandson?" she sighed once she was sure no one could hear them speak. The gravity of that thought hit her at once and she began to cry, lunging for Guido and embracing him so deeply, the tiny woman was on the verge of breaking the man in two, even though he was a foot taller than her and nearly twice her weight.

"You look so much like your grandfather. In nearly every respect you are the image of him at this age."

"I look like Fredo? The rapist? I always heard he was skinny and weak."

"Not Fredo, your *actual* grandfather," and Bella went on to tell Guido the entire story, about her past, about his grandfather, about her parents, about the lie, and the vendetta, about the heartbreak of leaving her son in Spain, and about how devastating it was to lose her cousin and Fredo's wife, especially because it was all her fault.

She asked Guido if he had come there to do her harm, but he assured her he was only there to confront her to try to understand how she could abandon her son and never return to Spain, even if only to console her aunt. She cried uncontrollably then, as if years of suppressed emotions broke through the levy. She hugged him again, only this time holding on for support as she sobbed into his chest. Her life had been incredibly difficult, beginning with the first moment Roberto Sr. caught her eye. She had worked so hard to restore her family and build it to what it had become. She endured a lonely marriage, while her husband discretely entertained male lovers for decades with her blessing. She raised four sons, expanded her business, and gained control of her family's empire. She had survived two world wars, a pandemic, and her homeland's reconstruction. And above all those obstacles she cleared, she also endured treachery and loss—the effects of her own bad judgment. She had been a foolish child, and she continued to pay for those sins decades later. She told Guido she wouldn't blame him if he took his vengeance upon her. She would almost welcome it to escape the life she'd built, but that wasn't who Guido was, nor who he is today.

Instead of destroying her, he told her he'd help her any way he could. He would deliver messages for her to her family. He would stand between her and those who would judge her, and he would help her make amends for her mistakes.

Bella invited Guido to stay at her home as her guest, and although her sons were suspicious of him, Guido never gave them cause to feel threatened. Instead, he spoke with them and learned from them. He was humble and listened. After only a little interaction, and at their mother's encouragement, they accepted him, all except the one he'd knocked on the ass, twice.

She kept their familial connection quiet, at first, but Guido convinced her that renouncing the lie would be her only path toward healing. Although she never went so far as to let Fredo off the hook, she did share the truth about why she had gone to Spain, how it wasn't to help her aunt, but instead was to deliver her baby. To her surprise, her children were more interested in meeting their half-sibling than in judging their mother for her youthful indiscretion, and a reunion between the two branches of Bella's family was arranged.

Guido had, in fact, helped Bella heal, and in the process had earned her trust and gratitude. The faith he'd earned, his sensible mind, and his obvious ability to handle himself physically inspired her to send him to America to stand guard over Al. He was to make contact, share the stories of everything she'd told him, and offer unlimited assistance—physical, financial, or otherwise.

Guido spent twenty years in America before Bella died. He was never again in her presence, but they spoke on the phone and wrote letters to one another often. Although he thought Al would welcome him with open arms, he was sorely disappointed. Al would neither trust nor forgive Bella nor anyone she sent, after what she had caused. She understood his reasons and unflinchingly wore his contempt. Regardless, behind the scenes, Guido invisibly ran interference for Al, creating a neighborhood network to support his business and keeping the entire bubble around Al's business and home safe.

And that is what differentiated Guido from other syndicated bosses in Philly. Mob guys, their goal is to grow an empire, gobble up territory and power, and become the top dog, defying anyone to topple them. Guido's motivation was simply to provide a safe haven for his charges. He didn't want to build an empire. He merely wanted to protect his fiefdom.

In the end, mob guys came and went, usually ending up violently dead, especially in Philly, or rotting behind bars. Guido lingered, and was likely to die of old age because he built all he needed and was content. There's a lot to be said for his way of doing things.

"Al wanted nothing to do with me, of course," Guido said. "Once he heard Bella sent me, he actually spit at me and threw me out of his restaurant. That was the one and only time I ever saw Al get angry, and that wiry little fucker was *pissed*. I backed onto the sidewalk with my hands up, palms facing him, trying to calm him down. I'd been sent to protect the guy, not give him a goddamned heart attack.

"We'd see each other around the neighborhood occasionally, but I'd always just wave and steer clear. He'd just glare at me, probably wondering why I didn't go the fuck away. In the meantime, without him knowing, I was running interference for him behind the scenes, negotiating good pricing for him with his vendors, arranging for neighbors to use Sonny's for events, stuff like that. I also kept an eye out for anyone trying to make trouble in the neighborhood and got rid of them. I didn't have a crew, at least not yet. It was just me, but at that age, I was more dangerous than a crew.

"One day, he saw me on the street and trotted across traffic to talk to me. I was expecting another confrontation, but he surprised me. Your Pop had been drafted into the Army and Al was drowning. He needed help in the restaurant, and he knew he needed me."

"He wanted you to work the kitchen? Seriously?" I asked.

"Fuck no. I can't cook. For fuck's sake, I burn water. No. He needed help, and not just menial labor. He needed a manager to help him run the place, but one who wouldn't rob him blind. He also needed help generating more business because he couldn't afford to pay a manager on what he was generating from the business already. It was a catch-22. He needed help, but couldn afford it, but if he didn't buy help, he'd go broke in short order."

"So he wanted you to be the manager of Sonny's?"

"No, not even close," Guido replied, a little frustrated by me chronically missing the point. "By the late-50s, Joe had a nice little cottage industry of horse-trading going on. He had become acquainted with powerful people who didn't know how to do basic things like carpentry, plumbing, stone work, etc., and Joe had South Philly neighborhoods full of artisans without political influence. Both groups needed one another, but didn't know how to get connected. Joe was the connector. Of course, Al had been watching Joe all his life and for the first time, found he actually needed his son's assistance, but he couldn't very well go to him, hat-in-hand and say 'Hi. I'm your biological father. Hug?'"

"Hmmm ... I would have paid to witness that conversation," I added.

"No you wouldn't. I saw it later, and it *did not* go well, but I'm getting ahead of myself.

"Al knew he had to bring something of value to earn Joe's assistance, and that something was me. On a much more local scale, I was doing what Joe was doing. In the neighborhood, I was getting complementary merchants to use one another, save money, generate business, and keep it all right here. I'd get the funeral home to get their flowers from the local florist. I'd get the florist to buy supplies from the hardware store. I'd get the hardware store to cut locals a deal in exchange for meals, or doctor visits, or whatever. Everyone in the neighborhood was using one another's services and also getting to know and support one another personally. In the most granular way, I was organizing a community, and I was keeping it safe. Suddenly, at a time when masses were exiting the city for the safer and newer suburbs, no one was leaving this neighborhood because besides their homes, their friends, family and business were all right here. They didn't want to leave.

"As good as Joe was at connecting, Al was better, because he put me and Joe together. After about eight seconds of me describing my operation to Joe, he was hooked. He agreed to give Al whatever he needed, because he and I were about to expand the breadth of both of our worlds and not only make life better for a lot of people, but make a *ton* of money in the process."

OUR SECLUDED RENDEZVOUS

We pulled into the parking lot a couple dozen minutes before we were due. Unlike the spin and hop one does to exit a minivan or truck, the climb out of the BMW nearly required an obstetrician. Once out, Guido ritualistically reached behind his seat for his sport jacket, stretched his arms through their respective sleeves, buttoned the front, "shot his cuffs," and *then* began walking toward the building entrance. Without looking back, he pressed the key in his pocket and the doors audibly clunked to lock with Teutonic precision. The alarm chirped. For a fleeting moment, I thought how fortunate some would-be car thief was that Guido locked the doors and activated the alarm. He locked it for their protection as much as his, because if they stole it, their brief victory of absconding with Guido's wheels would end very, very, VERY badly for them.

We parked away from the building, along the perimeter of the parking field to avoid attention, but it appeared Gio had other plans. His brand new, recently detailed Guards Red Porsche 911 was parked in a visitor spot fifty feet from the building's entrance. And it wasn't even a run-of-the-mill 911, assuming such things existed. It was one of the models more at home on the track than the street, with a massive wing perched a couple feet above the rear bumper. How did we know it was Gio's? Well, we didn't see him climb out of it or anything, but the car's personalized plate was three letters, "GIO," which was a solid clue. Guido walked past it, raised an eyebrow to me, and said "Nice car. *Discrete.*"

We took the elevator to the third floor, which was as high as it went, and made our way down the hall past all the other tenant entrances until we reached the entrance to the small law firm we sought. The reception desk was vacant, which is typical these days, but there were offices beyond it along the window line, some of which were occupied while others were not. The administrative cubes in the middle of the floor were mostly occupied, and a few people were milling around near the kitchenette and file area to the far right. There were probably a dozen people besides us in the entire suite, but no one paid us any attention. We weren't there to see them, so we were invisible, which was exactly why we were using their office. Gio called to us from an open doorway down the hall to the left, and we walked down and joined him, closing the small conference room's door behind us.

The old man stood up, acknowledged Guido, and extended his hand, a good start if the goal was to part later as friends.

"Guido, it has been far too long."

Guido replied, "Maurizio, your nose is a mess," and the old men both smirked and shook hands.

Then Maurizio covered his nose with his right hand and extended his left palm toward Guido in a faux plea for mercy. He laughingly replied, "Please don't punch me in it again. I'm finally getting used to the bumps you gave me. I don't need new ones."

Guido shook Gio's hand this time, and I leaned over to the old man and did the same. I added an apology for the way we left things the last time we were in one another's company, and he replied it was his fault for barging in uninvited and deserved at least as much as he received.

Gio and I politely acknowledged one another with a subtle wave and sat down.

Getting to meetings first can be strategically important. There are power seats to be had and images to convey. I remember catering a luncheon one time during my recent travels, and the guy hosting was the president of a company, but only about four and a half feet tall. He also wore an atrociously obvious wig, so you can imagine how self-conscious he was.

Some of the meeting members were his employees who already knew him, but the other half were potential strategic partners whom he'd never met before and he didn't want their first impression to be of him standing next to them, looking up from a powerless position. So, he insisted on being the first one permitted into the luncheon, and he had to be seated before his guests arrived. He selected a specific seat in the room at the head of the table with the window behind him, forcing those joining him to squint through the afternoon glare when they looked at him.

Placing others in discomfort was a power move.

To overcome his diminutive stature, his obvious shortcoming (excuse the pun), he had a one-foot-tall booster placed on his chair so he would sit taller, eye-to-eye with the six-footers in the room. He didn't get up when his guests arrived. He greeted from his seat, gesturing for everyone to sit down. Oh, and lunch was served, not set up as a buffet, because he didn't want to risk losing all his engineered "room power" by getting up and down from his chair and mingling with much taller guests.

During the meeting, I stood there with the rest of the help, watching everything play out, waiting to clear the table once the meal was finished, and I saw his counterpart drop his napkin during the meeting. He leaned over to pick it up, looked under the table at the man seated opposite him, and spotted his little size five dress shoes dangling a couple feet above the floor, like a five-year-old on a booster at Denny's. The guest snorted out a little chuckle, then grabbed his napkin and returned top-side with a straight face.

Mind you, there's nothing wrong with being short. We don't control such things as our height, and no one successful does business with someone else because of physical stature. Business partners are typically sought for their skills, unique knowledge, or strategic assets. This guy blew the deal because when the client saw him trying to be something he wasn't, he knew he couldn't be trusted, end of story. Anyway, my original point was: It's valuable to get to the conference room first to pick strategic seats, which will give you some slight advantage. Ordinarily, that means having one's back to the outside glass, but in this case, Gio and Maurizio chose the least powerful seats, with their backs to the door, ostensibly as a show of their commitment to finding common ground, not forcing their will.

As always, the old man was dressed like he stepped out of a fashion magazine for mature and successful European gentlemen. His jacket was tweed with a tapered cut over a starched white dress shirt, buttoned to the top, accented by a solid-colored purple silk tie and a matching square in the jacket's breast pocket. He wore a thick wool vest and matching slacks, both charcoal gray, and his shoes were handmade in Milan and looked like they'd never been walked in, like after he sat down, Gio pulled these shoes from a bag and slipped them on the old man's feet, taking the shoes he'd worn in and shoving them into the bag for later.

Conversely, Gio's suit was Armani silk. It was a dark shade and the jacket and pants were cut in a style that was at the cutting edge of fashion when he walked into the building and will probably be out of fashion when he leaves. He wore a black shirt and a black tie, and like Maurizio, everything was perfect. No hair was astray, no pleat was broken, no pressed line was wrinkled, and everything looked like it was custom made that morning.

Guido, of course, was dressed in a sport jacket that may have been as old as me, black wool slacks, a white dress shirt with the top button open, and a striped tie with pulls in the middle from catching it on the front edges of desks and conference tables because he always leans forward. He was also wearing shoes, which is about the degree of description they deserved.

I looked like a cook who wasn't going to work today—Levi's, Adidas Sambas (my black pair because I was trying to be dressy), and a collared shirt with sleeves rolled up to my mid-forearms. Maurizio and Gio both wore expensive watches—Maurizio, a classic Patek Philippe, and Gio, a very masculine TAG Heuer. Guido wore a Rolex knock-off, and I just relied on my cell phone for the time.

We were obviously all coming from different places, but we were trying to meet in the middle.

"We have air to clear," began Maurizio. Like his son, back before I shot him, Maurizio spoke at a relaxed pace and with a tone to match. He was confident, but not arrogant; in control, but not draconian. It was the sort of speech pattern one might expect from a calm parent explaining to a child why the family dog went to live and play at a nice farm in the country. It wasn't patronizing. It was conciliatory, but in an elitist sort of way.

"I would love to spend time together discussing old times, Guido, or talking about home, or sharing photographs, and perhaps we can do that soon over a nice meal, perhaps in your family's restaurant, John, but today we have business to discuss and the quicker we get to it, the more comfortable we will all feel."

Guido nodded and suggested Maurizio start. I was expecting Guido to be difficult, but there were no airs for him to put on, nor posturing to perform. These guys knew him. They knew what he was capable of and what would happen if they stepped out of line, so he didn't need to establish anything. He could just be himself, which also meant he leaned forward in his chair with his hands clasped in the gap between his thighs, and his eyes staring through Maurizio's head like he was studying the man's every word and mannerism.

"Instead of rehashing everything which has transpired over the past several months, a list of actions with which we are all uncomfortably familiar, I would like to first address who is missing at this table. Gina Gianetti was neither invited to this meeting nor apprised of its existence. Based upon some investigation by Gio and interviews with people familiar with various aspects of past events, the one common factor between everything is Gina. It has become glaringly apparent she is the one who orchestrated the plan to revive the vendetta. She manipulated my son, who so craved power he was willing to murder your entire family, John, to get it. She misappropriated funds to place the down payment on your restaurant. She nearly had you and your sister killed. She nearly got your sister's husband disbarred. She kidnapped your girlfriend's children and murdered Joe Acchione. She is too ignorant to understand how our family works, let alone how to build and operate a commercial empire, and if she was ever permitted any real authority, she would materially and quite possibly terminally damage our vast network of influence. I cannot begin to apologize enough for what she has done. I can only assure you we will end her reign immediately so her influence can be limited only to what has happened in the past. Guido, John, we cannot bring back Mr. Acchione, just as you, John, cannot bring back Stefano, but I sincerely believe holding the one person responsible for all of those losses accountable is the first step toward healing. Does that sound reasonable?"

Guido gestured toward me, and I simply shrugged and nodded my head. There really wasn't anything for me to say. Guido closed his eyes and sighed as he turned to Maurizio. Obviously, my response was not what he was hoping to hear, so he responded for us both, matching Maruizio's speech cadence and tone.

"Maurizio, more than sixty years ago, we met between the market and your family's home. We were impetuous and volatile and craving an opportunity to prove ourselves. You pushed me, but to be honest, I willed you to do it. We were adolescents and that's how we acted. I'm sure we would both like to believe we have matured since then. We don't react to situations in that way anymore, because we realize such reactions can make those situations worse. We use our brains. We use reason. We take deep breaths and we look to the horizon instead of the ends of our noses to assess the future. Everything was fine between us for the final fifty years of your dear mother's life, and for nearly fifty years since she has been gone, that foolish vendetta stayed buried where it belonged. All these years, we coexisted. I believe if we had gone a step further and cooperated, we would have been better prepared for Gina's coup, and would have worked together to quell it. The fact she played us against one another proves our relationship is not where it needs to be, and as members of the same family, we need to be better than that."

Maurizio closed his eyes and nodded, in apparent agreement with every word Guido had said. I, on the other hand, was spellbound again. This man who hadn't spoken a proper English sentence in my presence in my entire life, was not only cogent, but eloquent. Quell? Seriously? Who the absolute fuck was this guy?

Maurizio held up an old folded letter and told us all of its significance. We didn't have to read it, just understand it was written by Isabella, and contained her unburdened soul. She told the story of Roberto and Poppa, of her mother's deal with Bella's aunt, of raising her first son for six years and then abandoning him, and of the lie she'd created in the spur of a moment to protect herself, which ultimately cost the lives of Fredo's wife and Bella's cousin. She apologized to the family, praised them all for all they had accomplished together, and thanked them for letting the vendetta die upon little more than her assertion it was based on a falsehood. This letter was shared during *her* probate. Her sons, all of them including Roberto, were present and the eldest has always been entrusted with the letter to ensure it endures beyond each of their lives, protecting both families from any further consequences of her momentary cowardice more than a century ago.

Almost on cue, as he finished his statement, his pupils flared and grew from shock. In the window behind Guido, he could see the reflection of the conference room door opening. Before he could turn or say a word, Gina burst in and shot him in the back. She snatched the letter from his hand, then turned and fired at Guido. That old geezer is still quick as a cat and he lunged to the floor, knocking me out of harm's way in the process. Gio kicked his grandfather's chair (with him still in it) at Gina. It knocked her off balance. She dropped the gun so she could grab the edge of the table for balance, then turned and ran. Gio reached for her and missed but was at least able to grab the letter.

He who hesitates is lost. Reactions are innate. Some people freeze, while others respond instantly. No matter how diligently nor often Maurizio trained for conflict, when he spotted something happening, he stopped to think, for just an instant. Guido didn't. That's why there's a hole in Maurizio, and a hole in Guido's chair. In the moment, Gio responded like Guido. I'm not sure how I reacted, because before I knew what was happening, Guido had knocked me out of my chair. I'm afraid that alone tells me I'm more like Maurizio than Guido or Gio.

THE BAD PENNY

The good news about having a meeting in the suburbs is there's no security gauntlet to pass through to get to the office suites. Visitors can anonymously arrive and assemble without any record of them being within miles of the location.

Unfortunately, that asset is also the greatest liability of the lax security in the suburbs. Psychopaths like Gina can walk in unaccosted, enter any office, pass the unoccupied reception desk, and violate the sanctity of a private meeting. Doing so with a gun just makes it creepier.

Everyone in the office suite stopped what they were doing when they heard the first gunshot. They wondered if they had heard what they thought they had heard, but once the second shot was fired, they started running and screaming. Panic and more screaming ensued. Gina had counted on it. She was going to exit quickly and disappear in the panicked crowd to make her escape.

She had hoped to kill Maurizio, Guido, and Gio, drop the gun, and tell John she was going straight to the police to frame him for the murders. And while he rotted in prison, she'd burn the ridiculous letter, revive the vendetta, and destroy the rest of the Valmontis—but unfortunately for her, as Gina tends to do, she screwed up massively. The only thing she accomplished was murdering her grandfather, and there were three witnesses left behind. Now, instead of having a clear path to running the family business, she was out of it entirely, and on the lam forever from the family, Guido, *and* the cops.

She exited the building quickly, screaming about a shooting in a third floor conference room and how a man was dead, and then she climbed into the back of Umberto Roselli's car. He had been instructed by Gina to watch Gio and Maurizio and report their activity back to her. Roselli tailed them here from the Ritz, reported to Gina, brought her back, and was now on the run from the police with her. Even with Stefano gone, she still had Roselli on a leash, which isn't surprising for someone as manipulative as Gina.

Meanwhile, back in the conference room, Guido pushed himself up from the floor, shaking his head in disbelief and muttering "mother fucker." As the reality of what happened settled onto him, his muttering gave way to rage, and he yelled "mother *FUCKER!*" and slammed his fist on the table. He turned to me and hollered accusatorially, "GODDAMNIT, KID! We shoulda *killed* that bitch when we had the *chance!*"

On his feet now, he bolted to where Maurizio was slumped back against his chair. The old man's eyes were vacant, staring into the abyss. Guido lowered his own head dejectedly and closed Maurizio's eyelids, then straightened the grandfather in his chair.

As had been the case with Sophia nearly a century ago, the bullet had passed through Maurizio's heart, killing him instantly.

Suburbanites are not used to gunshots. The cops must've received fifty 9-1-1 calls, all at the same time. Once they made their way up to the conference room, we were all still there. The three of us corroborated one another's story, albeit in different rooms, to different cops. One of us, Maurizio, didn't say anything and instead served as evidence. We spent a couple hours at the scene and agreed to return to the station the next day to formally sign affidavits, which none of us were apt to do.

Meanwhile, an "all-points bulletin" was put out for the apprehension of Gina Gianetti for first-degree murder and attempted homicide.

As my family had done the day before, Gina immediately "went to ground," we hoped under a rock, never to surface again.

What a fucking week!

Joe Acchione

Somehow, amid all the murdering, we forgot we had made a late afternoon appointment at the funeral home to review and finalize Joe's plans. Guido insisted on joining me and wouldn't hear of rescheduling the appointment to a better time, because he wanted to get this done. He didn't want the arrangements hanging over his head any longer than necessary, and felt he owed it to Joe to be there.

We walked out to his BMW, which was now conspicuously alone in the parking lot. Guido wasn't his usual, storming self though. He shuffled out there, like he was sleep-walking, and handed me the keys as he quietly, sullenly climbed into the passenger seat without a word. He sat there the entire ride home, hands in his lap, sighing occasionally and staring out the window at absolutely nothing. There are only so many times an eighty-year-old man can watch his peers get murdered before he feels very, very alone. He no longer resembled a feral cat, counting the moments until he could pounce on an overmatched prey. Instead he looked like one of those house cats who gave up one day and wandered away from home to find a place to curl up and die.

Going to a funeral home was probably not the best way to get Guido's mind off death.

Once inside, he stood at the window, staring into the street with his back to me and to the mortician who was nervously trying to convince me which casket to use for Joe. I had never done anything like this before and was uncomfortable about starting now. I stood there quietly, unconsciously running my finger over the top of a bronze casket.

"You have wonderful taste, sir. That casket contains thirty-two ounces of bronze per square foot and is on clearance sale for only $12,000."

I withdrew my index finger immediately from touching the bronze box, as if the guy had told me it was radioactive. "People spend twelve grand on something they're going to drop in the ground and cover with dirt for eternity? That's *nuts*! If twelve grand is the sale price, what's the regular price?"

Before the mortician could respond, Guido, who never averted his eyes from the street, said "ten grand" in a very deadpan, sarcastic, and disinterested tone. Still gazing at absolutely nothing outside, Guido kept talking. "Mario, we're here about Joe Acchione. In his will, he mentioned he's already paid you for everything, so cut the crap and tell us what he paid for so we can get this over with and get out of here."

Mario had stepped in it, and he knew it. He tried to backpedal, nervously repeating "ahhh…um…Mr. Guido. I…um, Mr. Guido…" But after the third one of these, Guido lost his temper. He punched the wall a few inches to the right of the window, leaving knuckle marks in the drywall, and yelled, "STOP IT! GODDAMNIT! JUST STOP IT! Go get your *FUCKING* book and get back in here, *NOW*. I am *NOT* in the mood to put up with your *bullshit* today, Mario. *Capito?*"

Mario was a little troll of a mortician whose head was entirely bald at the crown, with bushy hair ringing his head like Saint Anthony. He was five feet tall, maybe, and portly. He wore a cheap black suit and cheap black shoes with thick rubber soles and a white shirt with what looked like a clip-on black tie. The man sold death, as well as ancillary bits and pieces that vulnerable widows and bereaved family members never knew they needed but were convinced they owed to their fallen loved one once Mario laid on his guilt-trip sales job.

He scurried off to his office to do as Guido had told him, and while he was back there, Guido yelled so he could be heard three buildings away, "And turn this bullshit, melodramatic music off before I rip these speakers out of the *fucking walls* with my *bare fucking hands*!"

"Unc," I said.

He didn't respond.

"Yo! *Unc.* You okay? You need a minute?"

He turned to glare at me for a second, and then dropped his shoulders down from his ears and shook his head and looked back out the window. "Goddamnit, kid. I am getting good and goddamned tired of seeing old guys like me die of *un*natural causes, and all at the hands of that little cu—"

"Here we are," Mario said as he strode back into the showroom, this time with a large white notebook in his hands, each sheet of paper slipped into a plastic sleeve with three holes punched in it, so it stayed secured in place by the notebook's rings. Guido turned back to looking out the window.

"I have Mr. Acchione's contract right here. When he was with us, I recommended he consider a package more befitting a man of his station, but perhaps you…," and he looked up from his book to see Guido's back tensing up and his hands gripping the window frame, about to rip it off the wall. "Ummm…on second thought, I'm sure the package is just fine. In fact, because you are such respected men in this neighborhood, I'll throw in $100 of flowers at no charge."

Silence.

"$250 of flowers at no charge…"

More silence, only this time with Guido now tapping his fingers hard on the windowsill.

"$500 of flowers at no charge, and complimentary use of our hearse."

"We need a hearse to carry a box of cremated remains, Mario?" Guido shot back sarcastically.

"Right. How about the complimentary use of our limousine to and from the church?"

"There's no church, Mario, and you should *know* that. *You* wrote the funeral plan in your *book*. Do me a favor. Take a moment to *read* what's in your book, and inform us what we're doing, so we can schedule this shit and get *outta here*! You've had all day to prepare for this appointment. What, don't I merit at least a *couple* minutes of preparation time? Do Joe and I command *that* little respect from you, Mario?"

Mario looked at me, and I greeted him with a shrug and raised palms, in the international "whoa" gesture, and shook my head. He had dug his own grave, and I was not looking to make it double occupancy.

We finally reviewed the plan Joe had paid for, signed off on the cremation with the Power of Attorney Tom had given me to make the arrangements, and scheduled a date and time for the services later in the week. Ordinarily, scheduling would be more complicated to ensure all the guests had ample time to clear their calendars, but in this case, to honor Joe's wishes, only immediate family would be present, even though dignitaries from far and wide would come if notified. That was one of the great things about Joe. He could have had a big affair, but he didn't need the ego affirmation when he was alive, and certainly didn't need it in death. Those of us who actually matter would be there paying respects, and knowing Joe, he'd have been apologetic about us having to take the time out of our busy schedules to do so.

Making arrangements was especially difficult for Guido. It's one thing to accept your best friend is gone, but it's little things like the reality of a funeral that bang the loss home like a two-by-four to the forehead. I took care of all the details and planning, while Guido never moved from looking out the window. I could feel his angst when I approached him. He was like an electric transformer buzzing with power. I put my hand on his shoulder and asked if he wanted to go back and see Joe, but he clenched his eyes shut and quickly shook his head. He never wanted to see Joe again, at least not in that state.

I patted the old man on the back and said, "C'mon, Unc. Let's get outta here. I've had enough of this place and that little ghoul who operates it."

When we returned to Guido's, the man who rarely imbibes in alcohol grabbed a fresh bottle of Makers from a shelf in the kitchen, informed me he needed to be alone, and passed me on his way up the steps to his bedroom.

We all deal with situations like this differently. Guido opted to be alone with his thoughts in his bedroom. Me? I grabbed my jacket and went for a walk. The brisk fall air on my face kept me in the moment, and walking helped burn pent-up anger. At this moment, I had enough pent-up rage to walk to the West Coast.

THE DINNER DATE

A couple blocks later, my nose was running, thanks to the cold air. I reached into my jacket pocket for a Kleenex and felt Rocco's phone in there. I had never given it back to him after yesterday's meeting at Sonny's. For some reason, the first thought to cross my mind was to call and tell him I had his phone, which obviously wouldn't work, since I *had* his *phone*, so I went with my second thought.

I had Rock's phone because I'd used it to save Gio's number. It was nearly dinnertime, and since Guido was checking out for the evening, I decided to call Gio to check in on him, see how he was holding up after the events earlier…you know, his grandfather being murdered right next to him and all…and invite him out for a casual bite. I figured the guy was in a strange town and could probably use a comforting soul to keep him company and help him deal with his loss.

Gio was a young guy, living the life of a rock star, except without the celebrity. His everyday car was a quarter-of-a-million-dollar pseudo race car. His clothes were custom fit—not just his suits, but his jeans and his body-tight sweaters too—and he only stayed in the finest rooms in the finest hotels. Like his grandfather, he was staying at the Ritz, in an owner's suite facing the glowing clock face on the City Hall tower, with a magnificent view of the city.

Beneath that flashy façade was a very bright, very diligent guy whose favorite relative had just been snuffed out right under his nose, and on his watch. When he picked up my call, he was a little weird, understandably, but agreed to see me.

I was already out walking anyway, so instead of hailing a cab, I kept going a couple blocks farther to Broad Street, where I hopped on a northbound bus and rode the mile or two to City Hall. Gio's hotel was right there on what is known as Penn Square—the square road encircling City Hall—and he greeted me in the main lobby bar, set within an absolutely spectacular circular lounge, at the center of a *massive*, marble-encased room with a hundred-foot-tall ceiling of the inside of a dome with an oculus at the top to view the night's sky. The volume of this room was breathtaking after passing through the human-scaled vestibule off Broad Street. This fortress of a structure was built in 1904, ten years or so before Bella made Guido's dad.

Gio let me know he made a quick reservation at one of the many steak places near the hotel and asked me to ride up to his room with him so he could get his coat and wallet.

His mood was somber, but gracious, and a little appreciative for having a wingman for the night—someone who understood his situation better than anyone else on the planet, and who could not only empathize with his feelings but appreciate the desire for revenge. There wasn't exactly a bounce in his step, mind you, but we made our way through the lounge and past the hotel's front desk to the marble elevator lobby without any drama. The hotel itself was in a renovated office tower adjacent to the domed lounge building. Both had been constructed by the Girard family—a big local banking family. An office building was constructed first, then the domed building, and then floors were added to the office tower around 1930 during an exhaustive renovation that included new elevator doors in the lobby, which were gorgeous, Art Deco bronze deals.

Remember the hotel in Pittsburgh where I left Gina and her grandfather? The only similarity between there and here is the word "hotel." This is where the gods from Olympus stay when they visit Philly, and I was being whisked to the top, to the best room in the best hotel in town. It's the room where Zeus would sleep when the gods were in town, except tonight, it's Gio's room.

We chatted lightly on the elevator up to his penthouse, and when we stepped into his suite, the first thing I saw was the massive, glowing yellow clock face on the City Hall tower. We were eye to eye with it, and it was impressive! Billy Penn's statue, which has stood atop City Hall for over a hundred years, was just a couple stories above us, and the street was nearly thirty floors below. Damned few people in this world have ever had the privilege to witness such a view, and I'm going to be honest with you here. Even as I stood there, I couldn't believe *I* was standing there.

The suite was so big, it had an expansive living room with a sofa and a couple chairs, plus a grand piano. The room had a goddamned grand piano in it—not a *baby* grand mind you, but a full-sized one.

Gio walked to the marble bathroom and mentioned how "tired" the whole place was and how he expected better from such a classy hotel chain.

"Seriously?" I asked. To my eyes, I felt like I was on a tour of Buckingham Palace.

"I know, right?" I guess he thought I was agreeing with him. "They actually have a landline telephone mounted on the wall next to the toilet. Who the fuck uses landlines these days?"

"Oh. I thought you were gonna say how weird it is for someone to be taking a phone call on the toilet."

"What? Why? You don't talk on the phone where you're takin' a dump or a pee?"

Somehow "dump" and "pee" seemed more vulgar than usual here. It was like cursing in church. I curse. I've been in a church. I don't mix the two. I didn't bother responding to his question either. Instead, I said, "My parents still have a wall-mounted phone, but theirs is in their kitchen…. I'm not sure anyone goes to the bathroom in the kitchen, though."

Gio didn't miss a beat. "Well, they're really old, so of course they have a landline, but old poor people aren't exactly the target market for a hotel like this, am I right?"

I had to give him that one. My folks were definitely *not* the target clientele for this establishment, and it had nothing to do with their ages. We're from so many rungs down the social ladder from this place, my family would be lucky to get a job in the Ritz' kitchen.

He grabbed his jacket and his wallet, looked in the mirror near the door to make a final pass at his impeccably coiffed hairdo, and gestured for me to walk into the hall first so he could close the door behind us. This time, as we stepped into the elevator, I addressed the elephant in the room.

"I can't tell you how sorry I am for your loss today, Gio. Your grandfather and I didn't exactly get off on the best foot, but I respected him once I had the chance to hear him out today."

"Yeah. I don't think you respected him much the other night when you spanked his naked ass and saturated his clothes in your hotel bathtub."

"Gee, thank you so much for graciously accepting that olive branch," I sarcastically responded as the elevator bell dinged and the doors opened to the main lobby.

"Are you kidding me? Don't get me wrong, he was pissed off like a motherfucker after you did that, but we laughed our asses off about it yesterday once his blood pressure came down. That was some funny shit, Johnny," and he slapped me on the back like we were heading out to hit a kegger at a frat house.

This guy was a flake. One minute he was literally sobbing, and the next he was ready for a big night on the town.

We walked about a block around the corner and stepped into a steakhouse chain in a beautiful old building that used to be a bank. Again, more elegant than anywhere I ever go…ever. "I really loved that old man," Gio shared. "He was definitely the boss, and I deferred to him accordingly, but he was also my grandfather, and always treated me like a son, sometimes even better. I had him for a long time, but not long enough. A guy that age should die of natural causes, not at the hand of some conniving asshole, but I guess you of all people empathize," and he left it at that as we stepped out into the chilled, autumn night air.

We reached the restaurant so quickly, we never had a chance to get cold, and Gio's personality changed just as quickly. When we opened the door to the restaurant, Gio instantly transformed back from his sullen, sincere self to a very jovial, flirty version. It was like watching Dr. Jekyll turn into Mr. Hyde, except this was Gio turning into Mr. Handsome, and when *that* guy approached the hostess station, he didn't have to mention a reservation. For all I know, he never made one. With a crowd of people in the lobby awaiting their turns to be seated, the hostess sat us immediately. We walked to a table near the bar, and Gio lightly touched her on the arm, looked in her eyes, and asked if we could sit somewhere a little more quiet because we had business to discuss.

The hostess was drop-dead gorgeous. She was *maybe* old enough to drink at the bar, although no bartender in the world would ask her for ID because he'd want her to linger at his bar all night. Anyone that gorgeous attracted other patrons to the bar like a flame draws bugs. She was probably five-seven, or five-eight, and was built about as close to perfect as god would permit any human to be. She wore a black dress that looked like lingerie and was designed for someone a couple inches shorter than her, if you can imagine what I'm saying. If she bent over, her dress would have ridden halfway up her back, exposing everything below to everyone in the joint. Beneath the dress were black stockings, but not thigh-highs, because her dress was so short, we'd have seen the tops of those stockings…and *then* some. She had long, black, poker-straight hair that actually shimmered as she passed the bar lighting, and the narrow heels on her shoes were at least five inches high. I mention all this because Gio is so damned good-looking, when he touched this example of female perfection, she nearly melted into a puddle on the floor and in full fluster responded to him with a breathy and rushed "Oh, sure. I'm so sorry. I should have asked before taking you here. Why don't you pick the one you want, and I'll be sure no one sits near you."

If I, on the other hand, had requested such an accommodation, she may have said the same thing to me she said to Gio, but it would have been one hundred percent sarcastic, and she'd have thrown the menu at me as she walked away. Of course, I would *never* have risked touching her, even lightly on the arm like Gio did, because she, the bartender, or possibly both would have punched me in the face. As it was, the hostess was probably going to go back to her station and sniff her arm to see if any residue of Gio lingered there.

… This guy.

Once we chose our table and sat down, the hostess asked if she could bring us tap, sparkling, or bottled water, and Gio artificially smiled and said, "You choose."

A minute later, she showed up with a frosty glass pitcher, leaned over the table to flaunt her goods (her top to us, and her bottom to everyone else), and poured us each a glass of the establishment's finest tap water. She made eye contact with Gio, smiled, and slowly walked away, in a *very* exaggerated fashion, maintaining eye contact with him for several steps.

Once she was gone, he tossed a slip of paper to me and said, "Here.

You want this? I don't fuck restaurant people." I opened it up and it was her phone number.

I replied, "I'm glad to hear you don't fuck restaurant people. I was a little worried what sort of quid pro quo you were expecting from me after dinner tonight, and the *nerve* of that little vixen trying to flirt with my date. I may have to have write a stern letter to her manager."

Gio laughed and wagged his finger at me and said, "You got a sense of humor. I like that."

Well, that made my heart go pitter-patter.

On schedule, the waitress showed up. The hostess had probably briefed her on Gio's handsomeness, so she tried hard not to stare. She didn't succeed, of course, as I sat there invisibly.

"What'll you drink, Johnny?" Gio asked.

"I'll just take a Diet Coke, thanks."

"Great and I'll take—what's your top-shelf gin?"

"We have Hendricks," she replied, trying to sound sultry.

"Hmmm…," he half-grimaced. "You got Monkey 47? I'd prefer that, but if not, I'll take the Hendricks. But I prefer Monkey 47. Bring me a double of that and a glass of ice on the side. You know what you wanna eat, John?"

I shook my head. I hadn't even looked at the menu yet, I was so enthralled with his entitled ordering.

"I got this," he said as he waved me off, then turned to the waitress and began his list. "We'll start with the seafood tower. We'll each have your Caesar. It has anchovies, right? Good. Then we'll each have a ribeye, bone-out. I don't feel like fucking around with a bone tonight. Medium rare, yes?" He looked at me. I nodded and shrugged. "And we'll have creamed spinach and potatoes au gratin as sides. We'll let you know about dessert later. Good? Good."

And with that, the waitress finished writing and Gio turned his attention back to me.

Once the waitress was out of earshot, I told Gio, if he ordered a drink that way at my bar, I'd probably pee in his Hendricks, and he laughed again, except I was dead serious.

I'm not a fan of elitists. Philly's not an elitist town, at least not most of it. Oh sure, there are bluebloods who don't believe their shit stinks, but most people around here are very real. We're not arrogant, but if we're disrespected, we can become very goddamned passive-aggressive, and you may not notice it until you drink our pee or pick something unsavory from your teeth after biting into your meal. I wouldn't say *I* would do something like that, but let's just say I've seen it done.

"What a day, huh?" Gio asked. His body language looked a lot like what I imagined Uncle G's looked like fifty years ago—leaning forward, bouncing up and down on his finely upholstered chair like his ass itched.

"That's one way to look at it," I said.

"I mean that meeting certainly didn't go as planned, but afterward *all* that time with the cops and their reports and affidavits, and then, I don't know about you guys, but by the time I got to my room, my day's agenda was shot in the ass. I had all these calls to make, letting people know what happened, how Grandfather was murdered by Gina…"

"I can only imagine those were difficult conversations," I said in a conciliatory tone. "Sharing such shocking and terrible news with family over the phone can be so emotional."

"It's disruptive is what it is. We hadn't planned on Grandfather vacating his role so soon or so suddenly. I mean, he was old, sure, but super frickin' healthy. He was a bull, right? You know, him and Guido being cut from similar cloth and all. And then, *bang*. Grandfather's shot." The glib Mr. Handsome disappeared for a second and the real Gio emerged long enough for his brow to soften and for him to gaze across the room at absolutely nothing, but as fast as Gio appeared, he disappeared again.

He got right back on the horse. "Now what?" he said. "It creates a huge power vacuum is what, especially without a clear succession plan. I mean there's a real risk of power struggles to see who's gonna take control. This is a multinational conglomerate, John. It's no longer watered-down driveway sealant and aluminum siding scams. We're hundred percent legit. We're a massive, multibillion-dollar international player—manufacturing, real estate development, high finance, you name it!"

"*Totally* legitimate? Is that why you kept those Neanderthals around, ransacking Sonny's and beating the shit out of me this past week?"

"There's always a need for muscle, to be sure, but that was Stefano and Gina goin' off the reservation. We're really not like that anymore. Honest."

By this time, the drinks had arrived as had the seafood tower.

If you've never seen one of these, let me describe it. A three-tiered serving tray is delivered to your table, and the bottom of each tier's tray is filled with ice. The trays are ascending in size as you go down—smallest at the top, largest at the bottom, and they are *loaded* with seafood—chilled lobster tails (plural), jumbo shrimp, oysters, Alaskan king crab legs (the really big ones), clam shooters, mounds of jumbo lump crab meat, and then some sauces for dipping. It stands about a foot and a half tall and is a whale's feast. It's enough food for…let's say *several* people, and we were going to attack it, just the two of us, and then eat a full meal afterward.

Holy shit.

I reached for a lobster tail and asked, "What about Gina?"

"Oh, we're gonna fuckin' kill her!" he said, very matter-of-factly. "She's toast."

"I thought you said your enterprise didn't engage in criminal activity anymore."

"Extenuating circumstance here, John. We're gonna make an exception for her. Hey, I'll trade you that other lobster tail for your crab leg."

"Deal. I'm not big on crackin' crab."

"Oh, you don't know what you're missin', my friend. I know you guys around here are really into those Maryland blue-claw crabs, but king is where it's at. It's the sweetest you'll ever eat."

"Have you ever tried 'queen'? It's sweeter than king. Snow is the sweetest of all," I said.

"Seriously? I never heard of it. It's that good, huh? Where can I get it."

"Seattle."

"Yeah? I never been."

"Me neither."

"So how do you know it's good if you've never been there?"

"That's not the *only* place you can get it."

"See? Now you're fucking with me. I like that too."

The rest of the meal was delicious and far too much. I could've waved the white flag of surrender before the salad, but one bite of that succulent steak entree, and I couldn't stop. I was seriously contemplating walking the thousand or so blocks home to work off this meal, and when Gio started to order dessert, I passed.

We talked a little more about the sudden power vacuum. And then he asked, so I told him the details of the past week. He was particularly interested in Indi, and what in the absolute hell I saw in Gina. I was prepared to make an argument about how she still looked pretty good for her age, but after everything she'd done to both families, I could no longer say those things with a straight face. The best reason I could give was "she was available, and I was horny."

Not surprisingly, that was a response Gio understood completely and accepted as being entirely reasonable.

Then Gio started asking real questions, with a purpose. "So, tell me about your business. It's a hundred percent legit?"

"Of course. It's a family-owned Italian restaurant. Spaghetti and meatballs, veal parm, normal Italian fare you'd find in this country."

"So it wasn't a front for drugs, or sex trafficking, or shit like that? No gambling in the basement?"

"*Noooo!* The fuck, man? You think my grandparents would do shit like that?"

"Why not? Mine did."

I crinkled my brow a little and let that sink in. Gio continued.

"Was the food good, or did you guys just endure all that time because it was good *enough* and reasonably priced?"

"I'll try not to be offended by that question, and I'll even try to answer it humbly, because at its root, it's a damned good question. The simple answer is yes. I think it was very good. The food was delicious. I mean, you know how it is. Everyone likes their own family recipes best, but judging by customer reactions, and our ability to retain repeat customers and their families for decades, I'd say the public spoke and gave us good scores.

"Our service was also good and attentive, like as if our staff was welcoming family in the door, instead of just mechanically taking orders and delivering food. A lot of places say they treat customers like family, but it really was our culture. We had 'regulars' coming in because our wait staff was with us for years. We were unusual. Our restaurant was run like in the old country. We didn't expect our customers to tip. The bill was the bill. We paid our staff a good wage and provided health benefits because we didn't want a revolving door of employees, and because these people had been with us so long, they really were like our family. We wanted them to live good lives, so we provided for that. Since servers weren't flipping tables for tips, guests were able to eat leisurely; lingering was welcome, almost encouraged. I think the combination of good, long-term employees feeling vested, providing good quality food, and not trying to be too fancy was another big reason we lasted so long. I think it's also the reason we'll do well when we re-open."

"So you're re-opening?"

"Yeah, why, did your family want to scuttle us again?"

"Ha!" and he laughed, which is the reaction I was hoping for, not the one where he punches me in the face. "No, to the contrary. I think if Sonny's is as good as you're describing, I should come back and try it, and maybe figure out a way to add a new business line to our portfolio. What do you know about franchising?"

"Absolutely nothing, and until I make sure the mothership is floating again and can make it to shore, I'm not planning on building a fleet, if you know what I'm sayin'."

"I get it. I get it. Look, my grandfather is at the mortician's, the one you guys used. Thanks for the recommendation, and once he's cremated, I have to bring his remains back to Italy and deal with a lot of corporate crap once the dust settles, but I'll be back. I'll stop in to see you, if you don't mind, and we can talk more about expanding. I like you…what, Mantelli? Valmonti? Which one?"

"I keep asking myself the same question. For now, let's just go with John, okay? And that all sounds fine. Stop by when you're back in town, and we'll see where things go. Maybe it's time for our families to prosper together, instead of threatening to kill each other."

"From your lips to god's ears, my friend. The only thing in our way is that old lady, Gina. She's a monkey wrench with feet. We'll find her, though. Trust me," and he looked me dead in the eye, and became dead-assed serious. "I *never* lose." And he sat back and finished his New York-style cheesecake with fresh berries and whipped cream (the latter of which I always thought was completely unnecessary with cheesecake).

If I hadn't seen it for myself, I wouldn't have believed it possible, but right before that last statement, he flicked a switch and went from chummy to threatening, just like that. It put me on my guard, for sure. This guy's got more faces than a diamond's got facets. I'll have to keep that in mind if we ever *do* discuss being partners. I can see why Guido likes him, but doesn't trust him. His sentiments perfectly describe my feelings, too.

We finished the meal, after he had a *couple* digestifs, and he insisted on picking up the tab, which was fine with me, because it had to be stratospherically expensive. We headed toward the exit and Gio nonchalantly pinched the hostess on the ass and winked at her, because he had consumed enough alcohol to both lower his inhibitions and standards by then. He told her to stop by the Ritz after her shift and ask the front desk to buzz Gio in the owner's suite and come up if she was interested. She blushed and nodded approvingly.

As we reached the exit, before I could utter a word, he looked at me, shrugged, and said, "She's available, and I'm horny."

I'd heard that somewhere before.

We stepped onto the sidewalk, and there was a big Mercedes S-Class sedan parked with the motor running at the valet stand. The car was gorgeous and immaculate—black, shiny, with dark-tinted windows. It was *exactly* what I would have expected to be waiting for Gio, who gestured to the passenger door. I got in and he strode to the driver's door, climbed in, and drove off.

"What happened to the Porsche?"

"Whattya mean?"

"Well, I know my cars. Earlier today you had a GT3 RS. Now we're in a brand-new S-Class."

"Oh, this isn't mine. I just like doing that now and then. The guy who owns the car is gonna be hyper pissed when he comes outside and it's not there," and he chuckled.

I looked at him incredulously. "What? We just stole a car? Whatever happened to that bullshit about not doing anything illegal?"

"You need to lighten up, my man," he said.

We sped down Chestnut Street until we reached Delaware Avenue, near the river, and turned up the street to one of the strip clubs. He actually handed the keys to a valet when we got there, but instead of walking into the club, we walked to another one down the street, so when the authorities found the car, we'd be nowhere to be found.

While Gio was paying the bouncer the entrance fee at the strip club—and mind you, these were *very* high-end strip clubs, not those smoke-clouded, cheap-booze-stained dumps the common men visit—I took that opportunity to call an Uber, on Rocco's account, since I was still using his phone.

Gio started to walk in, but I shook my head.

"You're not comin' in?"

"I got an early morning tomorrow, Gio, so I'm headin' home, but we'll do this again another night. And don't spend too much time in there. Remember you have that hostess coming up to visit you in a couple hours."

"Well, some wingman you turned out to be," he said. "And don't worry. There'll be plenty of Gio left for that raven-haired lovely when she comes upstairs later." Then Mr. Handsome took a break and Gio reappeared, grabbed my arm, sincerely looked me in the eye, and said, "John, no shit. I really appreciate you getting me out tonight. I didn't need to be alone. You're a good friend. Thanks."

Then he propositioned me.

"Listen, John. Guido's not gonna be around forever, and that's not a threat. Please don't misunderstand. He's amazing and scary and incredibly effective, but he's an old man, and he isn't getting younger. When it's time, help me roll his Philly business in with the rest of the stuff I run and we can run the whole show together. He's training you. Use that training with *me*, and we'll make a killing. Think about it. Think about our future, *your* future. Our family's can accomplish great things together."

Then he nodded to me, and walked back to the club with his arms stretched all the way out to either side, waving them up and down to get the bouncer's attention.

By the time my Uber, a ubiquitous Toyota Camry, showed up to shuttle me back to Guido's, Mr. Handsome was back and was hugging the bouncer, shoving cash into the guy's shirt pocket. Mr. Handsome was a player.

The Uber smelled like about a hundred of those air fresheners you buy at the gas station, and the music was very loud and featured some guy screeching Middle Eastern lyrics. Of course, I gave the driver five stars when he dropped me off because I wanted to be sure Rocco kept his perfect Uber score.

The ringing in my ears stopped after about a half-hour, but the air freshener odor was still lingering in my nostrils when I woke up the next morning.

ONE DAY AT A TIME

I woke up all by myself, to nothing. There was no one stirring me at an ungodly early hour of the morning. There was no one telling me we had a full day ahead. There was no one coaxing me out of bed to get going. There was no one tempting me with cooked breakfast meats under my nose. There was no one barging in on me during my shower, tapping on the glass with a damned pinky ring. There was no one at all. I woke up all by myself, at noon.

I kinda missed the disruption, but I welcomed the sleep.

I casually rolled out of bed, hit the bathroom to cover all my bases, put on some clothes, and climbed the steps to discover a vacant kitchen. There was no one around anywhere. There was no note. There was nothing.

Ordinarily, I'd welcome this. I'm a loner. I'd lived alone above Sonny's for decades. I set out on my own in my car when Sonny's was sold and traveled from town to town by myself, getting work, hustling and making my own choices. And yes, I briefly lived with someone in New Orleans, but although that went well, it wasn't going to last because I'm not used to living with someone else, compromising on everything. I like being alone.

The past couple days have been different. Living at Guido's has been like being part of a TV sitcom, like Oscar and Felix. It was collegial.

He finally opened up to me, after all these years. It didn't take long to grow accustomed to that camaraderie, and this morning it ended. I wasn't ready for that.

Guido was weird last night. I've never seen him drink any alcohol in my entire life, except the occasional glass of wine with dinner, let alone walk off to be alone with an entire bottle of Scotch. The trauma of the last few days, seeing my family come under fire from the Romani clan, losing his best friend violently, and then losing his peer and Romani counterpart in similar fashion right before his eyes had clearly shaken him. Guido never seemed so vulnerable…*human* before. He looked gutted last night, and not finding him here this morning was worrisome.

On a whim, I ventured up to Guido's bedroom area to make sure he wasn't in there. The door was open. The bed was empty and made, and the only thing in there was Scrotie, who lifted his head when I walked in, blinked, yawned, and, of course, farted. The dog is nothing, if not predictable.

Since I was home alone, I decided to take the opportunity to touch base with a few people to make sure the world was still clicking along, and to make sure I hadn't missed something important. For an instant, I had a twinge of panic thinking I may have slept through a day and a half and was missing Joe's service, but I found the newspaper in the kitchen trash can and as long as it was the current edition, I knew I'd slept twelve hours, not thirty-six.

My first call was to Ange, who assured me that she, Tom and the kids were all fine, and then insisted I stop asking her to install a nanny-cam so I can watch footage of the babysitter and the boyfriend in Ange's family room the next time she has a date night with Tom. I spoke to my mom and pop, because you can never talk to just one of them. What is it about old people and speaker phones? Finally, I called Raj. He told me he's fine, but that Indi had stayed home from work every day since the kids' abduction, and he was worried about her.

The sensible, smart thing to do would have been to leave Indi alone, but I'm neither sensible nor smart, so I grabbed my coat and started walking to her parents' place. On my way there I realized I was more worried about her ignoring me than screaming. Screaming exhibits fire, and fight, and passion. If she's like that, I know she'll be okay. If she ignores me, I'll worry.

I got to her parents' place. Mrs. Patel (Mom P) opened the door, and although she was hardly thrilled to see me, she agreed to let me in. She told me Indi hadn't left her bed in two days. Mom P called Indi's work to excuse her sudden absences, and she and Raj got the kids to school in the morning. Mom and Dad P collected the kids from school every day when it concluded to ensure the kids weren't alone, anywhere. Everyone's nerves were on edge, and no one felt safe.

Surprisingly, the kids seemed unaffected, but Indi was shattered. She had always been strong, unbreakable, but this shook her to her core. It's one thing to convince yourself you're not vulnerable, but it's another for someone to prove you're wrong.

I asked permission to go to Indi and went to her room. She was laying on her side on her bed, awake, staring at her door. She was a mess. She hadn't bathed in days. Her hair looked like a rat set up residence on her head. There were dark circles under her eyes, and she was wearing sweatpants, a hoodie, and sweat socks and had wrapped herself up tightly in a blanket. She was sweating up a storm, but she needed that constriction to feel safe, to hell with being overheated.

"Get the *fuck* away from me you *fucking* asshole," she hissed at me, her face tensed in a scowl.

Thank god she was pissed at me, and not ignoring me.

"I'm not leaving. You can hate me. You can blame me, but I love you, and I'm not going to sit by and watch while you struggle like this."

I walked around her bed and climbed in behind her.

"You have to be fucking kidding me. If you think for one *second* I'm going to have sex with you, you are out of your goddamned mind. I will *NEVER* do that with you again, *ever*! You *disgust* me!"

I put my arms around her from behind, even as she tried to fight me off, pulled myself in close to her, put my hand under her head, and pressed my cheek to hers, and in a very calm, quiet voice, I told her I would never have sex with someone who smells as bad as she did, and then I just hugged her and held her.

He body was tense for only a moment and then she relaxed and started crying, and didn't stop for a very, very long time.

I didn't say a word. I didn't go anywhere. I merely stayed there and held her.

After a while, a *very* long while, the crying slowed and stopped, and then, exhausted, she rested her head in my palm, and reached out from below her blanket and held my other hand, and we lay there silently for about an hour, and she slept. A little before three o'clock, I let her know her kids would be coming home soon, and asked if she'd like to get bathed and go downstairs to greet them, but she weakly whispered "no," and kept holding on. She fell back to sleep, and I slowly and carefully extricated myself and slipped out. I went downstairs and told her mom I'd be back tomorrow after Joe's memorial services and would keep coming back until she was back on her feet.

The walk home was sad, but I felt better than I did when I left Guido's a few hours earlier. Indi was devastated. Her babies had been kidnapped, and she was helpless. No one likes to learn we have no control. It's a bitter pill, and it can get stuck in our throat.

I got back to Guido's, and the house was abuzz again. Guido saw me walk in and asked me where the fuck I'd been. I told him I was at Indi's, trying to help her cope, and instead of hitting me with a smart-ass comment, he nodded and said we all have some healing to do.

I asked him where he was this morning, and he said he still had a business to run, and also had to make some additional arrangements for Joe.

We spent the remainder of the day doing our own things. We didn't eat dinner together or hang out with one another at the end of the day. Although everything was still strange for all of us, it was gradually becoming slightly *less* strange by the day. We were letting go and resuming our lives. Guido was running his business, and I was going to get started putting Sonny's back together.

It almost seemed as if life would become normal again someday, perhaps even soon.

UNCLE JOE

The ceremony was set for 10 a.m. There would be a memorial service at the funeral home, followed by a brief ceremony at the gravesite, and then a luncheon. When you break it down like that, it seems manageable and clinical, because that description is entirely impersonal.

To put the day's events an entirely different way, our family and close friends would convene at the funeral home to console each other, lean on each other, and share stories about Joe. There would be crying. After that, we would adjourn to the cemetery where we'd all stand around the gravesite, say a few words, awkwardly linger, and act like we're being reflective, all the while wondering how to appropriately leave, and then we'd all head to a local restaurant for lunch where we'd talk to one another, discuss ordinary topics, and act like someone we love didn't just die and leave us all alone forever.

Guido and I decided to take Mario the undertaker up on his offer of the limo so Mom and Pop would have a way to get from event to event without driving, since they didn't have a car. Guido and I rode together in one of his Caddies, with a driver at the helm and Rocco riding shotgun. Ange and Tom had their own car. Marilyn arrived on her own, and that was about it. Joe didn't have anyone else who was close to him, and although we could have filled the joint a dozen times over with dignitaries and bigwigs, Joe didn't want that, and today was all about him.

Once there, each of us had an opportunity to eulogize him. Angela spoke very briefly, gushing over his legal acumen and sphere of influence. Pop eulogized him as a nice man he had met a long time ago and who helped him and his Pop when they needed it. Pop's memory had become worse than I realized, and it was unraveling more quickly every day. I'm not even sure he remembered Joe, let alone Joe's name. I addressed the room as well, recalling what little I'd learned from him, about his time attending school, how strong his legs still were, and how he was happiest rowing. I shared the story of how my grandfather and I used to go to the Schuylkill River to watch Joe row, and how Joe never knew Al had done that. It touched him more deeply than I understood at the time, but it all made sense to me today, knowing what I know now. Finally, Guido batted clean-up, and for a man of few words, he held us riveted for nearly an hour.

Although we barely filled one row of the memorial room, Guido imagined every seat in the house was filled with the ghosts of the old man, and Marguerite, and Al and Sophia and the stagehands from the old Dock Street vaudeville theater who were all there, waiting to guide Joe to the next realm, and protect him. He imagined all the people Joe had assisted over the years, and all the contacts whose relationships he'd nurtured for decades were occupying seats. Finally, he imagined Joe himself, watching this all play out, humbled by the attendance and sentiments of the family he loved, and confident in their future, knowing they were all in good hands—one another's. Guido told story after story after story of his days with Joe, and gradually we all came to realize how much Guido loved Joe and how lost he was without him.

Once Guido finished, he stood at the lectern, lingering as if he didn't know where to go next. Mario recognized the condition. He'd seen it countless times over the years. He grabbed Guido lightly by the arm and gestured for him to take his seat, and then Mario asked everyone to return to their vehicles to accompany the family to the gravesite, where Joe's ashes were to be interred.

The time at the gravesite went as expected. The fall air seemed to hold an extra chill at the cemetery, and the dampness penetrated us all to our bones. The grass there had browned over for the winter, and leaves blew and scattered unimpeded across the property, occasionally getting stuck on a tombstone, or against the trunk of a tree. The air would be still until giving way to sudden gusts, then it would quiet down again, repeating the cycle over and over. We all stood around the grave, shielding ourselves from the elements, and trying desperately to look somber and contemplative when really, all we *all* wanted to do was leave. No disrespect to Joe, but the conditions and the occasion were almost too much to endure.

Only Guido seemed immune. He stood there with his overcoat open, but his suit jacket buttoned. Unlike most days, Guido was dressed formally. He wore an expensive black suit and white shirt. His Italian dress shoes were polished to a shine; his collar was buttoned and his tie pushed up. He didn't look feral. In fact he looked very subdued, saying goodbye for the very last time to the best friend he'd ever had.

After a few words were said, Joe's small cube box of ashes was handed to the cemetery's curator. The small crowd disbursed and headed to the next stop on the funeral train, but before Guido or I left, he grabbed my arm and asked me to stay for a moment. He had something to show me.

Once we were alone, Guido pointed to the grave next to this one, and I noticed the headstone. It was my grandfather and grandmother's grave. I hadn't noticed before that moment, probably because I hadn't been there in many years. The stone was inscribed:

Alfredo Valmonti 1898–1974
Rose Valmonti 1905–1978

Then he pointed to the stone above where Joe would be laid to rest, and it listed the following:

Vittorio Acchione 1860–1940
"The Old Man"

Marguerite Acchione 1875–1955
"Acchione the Greater"

Sophia Mantelli 1900–1926
"Loving Wife, Daughter and Mother"

Alfredo Mantelli 1898–1926
"Loving Husband, Son and Father"

Joseph Mantelli 1925–2021
"Acchione the Greatest"

"The old man bought adjacent plots years ago, because he wanted to be certain your grandfather could be with both families. They buried his empty casket with Sophia, but they buried him with Rose."

"I like what you had inscribed for Joe, Unc. He would have really liked that. It covered all the bases. Well done."

I patted my uncle on the shoulder and noticed tears running down his cheeks. He couldn't look away. He couldn't leave. Not only was he closing a glorious chapter of his life, he was beginning to realize his book would be closing soon as well. I put my arm around his waist and pulled him close. I told him I loved him and then I walked us both back to the car, because if I didn't, he'd still be there.

Guido's driver let him in the car, and Rocco grabbed my door for me as well.

"Can I ask you something, Unc?"

"Shit, at this point, you can ask me absolutely anything," he said, still trying to find his breath after the emotional moments at the gravesite. .

"Would you mind if we took a little detour on the way to the luncheon?"

"Where'd you have in mind?"

"Boathouse Row."

"Shit, boy. That's a fantastic idea," and Guido suddenly came alive. "Let's take care of Joe *before* we go to lunch." Guido leaned forward and tapped on the driver's seat. "Take us to Bachelor's Barge on Boathouse Row. If you don't know which one that is, ask Rocco to look it up."

This felt right. I think Guido felt it too.

Last Requests

According to Joe's will, he wanted half his ashes buried with his family, and the other half sprinkled into the Schuylkill River, where he rowed competitively through high school and college and then recreationally for decades thereafter.

He was appropriately proud of his professional accomplishments, and he loved his family, but his most profound joy came on the river. He said it made him a complete person. It cleared the cobwebs from his mind. It provided him with the sort of focus only solitude and physical exertion could bring, and it made him feel connected to nature—water, air, trees, and all the sounds that went with it. Standing on the dock at Bachelor's, one of the boathouses on Boathouse Row, and the one he used the most later in life, I got a sense for how he felt.

Boathouse Row, which houses the Schuylkill Navy, its governing body, is a string of Victorian structures lined up along the north bank of the Schuylkill River in Philadelphia's Fairmount Park. The area is surrounded with rock formations and walking paths and a multitude of large, bronze, outdoor statues. The part of town immediately east of the boathouses features the old Fairmount Park Water Works, the Philadelphia Art Museum, and the Benjamin Franklin Parkway, which connects the art museum district to City Hall a dozen or so blocks away.

That area is sprinkled with myriad museums and fancy hotels and the Catholic Basilica, and other churches and even the Free Library. The head of the Schuylkill River is famous in its own right for hosting some of the world's best river races, with men and women rowing in "singles," and "quads" and "eights" for clubs, high schools, and universities, not just locally, but internationally.

The boathouses themselves along the river are picturesque, and arguably the most photographed, iconic element in the city, even more than the Liberty Bell, Independence Hall, or even Billy Penn himself (or at least his statue atop City Hall). But as beautiful as the view of the boathouses is from the other side of the river, the view on the water's edge from the docks themselves is altogether different, and arguably more breathtaking.

Standing on the docks, your perspective becomes more personal. You're standing only a couple inches above the river on a floating platform, and your vantage point is on an entirely different plane than it would be from the roads beyond the opposing riverbank. This view draws you in. No longer are you gazing upon it from a distance. You're *among* the boathouses. It's like the difference between sitting in the second bleacher of a baseball game and sitting in the dugout. The view from the water itself was probably better still, like moving from the dugout to the pitcher's mound, or the batter's box.

Seated in a scull (the long, narrow craft one rows on the river), your hips are at the waterline, and your eyes are only a couple feet above. You look *up* at the boathouses instead of down, or across at them. You see what's surrounding you on all sides, and you feel the river's current beneath you. But don't get too complacent, because this section of the Schuylkill River may look civilized and tranquil, but if you let down your guard, you could end up in dire straits.

Only a couple hundred yards from the boathouse platform was a waterfall, and the current plunging over the falls used to push water into a pumphouse, which was constructed in the early 1800s to provide potable water to the citizens of our fine city. By the late 1800s, people started dying of typhus from drinking what had become heavily polluted water from upstream industry, and the dam and pumphouse stopped serving that purpose, but they both still remain in place.

That strong current pushes against you from west to east, and as it does so, you float toward a reservoir protecting the fresh water of the Schuylkill River from the brackish Delaware River. Just before the reservoir, the current gains strength, reaches, and spills over a diagonal waterfall, which is probably only a dozen or so feet tall but is 1,200 feet long. If a rower gets drawn too close, the result could be fatal. As a precaution, a wire is strung across the river a few feet in the air, from one bank to the other, and individual safety lines hang down from it, offering desperate rowers a chance at salvation before tumbling over the falls into oblivion—tying the dangling ropes to their boats to hold them steady until help can arrive.

Obviously, the falls are perilous, and a woman coach in the mid-1980s succumbed to going over when her launch (a motorized boat used for training, among other things) became entangled in the safety lines of all things, and once she freed it, the motor failed to restart and the launch floated helplessly toward the falls. Instead of heeding the directions of those sent to assist her, the coach must've panicked because she jumped from the boat and died in the falls. Proving their own point, when the rescuers launch *also* stalled and floated toward the falls (remember, this is Philadelphia where dumb, ironic shit like this seems to happen all the time), *their* boat went over the falls too, but they stayed in it and all aboard survived. The falls continue to churn today, and if the breeze is blowing just right, its natural sound drowns out the road noise of a heavy current of cars and trucks passing by on the roadways just beyond it.

Boathouse Row is a really big deal around here, and most of us know at least some trivial, anecdotal facts about it. For example, Bachelor's Barge was the original formal club to be formed here for this purpose in the mid-1800s, and it was so named because only bachelors could be members. Once a member wed, he got the boot. Well, Joe upheld his end of the bargain, even though those misogynistic rules were eliminated years and years ago. Regardless, Joe died a bachelor, and to Bachelors go his ashes.

I was contemplating all this, taking it all in—the sights, sounds, and nostalgia, imagining all the ghosts of rowers past circling about—as I stood there on the dock with a plastic bag half-full of incinerated Joe in my hands. Guido's car had dropped me at the sidewalk, and Guido encouraged me to do this alone, as Joe had wished. I was so deep in thought, I completely missed Gina walking up the dock behind me. When she called my name, a chill went down my spine and I turned around.

She completely got the drop on me.

There I stood, armed with only a plastic bag in my hands, while a gun was trained on me at center mass.

"Jesus Christ, woman. Not now. I swear to god, not now."

"Or what? What will you do, John? Will you kill me? I don't think so. I'm the one with the gun, and all you're armed with is a sandwich bag full of dead guy."

"The guy you killed, jackass."

"That's right, and I'm not planning to stop with him."

"Yeah, I was there when you killed the *other* old guy, remember?"

"Well, I *had* to break the tie. You killed one old guy, and now I've killed two."

She continued walking until she stood on the barge between me and the river. "Originally, I wanted to kill you all so I could take control of my family's company, but now I just want to kill you all because I *hate* you. You people have ruined *everything*! Because of you, Guido and that guy with the pretty hair and face, I have to run for the rest of my life before my family finds me and kills me. *Me*! I'm the rightful heir to my family's legacy. Isabella resides in me!"

She leaned in for this next part, the flickers of anger beginning to flash in her eyes. "I'm a direct descendant of Isabella. Did you know that? Because I *am*. I even *look* like her, but now that's all fucked, because of *you* people."

Every now and then, the wind kicked up and the leaves rustled. At first the breeze was coming off the river, but now it felt like it was shifting and coming from the road behind me. In all likelihood I was about to utter my final words among the living, so I decided to maintain my record for being relentlessly reckless and stupid and chose to make the person pointing a loaded gun at me as angry as possible. I started pressing. How could this possibly end badly?

"Are you telling me you're blaming my family for your failure? If you'll recall, you stupid twat, the only thing my family did was get wrongfully blamed for something your precious Isabella did. For fuck's sake, her lie and cowardice are the reasons my grandfather's first wife was murdered. Your family is a cancer, and you're the epicenter of the fucking malignancy. My family isn't the cause of your problems. *Your family's defective DNA is your problem.*"

Well, that worked. Gina's anger went from a spark in her eyes to a full-on raging bonfire. "Don't you *dare* say a word against my great-grandmother. That's all you men do. You blame women for what goes wrong, and you take credit for everything we do right! If it wasn't for Isabella, this family would have *nothing*! And if it wasn't for women, none of you would *be* here! We should be the ones running things, not *you*!"

Gina folded her one arm across her chest, kept the other arm outstretched with the gun pointed at me, tilted her head to one side, and asked me if I *really* thought insulting her while she had a gun pointed at my chest was a smart idea. Then she moved the gun down a little bit and said, "Nuts."

I may have struck a nerve, although the man-bashing sorta came from left field. I wasn't expecting that, but I ran with it.

The breeze kicked up from behind me again and I replied with more insults. Pissing her off was either going to get me shot or get her to fuck up. She had a track record, so I kept pressing. "Listen, psycho. You're gonna shoot me anyway, so why should I sugarcoat it? I'm sorry your life turned out so shitty, but frankly, that was entirely *your* doing, not mine or my family's. Stop blaming us specifically and men in general for your own failures."

And the bonfire turned into a nuclear mushroom cloud.

"What would you know about my life? You have no *IDEA* how much I suffered. While you had your family and friends surrounding you, I was a slave in my own home. My husband treated me like *garbage*! His brother *raped* me, and his parents treated me like their personal house slave. My own parents *abandoned* me, and it wasn't until my mother finally died I learned who I actually am!"

She just kept getting more and more angry, so I knew she was going to lose her focus. It would be like in that hotel room in Pittsburgh. I had an idea and slowly started to loosen the twist-tie holding the bag closed, and then I waited for my chance.

"You learned who you are? It took you that long? I could have told you who you were forty years ago. You're a cheap, uneducated bimbo who's only good for humping and vacuuming!"

She opened her mouth in shock or to scream, and as she did a gust of wind came up from behind me. I tilted the baggie down and Joe's ashes poured out. They blew toward the river, and directly at Gina. Joe covered her face, got in her eyes, filled her open mouth, and blew up her nose. She was so busy gasping for air, trying to process what was happening, I was able to take a couple quick steps toward her and shove her into the river.

Gina splashed and glurped and gulped for air. I grabbed a nearby oar and shoved her down below the surface and into the current, which grabbed her and propelled her toward the falls. Her arms flailed desperately as she panicked in the icy water.

It's important here for me to tell you a little bit about our local dialect. You see, some people contend Philadelphians have a very distinct accent. None of us locals hear it, but you all keep insisting. Anyway, apparently, *you* mispronounce the word *water*. The proper pronunciation is *wooder*, and at this very moment, Gina was drowning in it. As a friend's mother used to say, "Good riddance to bad rubbish." Gina wasn't a quitter, though. I had to give her that. She'd submerge for a moment and then pop up, gasping for air and yelling for help, then she'd dip below the surface again, only to breach again long enough to yell profanities at me, and then down under she'd go again. She kept floundering, going under water for longer and longer intervals each time she'd dip.

She was weakening, but the current was not. If anything, the river was gathering strength as it closed toward the pinch-point of the falls. The last glimpse I had of Gina, she was reaching for one of the emergency lines stretched between shorelines a few feet about the falls, but missed. That was her last hope. There was nothing left to keep her from going over the falls and being pulled down into the water (that's *wooder*) below, like that coach who died years ago.

Gina hadn't broken the water's surface for a while until her body limply popped up at the edge of the falls, floated face down over its edge, and then disappeared for good into the reservoir below. I have no idea how often the city dredges the reservoir for deer carcasses and other debris, because they don't submit that schedule to me for approval, but I was 99.9 percent sure they wouldn't perform this task soon enough to rescue GG.

Gina was finally dead, and hot-diggity-damn, Joe got her!

I started walking back to the road to get in the Caddy, and there was Guido, standing on the sidewalk applauding.

"You were here the whole time? Why didn't you shoot that bitch?"

"What, and deprive you and Joe of the pleasure of finishing her yourselves? I cannot think of a more poetic final resting place for Joe, than choking out the bitch who choked him out. *Fuck. Her.*"

Guido threw his arm around my shoulder and walked me back to the car. It was as though twenty years had just been lifted from his face. He was the old Guido again. There was an appearance of optimism on him—in his step, in his eyes, and in his posture. My man was back!

Lunch Is a Dish
Best Served Warm

We finally made it to the luncheon. It was a small affair, just our immediate family. They had all waited for an appropriate amount of time for us to show up before eating, but finally everyone got down to business when my dad, who's been having a lot of difficulty lately understanding the concept of time, became agitated because the food was there but no one was eating it, so they all finally dug in. That was actually okay, because the food would have been ruined if they waited much longer on ceremony, which we didn't ask them to do anyway. Once Guido and I arrived, they asked where we were, and we casually dismissed the question by saying we got sidetracked and spent a little extra time memorializing Joe.

We all ate lukewarm baked ziti and surprisingly good homemade meatballs. There was Sarcone's garlic bread, of course, and a little salad. It wasn't a feast, but it was fine. We reminisced, all of us together, and then started arguing about how I was going to spend Joe's money, which I kept telling them was none of their goddamned business. My mother, who cursed like a fucking sailor, told me to watch my mouth, and my father, who never cursed in his life, told her to go to hell, and we all laughed.

I did tell everyone that a portion of Joe's money was going to be invested in restoring Sonny's, and the first order of business would be getting our sign renovated and lit again. It had been extinguished in an attempt to disgrace us after Gina and her uncle gained control of Sonny's from the sale. That sign had been lit every minute of every day for seventy-five years, and if I had anything to say about it, it would be lit for another seventy-five, starting in a couple weeks.

We enjoyed one another's company, a good meal, and a chance to slow down and breathe. If Joe was there in spirit, and I hope to god he was, he and Al and Rose and Sophia, even Marguerite and the old man, would be smiling and nodding. We may not have been a big family, but we were a close and resilient one, and this time, we were pretty sure no one was going to walk in during our espressos and tell us someone *else* had been kidnapped or murdered, for fuck's sake!

Smooth Sailing

Guido settled the tab with the restaurant, and we all scattered back to our respective cars. The limo Mom and Pop were provided earlier in the day had long since gone back to its garage, after it dropped them at the luncheon, so Ange and Tom took our parents back home. Guido and I were heading back to his place, but I made an impromptu suggestion to stop at Joe's (now my, I suppose) place and toast him, to which Guido agreed without hesitation.

We pulled up to the front of the house, walked to the door, inserted the key in the ancient lock, and with one turn, we were in.

This may sound odd, but I believe homes feed on the energy of those within them. Last week, even though only Joe and Marilyn lived in this huge home, the place had a vitality and warmth. Maybe it was just the glow of the lighting. I don't know, but when we went in the house this time, with no one living inside, it felt like a hollow cave—lifeless, cold, and filled with only echoes. For the first time in probably 140 years, no one lived in this house. That would change soon enough. I intended to live here, at least until I got Sonny's back up and running and figured out a long-term plan, but for now, the house assumed the energy, or lack of energy, of its former owner and was lifeless.

We turned on some lights and wandered to the kitchen. Guido took a seat and I went to Joe's desk, which I noticed looked French and bore a striking resemblance to the desk Guido had described from the office above the old vaudeville theater. I searched its drawers to see if there was another bottle of Single-Malt hidden in there, but there wasn't. Rocco and I'd drained the last one with Joe the other night. However, on a table near the window, there was what appeared to be a Tiffany decanter, half-filled and surrounded by beautiful etched crystal glasses, on a beautiful antique gold tray.

I scooped up the entire tray and marched back to the kitchen with my prize in hand and held it up for all to observe.

It was a little after four o'clock in the afternoon, so we weren't going to make a big party out of this. That wasn't the purpose of our visit anyway. Rocco set down four glasses, one before each of us—Rocco, Guido, me, and Ant—but before I began to pour, Guido reminded me we needed one more for the guest of honor. I poured five shots of liquor from the decanter and put the cap back on it. We lifted our glasses, toasted to Joe, clinked one another's glasses as well as Joe's, which was set in the middle of the table untouched, and then poured the nectar down our throats.

I hate alcohol, but that's okay. For Joe, I'd have swallowed lighter fluid. As tradition dictated, we all turned our glasses upside down and set them on the table. Ordinarily, the glasses would be slammed down for effect, but these appeared to be precious and delicate, and we didn't want to risk damaging something that had withstood the test of so much time already. Then we reversed our path back out through the front doors, turning off lights as we went. I locked the doors tight and walked back to the car to head toward our final destination, and Joe's glass remained full and upright in the center of the table.

A little over a week ago, I was cooking creole in a restaurant kitchen in New Orleans, living with a nurse, and didn't have a care in the world.

Now I'm living with my uncle until I moved into my personal mansion, getting chauffeured around town, and being groomed to take over an operation I don't know the first thing about.

What a weird fucking week.

LIFE BEGINS AGAIN

As promised, once we reached Guido's, I let him and the others know I was planning to head to visit and support Indi. I knew I wasn't directly responsible for what happened to her, but if it hadn't been for our friendship, Indi would never have been targeted. Indirectly, her misery is definitely on me.

I spent a couple hours with Indi again. This time getting her as far as to sit up and chat and ultimately bathe—a major accomplishment for us all. She went downstairs to sit with the family and was there when her kids returned home from school. Her couple-days absence was explained away as a touch of the flu and everyone seemed to be healing. Things weren't great, and would never really be the same, but normalcy was in sight, and that was almost as big an accomplishment as getting Indi bathed.

Instead of heading back to Guido's, I decided to take a detour and walk past Sonny's. This was the epicenter of all of the craziness we'd all endured these past couple weeks. Standing there on the sidewalk in front of the place, with its massive and recently dented sign eerily dark and looming above the front of the store, and all the storefront windows filthy and dark, with no ambient light glowing in the restaurant itself, the whole place looked sad. What had been a thriving business concern just a few months ago, and had literally sustained three generations of my family for eighty years was now reduced to a dark, dirty husk in desperate need of revitalization before it caved in on itself. It was going to take a massive investment to restore our once-proud legacy, but thanks to Joe, and the money he left behind at my disposal, I was confident this Phoenix would rise from its ashes stronger than ever before.

I stood on our sidewalk for several minutes, just staring, imagining all the changes we could make, seeing those changes in my mind, superimposed over the building in its current state, when my phone blinged with a text, then three more texts in quick succession—bling bling bling.

It was probably Guido wondering where I was, so I reached into my pants pocket and grabbed the phone, rolling my eyes, resigned to being stifled by Unc's worrying for the foreseeable future. That wasn't so bad though. My grandfather never had anyone to watch over him, and on many occasions, he really could have used someone. I've been blessed with too *many* people who worry about me.

I gazed down at the phone, and … the texts were from Gina's number.

"What the fuck?" I yelled into the late-night silence. In that moment, I completely forgot about Sonny's and its future.

She said:

"Thanks 4 swim"

"and mouthful of Joe LOL"

"How's Sonny's?"

And then she added four laughing emojis.

I turned around to scan the neighborhood, to see if she was watching, then another text arrived.

"BTW, Ka …"

"Ka??? What the fuck is *that* supposed to mean?" I asked myself out loud.

And that's when Sonny's exploded.

BOOM!

About the Author

MICHAEL ATTIANI is a second-generation Italian from Philadelphia. His grandparents all landed here by boat, but one of them was born a few months after she arrived. The family always assumed she was patiently waiting to see how things were going before coming out.

Many things can happen to someone who is born and raised by Italians in Philly, and one of those things is writing a fictional account of Italians in Philly. That's exactly what Michael has done.

Sonny's Revenge is the second installment of a trilogy about the Valmontis, an Italian family in Philly – South Philly, to be specific, since that's where the city tends to keep its Italians. Although the series is entirely fictional, many personal memories, some familiar characters and a lot of satirical wit and sarcasm have combined to shape the tale. So far so good for the book series, because Michael's bio doesn't include any account of his sudden "accidental" demise, nor any news of his excommunication from his family … at least not yet.

Growing up, aside from a brief stint in a public elementary school, Michael ended up where most Italians do: Catholic school. He endured that excruciating form of purgatory from 8th grade through college graduation, shrewdly compacting an entire lifetime of Catholic obligation into the first twenty years of his life. Once he was paroled from academia, he spent three decades pursuing a career in commercial real estate and continues to do so today.

Along the way, Michael somehow convinced a beautiful woman to marry him and produce two sons. Then they added four dogs because two boys don't produce enough mayhem and mess on their own. In addition to his family and career, Michael enjoys spending as much time as possible with his friends, writing, drawing, skiing, traveling and doing pretty much anything with cars. Oh, and eating, Michael does a lot of eating. If he hadn't married his wife, he'd have probably married his fork.

Food, after all, is the hub of any Italian family, especially one whose spokes include humor, storytelling, love, affection, too much hugging and a smattering of judgment and guilt. Sarcasm and wine keep everything well lubricated.

Learn more about Michael and his books at www.sonnysvendetta. com, or contact him through the *Sonny's Vendetta* Facebook page, @ SonnysVendetta.